HOLTGART

Book One of the
Harkentale Saga

by

Jeremy James Smith

hp

Published by Harkentale Press
Copyright © 2020 by Jeremy James Smith
www.JeremyJamesSmith.com

Cover art and Artemus' Map by Angela Rickerson

This book is a work of fiction. Names, characters, places and incidents are products of the author's imagination or are used fictionally and are not to be construed as real. Any resemblance to actual events, locales, organizations, or persons, living or dead, is entirely coincidental.

All rights reserved. No part of this book may be reproduced, scanned, or distributed in any printed, electronic, or audio form without written permission.

Printed in the United States of America

10 9 8 7 6 5 4 3 2 1

First Edition

Acknowledgements and Dedication

Holtgart represents a journey of well over a decade and would not have been possible without dozens of readers, mentors and coaches to help develop the story and hone my writing. I would like to thank a few specific folks who gave a tremendous amount of time and effort, starting with my brainiac wife Sheena, calliopist Lauren, editor E.G. Moore, and heroic beta reader Joey.

I would also like to thank the members of the Coeur d'Alene and Sandpoint chapters of the Idaho Writers League for countless critique sessions and excellent writing advice. I hear your voices anytime I edit now and will carry them throughout my career.

J. Elliot Young helped me with the original character development decades ago. Never did either of us expect Angus to be part of a commercial enterprise. Thank you for challenging me to get outside my comfort zone.

To my patrons, starting with my own kin, thank you for smoothing out the bumps and allowing me to accompany Angus on his journeys. Wherever they take us, it is only because of your support.

That said, I must dedicate Holtgart to my wife and best friend Sheena. Your faith and support throughout this venture have been fantastic, and I appreciate the occasional and (oft-deserved) swift kick in the behind to get this out the door.

Prologue

Raiding the Roost

*"In granite stone we place our trust
And as we tunneled through that crust
One errant rock nigh 'trayed our crew
Yet patience 'low'd us to break through"*
- Argent Origins

----- -----

Dragonlord Thykskaal paced through the cavern, searching for the source of the sound that disturbed his long slumber. Finding only a single fist-sized rock calved from the solid stone wall on the north side of the chamber, he sent it skittering down an unused tunnel before returning to the pile of gold and silver coins that served as his bed. Using his massive, scaly, trefoil tail, he caressed the mound after he settled, putting the pile back in perfect order.

He shared his chambers with several beautiful dams and dozens of their eggs, coated in semi-molten silver and containing his brood. Another hundred years of careful incubation and they would be ready to hatch; the next generation bearing his trace. He chuffed with pride as he surveyed the scene.

No sign of men or dwarves crossed his eyes or nose. The smell was telling, of course; humans smell sour to a dragon, and dwarves are even worse. But offensive as they may be, identifiable scents make for a good early-warning system. Awake and aware, Thykskaal was nigh-invincible. Asleep, even mighty dragons are somewhat vulnerable.

Dragons can *see* residual heat, even through walls in some circumstances. He scanned *beyond* the room for threats before settling fully. He saw nothing to cause alarm, no telltale hotspots aside from his family. They were safe.

He stretched his powerful, sinewed wings, touching both sides of the chamber. His cavernous maw opened in an extended yawn. Confident again of his unassailable position, the dragon curled up like a sleeping dog on his pile of precious metals and stones. He tucked the tuft on the end of his tail behind his scaly lips; paying homage to some primal, suckling need. Sleep soon overwhelmed him and he did not wake. For the first and last time in his long life, Thykskaal dreamt of tunneling dwarves.

----- -----

A lone stone fell inside the dragon's bedchamber, dislodged by the dwarves' adjacent work.

"That was close." Dannl's voice was a mere whisper. "No mistaking, we've a dragon on the other side of that wall. And he's big." Dannl Steelpike was a dwarf in his prime; stout and muscular. He stood nearly five feet tall and held a funnel-shaped listening device between his ear and the freshly worked stone wall.

"Aye. We're almost through." Young prince Artemus pressed his ear to the cold stone wall, listening. "We'll sit here 'til he's asleep again."

One impertinent pebble nearly derailed years of drilling and tunneling. The company of dwarves waited for hours before moving, then started the achingly slow process again. The diggers masked their presence from the dragon by constantly splashing water from the spring on the walls in front and around them. Cool stone made their body heat undetectable.

Not much longer now, and they would be ready for the strike. It was critical that they come upon a sleeping dragon, as those awake put up much more of a fight. Young Artemus would be there, but would not be the first to take a swing. Despite his royal blood, he had not yet earned the right to attack a creature like this before the worthier dwarves had made an attempt.

Young Artemus was a big believer in tradition.

*"We breach'd the wall and silent sped
'cross t'the Dragon, pierced and bled;
We slew his dams and cool't his eggs
Leaving not the slightest dregs."
- Argent Origins*

Roughly a thousand years later...

Chapter 1

A Simple Name

As a young dwarf of ninety years, Angus embarked upon a military career. Being inducted into the Holtgart meant the first step in a life path that would culminate in an honorable retirement after only a half-millennium of service. His was a rather inglorious job, raising and lowering the gate, but it was a start.

The post was an accomplishment for Angus, born of a poor family of laborers. While he was still working in the mines, some of the more fortunate dwarves were free to concentrate on higher education - like combat training and liver development.

Back in his forties, he apprenticed in several more skilled trades; but each position lasted less than a decade before the trade master terminated the apprenticeship. He worked with miners, alchemists, smelters, metalworkers, and stonemasons. His time as a brandy maker was the shortest; his propensity for sampling the product likewise guzzled profits.

Dwarfing the front gate controls was probably the best post for him until he calmed down from the carousing, unfocused ways of his youth. The entire job consisted of staying awake and listening for cues from the watch commander. When the command to open the gate came, there was a certain series of levers to be pushed to start the unseen flow of water that powered the whole affair.

In fact, the worst part was being rooted to the 'dead dwarf's pedal' any time the portcullis was open. If weight was lifted off the pedal while the gate was open it would come thundering down and would not open again until the pedal was pushed, and the proper lever sequence entered. The idea was to ensure that the gate was only open when there was a living, conscious dwarf in control.

Angus' beard had not yet changed to the shades of white, grey or silver that signified adulthood among his race. This was, in fact, the only remarkable thing about him. It led to his first byname,

'Redbeard'. He longed for the day he was no longer called 'Redbeard.' But Dwarves don't get to choose their names; the name chooses the dwarf.

Dwarven names spring into being from deeds, attributes, or even sometimes mistakes. Trademasters usually have bynames that discuss their signature item while laborers often derive their names from more mundane descriptors; such as Perfectedge the bladesmith or Strongback the digger.

Heroes, on the other hand, usually are named for their great deeds. For example, Damon Orcgrappler once bested an orc barehanded in a prolonged fight that went to the ground before the end. Damon actually has several other names, but Orcgrappler is the most outstanding, hence the name that is used. As Dwarves go through life, they may be known by a dozen or more names.

Dwarves enjoy an entire sub-culture built around being a 'bane'. Any enemy that is formidable, monstrous, or otherwise remarkable is allowed into the group; but there are certain names that are more coveted. These generally fall to the very rare and fatal enemies – opponents that no dwarf in their right mind would engage. This works for dwarves, as they have usually left their right minds behind by the time the fight comes around.

A Bearbane would be respected, as long as the bear was slain in close combat. Stories would be told about Lichbanes and ballads sung of the dwarf who slew the elven king. But the stuff of Legends? That takes something big, like a Dragon. No living dwarf has the Dragonbane moniker, for two reasons: Dragons don't attack dwarven Holts very often, and when they do, they generally win.

Like many young dwarves, Angus secretly fantasized about becoming a Dragonbane, but he didn't dare utter the thought aloud for fear of ridicule and the resultant mocking nickname. But he did keep up his practice with the spear, just in case the opportunity was to present itself. Angus often held spirited discussions with the young bane-hopeful crowd about the virtues of the spear, which he held as critical to the dwarven style of fighting.

"If you're in a tunnel that's just wide enough for one," he would say, "a well-trained dwarf with a spear is nigh undefeatable. The enemy can never get close enough to touch you." The arguments ran for hours, with each participant sure that their weapon of choice was the best, but those talks - fueled with strong ale and good dwarven brandy - were some of Angus' favorite memories.

The young dwarf took his spear everywhere. It measured six feet tall, with a thick shaft made from a particularly dense mountain oak. The broad spearhead had an oval shape to it to keep it from sticking in the opponent. A stylized steel counterweight was fixed at the butt, polished to a mirror shine. Angus was proud of that spear.

Chapter 2

The Big News!

Vern and Ylus were still a long way off when the forward lookout saw them. Had they been enemy scouts, they would have come no nearer – Bary Thunderclub was a genius with a four iron. But these men were known to the dwarves; they were local farmers who made annual visits exchanging barley, oats, and hops for quality steel tools and silver coin. After observing from his hidden outpost for a few moments, Bary scrawled a quick note onto a tiny lead sheet, attached it to one of the messenger rats' harnesses, and set it running along the ancient tunnels towards the gatehouse.

Kelly Siegebreaker held command of the Argentine Holtgart. When the rat delivered its message, it was Kelly who got the news. "Angus! Open the dwarf-gate!" He continued to bark orders to other guards as he made his way to the offices of Artemus, the Mountain King. Even traders were an unusual occurrence, drawing crowds of dwarves hungry for news of the outside world. But today was not a scheduled trading day. Soon, the open plaza just inside the gates was lined with hundreds of the stout folk, many standing on crates and barrels to get a better view.

By the time the men came within sight of the dwarf-gate, the commander assumed his place on the turreted balcony just above the main gates. "Who approaches the hallowed halls of the Argentine Holt?" he intoned. The balcony had been cleverly placed to cause Kelly's voice to reverberate and boom with authority. It had the desired effect. The men's mounts shied and reared, and they exchanged nervous glances.

"We come with news," replied Vern. "Usually it could wait until our next trading day, but this we thought you should hear right away." His voice was audible from his vantage point but seemed only a weak, wavering whisper compared to Kelly's rumbling reply.

"You may enter as friends of the Argentine Holt. Please, come in, share a drink, and tell your tale!"

They started in before the invitation was complete, with an urgency akin to the desire to come in out of the rain. Ylus kept looking over his shoulder – at the clear, spring sky. Both men dismounted at the five-foot-tall gate, stooping their necks to pass. Watching the horses crouch-walk through the too-short door was almost comical. Once inside, a dwarven groom took the horses to the stables. Thanking him, the men walked on to stand before the Mountain King.

"Bring us some stout!" Artemus bellowed, sending a half dozen dwarves scrambling. "Come! Sit with me and tell us of your news!" Two short stools, properly sized for a four-foot-tall person, were brought in front of the dais. The men sat with their knees high and backs curved, looking very uncomfortable. "What brings you here on this fine High Lode[1] morning?"

Vern started right in. "Well your highness, there is a problem you should know about. It started with livestock disappearing in the night. First old Dolen's cattle, then others. We thought it the work of bandits in the beginning, but then we found tracks. Rather, we found where the tracks ended. A hundred stone cow could be tracked through a wet field, then the tracks just vanished." One of the dwarves arrived with a pair of lacquered pewter tankards; Vern set to the business of draining his in one draught. Ylus started to

---

[1] Dwarves spend most of their lives underground. They learned long ago how to cultivate moss, mushrooms and other plants that don't need much light. The eyeless fish native to the pitch-black pools and the half-wild albino boars that subsist on the refuse piles provide all the protein they need. The temperature inside the mountain remains constant. All of this makes what humans know as seasons somewhat irrelevant; so dwarves discovered other ways of marking time. They found that subtle variations in the earth's magnetic field could be measured by marking where a magnet pointed. This was accomplished with a spherical room with a perfect cone standing in the center, the 'Lodebeam' balanced atop it. The Lodebeam is a long, hollow rod carved from natural lodestone. It is fitted with a gemstone lens at either end; when backlit with an oil lamp it focuses a narrow beam of light at the exact distance of the wall allowing for very precise measurements. The northern wall where the beam is focused is home to a very rare and valuable form of lichen that stores light – where the beam falls, it glows for weeks afterward, leaving a radiant record of the recent movements. The result is a system for marking time which is regular yet has no dependence on the sun. High Lode is the time when the Lodebeam shines on its highest point; a natural time of celebration for dwarves.

look pale – he had heard rumors about the potency of dwarvish stout. Dark, flavorful and almost thick enough to stand a fork in, they said. This being the first time he had been offered a drink, he felt stuck between not wanting to offend his hosts and wanting to keep his liver healthy. Ylus was roused from his silent reverie when Vern finished and came up for air.

"Oh! Yes, that helps. Yes. Where was I? Oh – where were the cattle – that was the next part." Vern wiped the remnants of the frothy head from his moustache. "It took some time before we figured it out. Some said there must be witches, others suggested that it was all a prank put on by bored youngsters – but the truth presented itself two days ago.

"It," he began, eyes flitting from one dwarf to the next, all in rapt attention, "was… it was…"

Vern forcefully traded his empty tankard for Ylus' full one. As he chugged a second quart of dwarven stout – a mighty feat for a mere human – a concerned murmur rose from the assembly. What would cause him to have such a hard time telling his story? What could it possibly be? They daren't hope…

"Two days ago, a dragon flew into the town square. A *Dragon*! He just flew in, landed, ate Bradley the baker in a single bite, and then he – he – *spoke*…" Vern paused, pinching his upper lip with a quaking hand and staring off into space. Ylus sat looking at the empty tankard in his hand, considering whether he should have drunk the stout after all.

"He actually *spoke*," Vern continued, "and made sense. He delivered a monologue. None of us knew they could do that! We thought they were dumb, murderous animals, and that was it!" There was a collective chuckle from the dwarves; as an adult might when a child learned that the tooth fairy looked suspiciously like their mother.

Vern went on. "He told us that we were to help him. If we did, he would leave us alone and let most of our livestock live. If not, he would be back to eat us all and burn the village to the ground; and he said he'd find out what he wanted to know anyway." He raised his empty tankard and rocked it to indicate the need for a refill. "He gave us a week. We are simple farmers, not warriors. We don't have a king or country. We've always kept to ourselves and are generally left alone. But this," he waved behind him in the direction of the gate, "is happening. So we came to you first."

During the telling, Artemus moved progressively from his usual semi-reclined state to leaning full forward, hands on knees in anticipation. His tankard had not been touched. "Well! This is good news! Great news! And to come on High Lode – it portends well! We shall rid you of this foul beast at once. Do you know where it roosts? Can you describe it fully, so we can properly prepare?" He spoke in a matter-of-fact tone, as if this were a broken plow to be fixed, with no danger involved. There was no doubt that it could be done, not a trace of hesitation. Several of the dwarves cheered, and everyone murmured assent.

Ylus had had enough. "This is madness!" he snapped. "We haven't told you what it – he – wanted! There is more, you know!" He lowered his voice and continued. "This is a beast of epic proportions. Truly immense. Dragon is an appropriate term. If he were to stretch his wings, he could touch both sides of this chamber! He called himself Szicthys and said he had come for a Reason. He said he had returned to reclaim his hereditary nest and would lure a harem of she-Dragons with news of his glorious victory. He intends to make it his stronghold, a new capital for Dragonhood here in the land of plenty." He took in the dwarves, scanning right and left. They grinned one and all, whispering and murmuring with each other. Their continued giddiness put him off balance.

Ylus stood now, breathing hard and sweating. But he kept on. "He said that his forbears had been defeated here - right here - over a thousand years ago by a treacherous tunneling army. His father and the rest of his family were slain, and his mother forced to find a new home in the eastern wastes, where he was hatched. He said he has made himself ready for battle and is sure of success. You didn't ask what he wanted. He wants directions. To the Argentine Holt! He isn't here for us, he's here for *you*."

A full second passed without a sound. Then it happened; the thunderous roar of applause, cheers, and tears of joy. The dwarves surged forward, closing the gap and raising the men on their shoulders, dancing jigs and singing songs. Ale, stout and dwarven brandy appeared as if from nowhere, and the party went on for hours…

…Except for Angus. He was still dwarfing the gate. He did hear the humans' story from his post, however, and his mind raced with the possibilities. It was a lot to take in. The spell was only broken by the sound of dwarven boots thundering up the stairway; for a moment he wondered if the Dragon had come on cue. But the four dwarves who burst through the door were carrying a portable party; a large roasted boar haunch dripping with fat, a freshly tapped keg, two bottles of brandy and five ornate steins. They were Angus' oldest friends; about the same age, they had grown up together.

Dylaen, Flannan, Neill, and Gierman were smiling and laughing, having already enjoyed a full share of the libations. "What would a fellow do without fellows like you?" Angus asked rhetorically, returning his friends' mirth. They set about setting up, using whatever they could find to make a circle to sit in, the keg dead center with the bottles and food on top like a bistro table.

When they had settled in, Niell spoke first. Diminutive even for a dwarf, he was well into his first century as the apprentice to the Chronicler. After another hundred years, he might be allowed to write something down! "Well lads, I have to say there is nothing quite like a Dragon to give one a true sense of purpose." That brought nods all around. "I've been going over the names of the heroes most likely to strike a killing blow. I've got a good guess; I don't suppose you lot would like to set a wager, would you?"

"It wouldn't really be fair, Niell. I'm going to kill the Dragon." Indeed, Flannan might possibly do it; he was a true prodigy with his unique sword. Were he a bit older, he may have understood that when the elder swordmasters said he fought like an elf, it was so. But Flannan, like all five of these young dwarves, had never even met an elf, much less fought one. Flannan may have been on Niell's list, but still not near the top.

"I'm afraid not, Flannan. Unless you plan to romance the beast, I think Angus would stand a better chance with that bloody great spear of his." Everyone laughed at Niell's jibe; Angus would be locked up in the gatehouse where he would see none of the fighting.

Gierman chimed in next. "I think maybe Hamish could bash its brains in with his great hammer. Brute force may not be as fancy as that Elven swordplay of yours, but you can't argue its effectiveness. My money is on Hamish." Gierman was often of the opinion that a bigger hammer could solve most problems. If nothing else, they made the problems flatter.

"I like the diggers' chances." If anyone were to stand up for the simple miners, Dylaen was him. As always, he had his father's gilt pick leaning against his chair. "I'm not saying that it'd be a pick, mind; just a digger. Blasting powder may be involved. I'll get in on the bet if I can say that any active digger could do the job…"

The talking, drinking, and haggling over odds went well into the night. In the end, Niell had a scroll with several dozen wagers and two possible results. Either one dwarf would win it all but pay for an evening of fun out of his winnings, or the pot would be spent in the same way – with a strong commitment to spend it all in one night. All five dug deep into their savings for the wagers; one way or the other, there was a party coming!

Chapter 3

Here's the Plan

The sun was high in the sky when Vern and Ylus dismounted to eat a bit of lunch. Their hosts had put on an amazing party. How they could drink so much and remain functional seemed at odds with dwarves typically diminutive stature. When the men came to in the late morning, one of the dwarves handed them meat pies for the road; a polite way of suggesting they leave.

As the men ate the pies right out of their cleverly folded foil wrappings, Vern looked back. What he saw would be described as looking at an anthill from four feet away, but this was no anthill. The mouth of the Argentine Holt was crawling with dwarves preparing for the coming battle. Mostly younger dwarves were scaling the bluffs that competently hid the yawning cavern mouth which housed the entrance to the Argentine Holt. Try as he might, Vern didn't understand what they were doing, or how it would help with the recent Dragon problem. Yet he continued to ponder while chewing his pie.

Ylus broke the silence first. "Quite a party." His delivery was as dry as the desert in late summer. "If I didn't know better, I'd think they were excited to have an undefeatable, mythical beast over to visit."

"They aren't human, Ylus." Vern's voice betrayed the resignation he felt heavily. "Dwarves don't think the same way we do. I don't understand them either, but they've always been our allies, and those I have known personally are true friends. I have no idea how they intend to do it, but they seem convinced that the problem is well in hand. I will agree with you about the party though. I've got the headache to stand witness, too!"

"That's another thing," Ylus said, "after all the drinking, joking, and incessant bungled attempts at song and dance, how are they all so chipper? By the time we roused, they were already in full swing! It can't be healthy!"

Vern sighed. "The Creator didn't grant them good looks, beautiful voices or even a modicum of grace. I guess we can't begrudge them their extremely resilient constitution. They've got to have something!" They both laughed and turned back towards the Holt to watch as they finished eating.

The men missed most of Artemus' speech, but here is what the dwarven king had said to the assembled people early that morning:

"Good people of the Argentine Holt hear me! I stand in awe of what we have accomplished here. A mere twelve hundred years ago, these grand caverns were nothing more than a dark, dank roost for the filthy, useless creatures we call Dragons. The very spot I'm standing on right now marks the highest point of the pile of silver and gold they used as a nest; their unholy spawn incubating here and there, encased in the soft, semi-molten metals they were coated in. It was twenty years after we arrived that we finally had the spaces cleared of bones, feces and other discards. Only then did we have a full understanding of how glorious this place could be. And here we are, more than a millennium later; one of the greatest Holts in the world!

"Now we are told that we missed one; that one of the Dragon dams escaped, still forming an egg as she fled. That egg was tended, and the hatchling has grown, learned of his past, and returned to claim his birthright. He says this place is his; what do we say to that?"

An echo of the previous night, the dwarves as one shouted, laughed, jeered; the clamor reverberated throughout the great hall. It was hard to make out any one voice, but the message was clear: "Go ahead and try it, Dragon. See what happens. We dare you." As the noise subsided, Artemus went on.

"Will we prevail? Absolutely. But we will need to plan carefully, prepare diligently and execute brilliantly. We were victorious in our last meeting only because we found a secret way in and ambushed the Dragons that were roosting here while they slept. We don't have that luxury this time, but I have a plan that should give us a similar advantage. This Dragon has been marauding as his way of getting ready for a fight with us; we don't want to meet him out in the open. Not even just in front of the gates; he might still get away.

"We need to take away his advantages. We will remove the option of flight. We will make his bulk a liability. And we shall take his fire from him. How can we do all of this?" Artemus' serious face turned wickedly amused, a half-sneer, half-smile showing teeth through his silver beard. "We let him in."

There were a couple of muffled gasps, but Artemus let the idea sink in. He had been a leader for a long time and knew that a thoughtful silence from the audience could be as valuable as a howling crowd on the edge of sanity; sometimes even more so. When enough of the wondering faces turned to knowing smiles, Artemus outlined the rest of the plan.

"We will clear the atrium. We will seal the doors and windows of the shops and homes that line the mall. We will close the connecting doors. We will let him enter, and when he is in, we shall drop the portcullis behind him. The atrium is too small for him to fly, and he will not be able to flee.

"The stone floor will be sown with flour, half an inch thick. When he is in and realizes his predicament, we break open the upper cistern to create a flash flood - which should quickly turn the flour into a slippery slurry. That is how we turn his bulk against him. If things work out right, we might even be able to douse his fire; but at least the amount of water should make it easier to get out of trouble if things get heated.

"This is where our champions will enter the fray. With special cleats designed to navigate our slippery, slurried floors, they should have a solid base from which to mount an assault. I invite anyone ready to do battle to participate, but a dozen pair of cleats are reserved for our most distinguished warriors.

"Mungan Longspear will have a place front and center; all he needs to find is one chink in the Dragon's armor, and we'll have lizard shish kebab for supper! Steafan Silvernose will be at his side, of course; mind you don't get your pick stuck this time, Steafan... ah, and Uspaig Ogrebane will be out there, starting trouble; Stiubert has promised to bring out that ghastly longsword he got from the traders; it's crude but effective... I'm hoping to see some of the longbeards get into the action, but I wouldn't presume to assume; who knows, maybe I'll be inspired to take a swing!

"Everyone will have the opportunity, in proper order. I've talked with our noble tradesdwarves and looked into the treasury, and we've come up with some rewards. First, we've put together a large chest of silver coins. These coins are to be split between any dwarves that manage to get close and take a swing. Also, a chest of gold coins will be divided among those that make solid contact. A panel of longbeards will be watching and will make the awards. Those that do visible damage will get some of the gems from this sack, but the real prize will go to the dwarf that issues the killing blow.

"That dwarf will receive a customized suit of Holtgart Armor. It was last worn by Dannl Dragonbane and has been on display since his peaceful passing three hundred and sixty years ago. Also, one of Yuri Stoneblade's coveted Blood Onyx axes – said to absorb blood from your opponent, each Blood Onyx weapon gains color and character as it is used.

Lastly, the brandy makers have put together a wagonload of their finest vintages; it should last at least a week! I'll also put in one of my favorite siege bows for good measure.

A buzz brewed amongst the dwarves since the armor was announced. Tried and tested technology like mithril plate appeals to dwarves, and this Blood Onyx was still too new for some to be sure of. Everyone, however, enjoyed the promise of brandy.

Chapter 4

You Can't Argue with Success

The Argentine Holt was built into a natural cavern system, the mouth hidden by a deep, curving canyon; which in turn was hard to differentiate from the hundreds of other small canyons that issued from the west face of the butte. Indeed, the Holt's greatest defense was the fact that it was hard to find, and only a few farmers and traders knew how to navigate the foothills, creeks and scattered copses of pine and oak. To further keep the secret, each authorized visitor had been taught his own path; by rule not shared with others. This meant that there was no well-established trail or road in.

Now the dwarves wanted to advertise their location to attract a Dragon. Generations of work to hide the entrance was likely to frustrate their plans. They needed a way to stand out. The solution was provided by old Yoric Shadowhand. His propensity for shadow puppets had always been regarded as little more than a diversion for dwarf children, but now he put it to work. Yoric brought out the largest Dragon skull from the museum, that of the last male Dragon to live here. He set about using the canyon walls and a bonfire to make an all-night shadow Dragon show. The hope was that Szicthys would be flying at night, and would see the flickering flames from the bonfire, and if he got close enough, he would see the skull-shadow and become enraged.

Inside, it took all of the flour stores in the Holt to make the slurry trap; quite an expensive plan indeed. Hours of spreading and smoothing left little evidence that anything was out of the ordinary - until tread upon. The humans had been sent with bags of silver coin to secure new supplies. They had been pleasantly surprised at the large order and seemed to understand the pressing need. After all, Dwarves were known for their affinity for baked goods.

The cistern had been rigged to drop tens of thousands of gallons of water in one swoop; a makeshift spout with an upturned lip was the best they could manage to try to get the water to hit the Dragon's face. The doors and windows, and most of the connecting tunnels had been sealed with clay and wax in an effort to keep the water in place; the tapestries and all other water-vulnerable items had been moved out as well.

Every smith and cobbler in the Holt worked on turning out as many sets of cleats as possible. They consisted of dozens of quarter inch long, pointed spikes set into a hard leather sandal, intended to be strapped on over boots or sollerets. In order to gain traction on the smooth stone floor, a very high-carbon steel was utilized, with all its involved processes. Hundreds of sets had been produced by the end of the day and distributed amongst the warriors and longbeards. Angus, of course, did not receive a set.

Every single dwarf in the Holt did his or her part to make the plan a reality; most not sleeping for the duration, working non-stop. The cost of this one attack would be the most expensive in dwarven history, and its success would earn the Argentine Holt a place in the annals of legend. By extension, each dwarf in the Holt would be able to say that they played their part in slaying a Dragon; a rare and wonderful opportunity.

Angus' part was to dwarf the gate. The first task was to check and maintain all of the machinery for the gate mechanism. Like the other dwarves of the Holt, Angus took his job very seriously and inspected every part. Everything was cleaned and oiled, tested and rehearsed. He wouldn't get a chance at the Dragon directly, but he would play his part at the beginning of the battle; it would be his closing of the gate that trapped the Dragon. That would make for a tale worth a few beers at any other Holt, to say the least. He did have his spear with him. He thought he might throw it at the beast if he got a good shot at it; but only after it was inside, and after those dwarves who really deserved the right to take a swing had done so.

As night fell, the dwarves began to take their places for combat. Most of the warriors packed the stairways leading up into the galleries and even the gatehouse. The idea was to wait for the trap and the flood, then spring out from all directions at once, after the Dragon was closed in, doused and on unsure footing.

Thus began Angus' long waiting game. Until the Dragon arrived and entered, he had to keep his foot on the pedal to ensure the gate stayed open and the portcullis remained raised. He dutifully stood rooted to the spot. Several dwarves were assigned to keep the bonfire burning brightly, and scouts were hidden out and about on the landscape to warn of Szicthys' approach. Hours passed.

----- -----

Szicthys lifted off from the pasture with yet another bovine morsel in his maw. It mooed, yet it didn't struggle much. Domesticated. It just wasn't any fun to take an animal that looks at you when you approach, as if to ask, "have you brought food?" No chase, no struggle, just this inane mooing. He tossed the cow high and in front of him, and as it fell, he swooped, jaws wide, and swallowed it whole. He had finally reached his full adult size, and he really didn't need to eat as much as he had been, but he felt it important to instill terror in the humans below; he certainly couldn't let them think they could fight him.

Soon, he would rule these valleys and hills. Farmers would leave out animals for his sustenance. This would be just part of the required tithe, of course; the occasional virgin strapped bare to a rock could mark the summer and winter solstice, for instance. Who knew? Maybe he would demand a statue to his greatness in the larger towns.

His fame would spread over time. Dragon dams would flock to compete to be his mate. Over several hundred years he would settle on a few prime specimens and eat the rest. And with the roost reclaimed, they would use the same gold and silver to coat their eggs, the old way; the way of his ancestors.

Along the way, he planned to enjoy the dwarvish snacks that would sneak in. The Dragon counted on dwarves' inherent disregard of reason and personal safety to help him in his victory. After he had taken the roost, they would sneak in to attack him in his sleep for a while, but he was in his prime; he really didn't need to sleep. Still, he would pretend, and build his legend as the undefeatable Dragon Szicthys.

He gained quite a bit of altitude as his thoughts wandered when something below caught his eye. Distant yellow and orange lights shimmered and flashed from far to the west. Fire. His first thought was territorial. If there was another adult male dragon in the area, he would need to be dealt with first. He could have glided in, being so high; but fierce competitiveness drove him to fly faster. Within three powerful wingbeats, his speed was so great he had to close his clear inner eyelids for the buffeting by the wind.

Velocity was his. Only a few minutes had passed, and he had traversed miles. Szicthys had truly become a fearsome dragon; he had slain two of his own kind already. His fighting style was aggressive and ruthless; and as soon as he knew he had won, he tended to toy with opponents before finishing them. He had taken individual humans and destroyed small towns that dared to attack him in return.

Over six hundred years passed since his hatching. After enduring centuries of incubating encased in soft metals that his mother kept warm and pliable with her breath, he was raised in squalor. His mother shamefully hunted at night, trying to keep their presence a secret for decades. She had died when he was still young, defending him from residents of a nearby town when they discovered where their cattle had been taken. Szicthys had cowered deep in the cave at the time, not yet ready to fight. His revenge came some eighty years later when he cooked and ate every resident of that town; many of them the grandchildren and great-grandchildren of the men who killed his mother.

Revenge was close again now; he would find these dwarves soon. Some would die immediately, but he looked forward to years of stragglers. They would suffer greatly. They would suffer as he had.

As he neared the butte, a recurring image appeared on a cliff face, framed by firelight. It was reminiscent of a Dragon, but not quite right. Drawing closer, he saw clearly - a skull, illuminated from behind. A great Dragon skull! It was probably being used in some unholy ritual; he would see that it was properly burned to ash, and the desecrators punished.

Circling overhead, he saw a couple of people feeding the fire; but not the number he expected. He descended to see more clearly and realized that the people were dwarves. As he hit the northern apex of his wheel, the cavern came into view, with the dwarvish wall and gatehouse closing it off – the gate was open! Not wanting to waste the opportunity, he dove towards it, aiming to land just in front of the gate.

This was too good to be true! He had prepared speeches to taunt the dwarves into opening the gate, practiced throwing boulders from flight to try and bash the walls down; and here was the gate sitting open! He would land and run straight in, taking them all by surprise!

----- -----

The shouts came in rapid succession; "He's coming!" and "He's here!" – and Kelly Siegebreaker howled for Angus to hold his position. Angus had a front row seat and was taken aback at the sheer size of the beast. Brown, almost bronze skin covered the thing; taut, bulging muscles worked visibly. Scars from untold battles marked the entire body. It landed and folded its wings immediately; it was taking the bait! As the dragon swept the walls with great gusts of billowing flame, the dwarf took a half-step back from the outer arrow slit.

Extinguishing a small patch of burning red beard with one hand, Angus' mind went in several directions. Part of him thought of an escape, another felt a deep respect for this creature, and how rare it was. What a time to live in, to see combat with a full-grown Dragon!

Szicthys started right in towards the now-smoking gate, and Angus realized he wouldn't be able to see the action until he dropped the portcullis; his mind worked quickly to come up with a solution. His spear! He set the heavy butt of his spear on the pedal and took a step toward the inner arrow slit for a better view. Angus maintained a firm grip on the shaft to ensure the pedal stayed depressed. The dwarves in the stairway were buzzing; this was the way it should be. Everything working exactly as planned. It never went this well. They were sure to win!

Looking down through the interior arrow slit, Angus saw the nostrils peek through, serpentine tendrils of smoke rising lazily from them. The Dragon's eyes came into view; glossy dark protrusions, ovoid irises dilating clearly. Szicthys turned his head from side to side on that long, muscular neck, then moved his ponderous bulk forward. Angus was mesmerized by the power, majesty, terror that radiated from the creature. He likely would not have enough control to even hold his weapon, were he face-to-face with this dragon.

It was right at that moment that the butt of Angus' spear slipped, triggering the dead dwarf's pedal. He sprang to engage the safety, but it was too late. The several-ton steel-and-silver portcullis rumbled down, faster than thought. Szicthys tried to look up at the noise, but his head was forced down as the heavy portcullis fell onto his neck with a sickening crunch. While the impact didn't quite sever the head, it did break the Dragon's neck and smash several vital veins and vessels.

The dwarf that was stationed at the cistern heard the rumble of the portcullis and did his duty. One swift blow with a sledgehammer and the release valve was severed from the tank. The vast volume of water that was the dwarves' main water supply burst out and flooded the main chamber; kicking up flour dust as it hit the floor. A keen observer would see that it did, in fact, make the intended slippery soup; but the dwarves weren't really paying attention to that.

They were listening for the signaling sound of rushing water; upon hearing it, they as one leaped out of the stairways, battle cries and curses for all Dragon kind on their lips. To a dwarf, they all knew within a dozen steps that it was already over. Confusion was the first emotion to come out, followed by countless tirades of colorful dwarvish phrases and epithets.

The last thing the great Dragon Szicthys saw was a flood of water raising an odd powdery cloud in front of it; like laying on the beach, watching the foamy after-wave running along the sand, mist rising. There was a percussive steamy hiss as the water crashed over his captive face and doused his smoldering flame sacs. As his vision faded, he knew his mission of revenge had failed.

The foul-mouthed cacophony lasted half a minute before being broken by Artemus, who was watching from one of the galleries. "Angus Redbeard! Get out here!" Angus was reluctant to comply – he would have to get by a very upset Kelly Siegebreaker first. He picked his spear up and ran out anyway; avoiding eye contact as he passed Kelly. As he entered the main hall to stand before Artemus, he saw that Kelly wasn't the only angry dwarf present.

"Yes, sire?" Angus hadn't spoken directly to Artemus very often and wasn't comfortable in front of a crowd. He dreaded what was to come.

"Angus, you have done something," the Mountain King fought to maintain his composure, "Something that is hard for me to come to terms with. The dwarf in me is outraged that you would dare to take this honor from so many deserving dwarves." A murmur of assent rose at that, including a few "hear, hear's" and one "hang him now!" Artemus continued. "Here you are, approaching the end of your first century - barely an adult - in the company of veteran Holtgart, proven heroes, and even some who were here the last time we faced dragons. According to our custom, you had no right to take the killing blow until all worthier dwarves had made an attempt." More noises of assent; his description was truly fair.

Artemus let his breath out noisily and pursed his lips while taking a deep breath through his nose. He licked his lips and squinted, tilting his head a fraction. He continued; every word meted out with exaggerated enunciation. "But the King in me is astonished. Not at the audacity of being out of order but recognizing that you were inspired at the last minute with a better plan and that you had the presence of mind to execute it perfectly. The King in me says that you are a true hero." Angus tried not to squirm; no one had seen how it had actually happened – could he pull it off as being the way Artemus had portrayed it? It occurred to him that this might be his only way to avoid prison, or worse.

Chapter 5

Into the World

Cleaning the floors and reopening sealed doors and windows took any time that might have led to a party. The ale and brandy flowed, to be sure, and a few songs rose; but it was more of a work party than celebration. The flour was the worst part; as the water drained and evaporated, it left behind sticky glue on every lower surface. This was shoveled into barrels and loaded onto wagons to be taken down to the boar sties. Subterranean boars are not, as a rule, picky eaters.

The Dragon was left where it lay overnight. Several artists had been commissioned to capture the moment, busily sketching the scene while apprentices were taking copious notes. In the morning, it would be butchered. There were in the world a number of cultures that prized certain parts of Dragons for medicinal or ceremonial purposes, and those would be preserved and sealed in jars and barrels for sale. The bulk of the bones would be used for weapon or tool handles, and some of the less useful bones would be ground into 'dragon-bone powder' which would also fetch a high price.

The dwarves also harvested the Dragon's scales to be used in armor-making, and its horns and claws would find new uses as well. Most of the meat would be set aside for salting, with the most tender cuts (as tender as one can find on such a long-lived beast) being cooked for a dinner in honor of the Dragonbane. The defleshed skull would be added to the museum, next to the largest one that had attracted the Dragon. A golden plaque would be affixed to the snout, inscribed with the story as told by Artemus. Angus' place in history was certainly assured.

Angus did his part of the work with the rest. He was eager to do anything he could to feel like he was still just like everyone else. It would never be the same, however. Angus was now - officially

– a Hero. The fact that it had happened by grand accident instead of skill and perseverance dampened his enthusiasm for his new name greatly. He shoveled until there was no more to shovel and helped with the doors and windows after that. When he finally turned in the only dwarves still going were the artists; not much he could do there. Angus also avoided being posed with the Dragon; that would have been just too much for him to bear.

He trudged back to the alcove he shared with his father, with his still unproven spear across his shoulders like a water bar. Only a few oil lamps still burned, and the way was dark, but dwarves have excellent night vision, and Angus could have made his way in almost total darkness. He opened the latch and lifted to take the weight of the door off the floor – the wood was slowly rotting and needed to be replaced. Inside, Floin Thunderpick sat in his padded chair, smoking his signature long pipe thoughtfully. "That was quite a thing you did today, boy."

There was no way around it. When Angus' father wanted to talk to him, it didn't pay to let him stew. Angus moved a three-legged stool to make a place for himself in front of his father, poured two tall mugs of mulled mead from the cast iron vessel Floin had placed on their small, pot-bellied stove, and sat down, handing the second cup to his father. When Floin had taken a sip, Angus did the same. Floin tossed his son the leather scrip of pipeweed. Angus nodded as he caught it and produced his own pipe from his vest. He completed the family ritual by taking a few puffs, then giving Floin his full and undivided attention.

"I'll start by saying I'm proud of you, boy. I'll not pretend that it's as I expected; I don't suppose anyone can say that. I've never heard of a Dragon being slain by portcullis, and once word spreads, I doubt it will ever work again. Personally, I had great faith in Artemus' plan, but we'll never know now." Floin took a long draw from his pipe and puffed it out rhythmically, making a series of circles, each within the next. "I've been wondering where you got the inspiration to take matters into your own hands. It's not a trait you've shown before, and you certainly didn't get it from me."

Angus shrugged. "I can't really explain my actions, Da. It just sort of happened before I knew what was going on." His fingers moved uncomfortably over the scrimshaw carvings on his pipe. "I can only assume that a deeper power was at work."

"That sounds like something your mother would have said, boy. Things just seemed to 'happen' around her, too. Not always for the good, I'm afraid." Floin's voice remained stable, but a tear formed at the corner of his eye. "I still don't understand why she fell. Thousands of pits in this cavern system, and she finds the only one without a bottom to fall into!" Angus could see the memories flashing through his dad's mind; he let Floin reminisce in silence while he tended to his mead.

After a few moments, Floin returned to the present, a slight smile in his eyes. "Tell me. How did it feel, boy? Knowing that you had done what no dwarf had in over a thousand years? When you heard the foul beast's neck pierced by your portcullis, what went through your mind?"

"I guess I was in shock. I hadn't expected to even be in the fight, and then I had killed it, with barely the blink of an eye in between. I couldn't predict it myself. That shock hasn't worn off, and it has been joined by a bit of mortification that I had acted out of turn, and in so doing, taken the chance from the real Heroes. Da, I don't know where I stand anymore. Yesterday I was the lowest of the Holtgart, a youth with only a hint of direction. Today, I am a Dragonbane. *The* Dragonbane, Hero of the Argentine Holt. I'm ninety, Da. I'm ninety and I have no greater deed to look forward to!"

Floin stroked his beard and sighed deeply. "You understand my concern then. I would have felt the same way. But what you should do – must do – is to find something greater to aspire to. I can't think of what that might be, either. You've slain a Dragon, boy! Enjoy the moment and look for a greater. Now, let's finish our mead and call it a night. I understand Artemus will want to talk with you in the morning."

The morning came too quickly for Angus' taste. He got cleaned up and dressed for work before breaking his fast quietly with his father. When he stepped out onto the underground avenue, the Holt buzzed with everyday life; you might not know that a Dragon was being butchered at the main gates. Not wanting to have any more uncomfortable conversations, he took a somewhat circuitous route to avoid the more crowded areas. He even entered the gatehouse from the far side when he saw some of the Holtgart clustered around the rapidly shrinking bulk of Dragon.

Climbing the stairs, Angus walked all the way in without being stopped. The last thing he expected was to find his cozy work area in the heart of the gatehouse occupied by none other than Mountain King Artemus. Standing with his hands folded behind his back, Artemus was looking into his mountain fortress, through the very same arrow slit Angus had stood at the day before. He tilted his head downward as Angus entered, looking at the still-whole head of Szicthys – it still lay where it had fallen.

"It was an accident, wasn't it?" Artemus' tone was rhetorical. "I saw you from my balcony, standing here as it happened. The only problem with that..." he trailed off and looked over his shoulder at the dead-pedal – a full six feet away. "You must have used the butt of your spear to hold the pedal down and come to stand here to watch the battle unfold. A very clever way to watch the battle; with an unintended consequence. I suppose I might have done the same, a long, long time ago."

Angus stepped over to the workbench and laid down his lunch sack. He had no idea what to say. Artemus had the truth of it; nothing he could say would make the situation better. He decided that speaking could make it a lot worse. Turning back to Artemus, he assumed his best soldierly pose and waited for Artemus to continue.

"Don't think you can convince me that you will follow orders by standing at attention after this. Taking your foot off that pedal before Kelly gave the order was at best dereliction of duty, and at worst, treason." He let that last sink in for a moment; it was not something to be said lightly, nor did he mean it so. Angus wisely remained silent. "Understand fully that the next time you disobey a direct order will be your last.

"On the other hand, to call you down for this publicly would not benefit the Holt. The people have a victory, if not in the way they had hoped, and I won't take that away from them. They will have the illusion of your tactical brilliance and composure in the heat of battle. It will be incumbent upon you to realize this notion; you must become the great dwarf that your recent credentials declare you to be. Are you willing to accept this challenge, or would you rather face charges?"

Angus didn't hesitate. "I am willing, my lord. I am a loyal King's dwarf, and your wish is my command. Being honest, I'm afraid I don't know what to do or how to go about being a great dwarf."

"I'm glad you chose the right, Angus Redbeard. It is difficult to be a person of note; it took several hundred years before I had accomplished enough to be taken seriously by the longbeards. Even though it is mine by right of blood, I had to prove myself to my subjects first. Your great deed is dubious at the moment, but with more deeds to back this one, it will gain legitimacy over time. You have perhaps a year to cement your standing as a hero in a way that would normally take half a lifetime. So, we will create a framework of potential; trials that you will face with your actual talents as they are now and as they will be in the near future."

Angus imagined the Games as the framework; a series of physical challenges to be met in public. He had never done well in the Games, with a middling performance in most cases. It just didn't seem feasible.

Artemus took up his monologue again. "You will leave the Holt for a time. The Chronicler approached me late last night and reminded me of ancient treaties from a time when Dwarf and Elf and Man were united in a common cause. They are long past, and very few will even remember them, but they provide us with a Reason for you to leave the Holt and visit cultures that we lost contact with long ago. One of the common provisions of these treaties is the relation of news. When an event of great importance happens, one of the people involved must bring news to the other peoples. This must happen quickly before rumor spreads and the truth of the matter is misunderstood. It can be argued, Angus Dragonbane, that you are the only person who was actually involved; ergo the only one legally able to fulfill these treaties. And the only one legally bound to the same."

Leave the Holt! Was Artemus mad? Angus still had a full, red beard – as a rule, no dwarf ventured farther than a few miles until fully grey!

"My Lord," Angus began, but Artemus interrupted him.

"I am not finished with you yet! I cannot bring myself to leave your mutinous behavior unpunished. I will have your spear since you cannot seem to hold the butt end of it still. Moreover, you are not to touch a spear again until I so order it!"

Angus gasped, wondering briefly whether a swift execution would be a preferable resolution. No, he decided quickly. But he did feel that his most prized possession deserved better treatment than to be tossed across the floor carelessly. With great ceremony he lifted his spear, knelt and offered it to Artemus. "It shall be as you desire, my Lord."

"You will wait here until your relief arrives. He will have something for you to do. Do it immediately, and then instruct him in the essential operations of the gate. When you are finished, make your way to the Armory to be outfitted with your new gear. After that, go back to your home and pack whatever else you deem necessary to your journey on the wagon that will be waiting there. You leave before nightfall, for the Old Forest southeast of here. Do you have any questions?"

Angus did not.

"Fine then, it is settled. I'll see you off this evening."

Angus stood agape as Artemus strode out. He had to leave the Holt, alone, tonight. No spear, ever. That stung; he would have a hard time explaining the missing spear to his friends. Mind swimming, he waited for his relief. When it did come, it came as a properly grey-bearded dwarf, already a seasoned member of the Holtgart. He handed a plaque to Angus, and said simply, "The King wants this put in an appropriate place." Angus read it quickly and hung it over the portcullis station. He gave terse instruction on gate operation and protocol, then started down the stairs. "'No polearms allowed in this room', eh?" he muttered, following it with a string of barely audible but very colorful curses.

He arrived at the Armory only a few minutes later. It had always been one of his favorite places; it contained an entire wall dedicated solely to spears. This visit, however, he ignored that wall completely and moved on to the armor master's bench. Odhar Freeplate was one of the best armor makers in the craft and had worked through the night to customize a special suit of Holtgart armor for Angus. It was made largely of overlapping, cleverly contoured mithril plates with a light mithril chain shirt underneath. Head to toe, it moved well while protecting excellently. Further, it was worked with Dragon inspired themes which culminated at what Odhar called a 'Dragonmaw Helm,' complete with articulated visor. With the visor closed, it looked much like a miniature, silvery dragon's head; with the visor raised, it appeared as if Angus' head was sticking out of the gaping mouth. It had been modified to fit him exactly, though it was several generations old.

Mithril itself merits discussion. It is an exceedingly rare metal, with no mines actively producing it. In point of fact, hundreds of years passed since the last vein was mined out. Other than its scarcity, the innate qualities of the metal are beyond remarkable. As strong as high-carbon steel at half the weight, it makes for excellent weapons and armor. It does not corrode and can be differentiated from other precious metals by a slight bluish tinge. In sunlight, mithril reflects and refracts with an oddly gem-like quality. For a dwarf, the feel of mithril against one's skin is akin to how a human might enjoy a fine fur.

Angus was also given one of Artemus' famous siege bows. It was a large crossbow with three bows stacked, activated by three sequential triggers, and a lever-operated cocking system to allow it to be reloaded while mounted. A very loud and powerful weapon, Angus was warned against traveling with it cocked because it might wear quickly, and possibly – not that it had ever happened, of course – might just fire on its own if it were to be jostled. He had seen Artemus fire one before; three bolts striking a bolstered target dummy in near unison. Angus may not be an expert marksman yet, but just the act of cocking the contraption was known to drive enemies off in fear. Angus nodded in satisfaction as he set it aside for the moment.

Yuri's blood onyx axe was very interesting; this one was new, the blade a black deeper than the darkest of the Unseen Pools. It would gain color over time, he was told. The handle was three feet long, an impossibly sharp stone blade on one side with a mithril pick on the opposite end. It was a beautiful weapon, to be sure; crafted by a true master. This axe represented the sum knowledge gained by dwarven smiths and warriors since time immemorial. It was obvious that Yuri had spent a great deal of time planning this particular weapon. Details such as the groove on the pick side that had another piece of blood onyx inlaid but set back from the point made the whole assembly look fearsome and artistic in the same glance.

Angus took it in his hands and shook his head. "No polearms. I have spoken poorly about axes all my life, and now I find myself owning one so fine that I would be a fool not to embrace it." Angus looked over at Yuri and bowed his head a bit in respect. "If it takes centuries, I will become worthy of this weapon. It will be difficult, but I'm ready to take an honest swing at it."

When he arrived home a short while later, Angus found a stout two-wheeled wagon hitched to a sturdy dwarven pony. Several big bags of oats and four casks of the promised brandy were on board, as well as the chests of gold, silver, and gems. Those he took inside. He was dismayed to find that his father was not there. Not deterred, Angus fetched several empty leather bags and filled one each with the precious metals and gems. He really had no idea what things cost outside the Holt, but he was sure that chests like those would make him a target. He would leave them and most of the wealth here. He gathered the other things he needed for a journey; camping gear, water bags, pipeweed, and pipe – all of what he considered essentials. Leaving a note for his father, he loaded everything on the wagon and led the pony out toward the gate.

The corpse of the Dragon was more than halfway through the disassembly process when he arrived at the gatehouse. The portcullis was in the raised position, and the head was being dragged whole toward the preservation chambers. A path had been made through the open gateway, but most of it was still blocked by the massive body. Angus had to wait for two of the still-wet rib bones to be removed before he could get his wagon by, and even then the wheels scraped on the neighboring ribs.

Waiting at the open end of the cavern were Artemus, Floin and Kelly. He was glad that there weren't more people there to see him off. The less discussion there was right now, the better his chances were for keeping his secret. Angus was almost relieved that he would miss the party. He was, however, a bit disappointed at the absence of his friends. "It seems that I'm off." That was not the great parting line he had intended.

"We know, son. You've always been a bit off." The older dwarves chuckled with Floin. "But now you've got a great adventure ahead of you. Make me proud, but please come back to tell the story!" Kelly nodded along with Floin's comments. His anger seemed to have dissipated since the night before.

Artemus spoke next. "Here are your declarations. You are to show them only to the following people: The Elven high council, the southland emperor (known as the Ivon), The Queen of the Veyns, and the Dwarven King of the Smaragdine Holt. After that, you shall take them to the Historians at the Aureate Holt, for entry into the Annals. This," he said, handing a large, leather-bound scroll to him, "is your map. It shows, in general terms, all of the locations that we are bound by custom to send you to. Bring the news of these events to the leaders of these peoples. Not all of them will welcome you with open arms, and some may have lost the knowledge of our ancient alliance entirely. But we remember, and so must do our part.

Artemus' Map

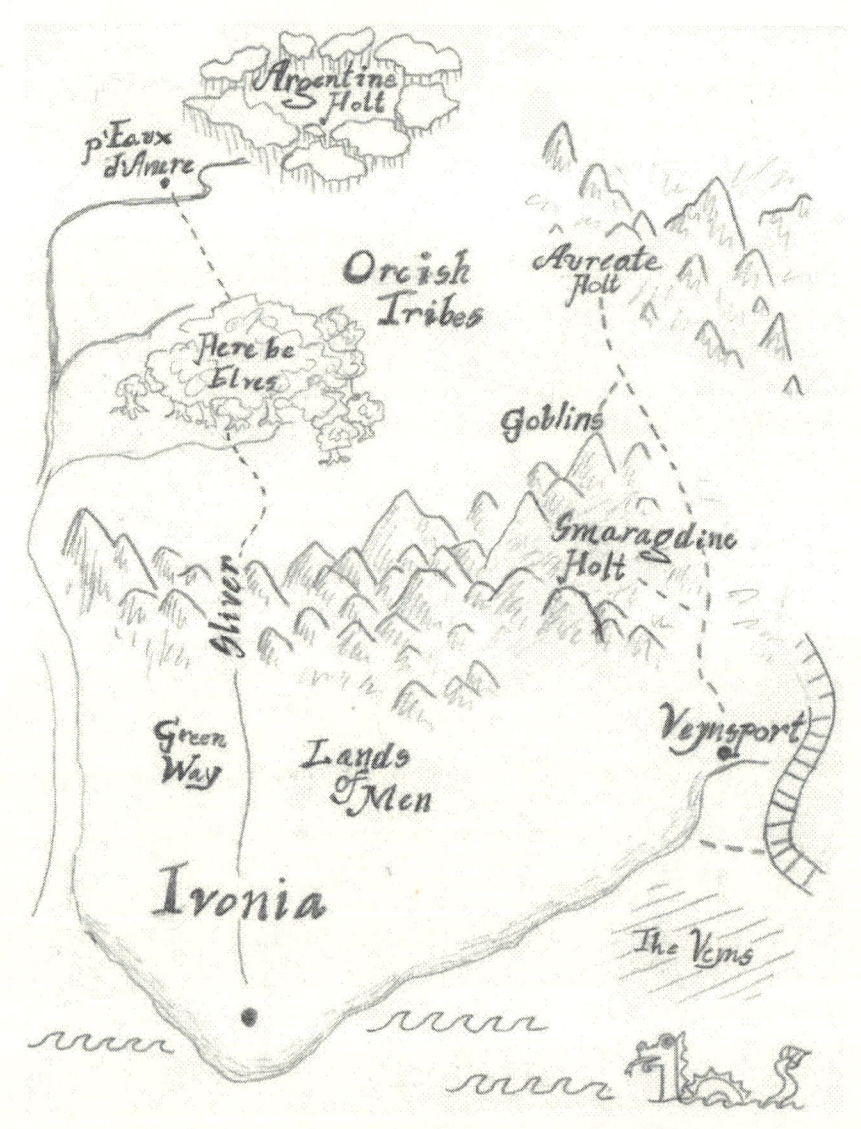

HOLTGART

This bag contains several of the beast's teeth and claws. You may find them useful if anyone doubts your story." The dark leather bag was heavy, with a thick strap. Angus looped it over his neck and tucked the bag neatly behind his blazing red beard.

"Angus Dragonbane, this is your charge and yours alone. You must act quickly, for arriving after the news has spread on its own may be cause for serious embarrassment. Travel fast, making sure the people you meet along the way have the right of the situation. When you return, we shall have a feast in honor of you and your service to the Holt. Fare well, Angus." He clapped the young dwarf on the back and shook his hand.

Feeling a little stunned by the abrupt send-off, Angus turned back towards the wagon. Still wearing his brilliantly shining Holtgart Armor, he climbed up and settled in to the simple wooden bench. "For the Holt!" came from his lips, and he realized that his right fist was raised in an automatic salute to his elders. Giving the reins a quick flick, the pony and wagon surged forward. It wasn't a grand exit or fast, but it did fit with the way Dwarves tend to do things.

Only a few miles away Angus stopped at the little farming town of p'Eaux d'Ancre to stay the night in an inn called 'The Rosy Cheek'. Instead of pulling up to the door, he led his pony around back to the stable yard. Jean, a lanky, pubescent stable boy stepped forward to take the reins and Angus offered the following words: "Jean, I know you are as good a man as your father, who stabled my pony when you were just as high as me. He did an excellent job of keeping my belongings unmolested. If you do the same, there will be a Holt-minted silver coin in it for you. However, if I find anything out of place in the morning, just try to remember this – I have slain a dragon just because it smelled bad. Try to imagine how a stable boy would fare if my pony were less than happy, or my gear missing. Do we have an understanding?"

Jean's mouth could not go any more slack, nor could he find the words to respond. Angus reached up to close his mouth, then helped Jean to nod his head. "That'll do, boy. I'll see you in the morning." Still in his armor, Angus grabbed his axe and started around the building to enter properly. He stepped in with his helm under one arm and the gleaming Blood Onyx axe held at his right side. He took in the scene of a few dozen patrons having dinner, then announced loudly, "We took care of your Dragon problem."

The message was repeated at every table, followed by applause and shouts. The band struck up a celebratory tune, and then there was a fancy porcelain stein in his hands, delivered by the portliest of the smiling serving girls.

"This should go to Bradley's widow." He held up his hand with one of the Dragon's smaller teeth perched atop his fingers. "She deserves something for her loss, and it seems fitting that it comes from the Dragon itself." Authentic Dragon's teeth were very rare and quite valuable. He tossed it to the innkeeper over the bar he had been wiping; the pudgy man dropped the rag and fumbled to catch it.

"Can I assume you would like to sit with your friends, sir? They are already here." He indicated a table at the far end of the common room, where four dwarves sat smiling from behind great grey beards. His friends had been so notably absent after the fray, he had wondered if they were upset with him. Seeing them here made his heart glad; both for the camaraderie, and the remembrance of their wager. It seemed he would have a party after all! He approached the table with a mirthful chuckle.

"We've saved you a chair, Dragonbane!" Flannan cried out, the others laughing and gesturing. "Marcel knows to keep the food and drink flowing, so order what you like!" The innkeeper nodded eagerly; dwarvish revelry promised a profitable night. Angus belly-laughed when he saw the chair – painted wood to look as if it were gilded, clearly a prank to make him uncomfortable, which he would, normally. Not now or here, however; this was not the Holt, and he was in a human town - one that he saved from a marauding dragon. He summoned his best pomp and strode to the chair like a king. He set the Dragonmaw helm on one of his chair's finials. He drained his stein before sitting, then hollered "Marcel – I seem to need some of your best stout – something so gritty that I'll need to pick my teeth after drinking it! And some of your roast beast du jour, if you will!" It was shaping up to be a good night indeed. "What do you say, Niell? Who won the wager?"

"I'm embarrassed to say, no one. If I had followed up on my jest to Flannan, it would have been me – so it seems that we now need to test Master Marcel's stores. Argents stretch quite far outside the Holt, being so much purer than most mannish coin. It took me a while to convince Marcel that we didn't want a complimentary dinner in honor of our – your – feat."

"Can you imagine a business owner trying to turn down business? That's as likely as an Orc who won't fight!" Gierman got only chuckles for that, but the inevitable cascade of orc jokes had just begun. The Holtgart Sapper continued. "Did I tell you about the new orcish siege technique we've heard about? They choose their biggest warrior, line him up with the wall or gate in question and have him run full speed – head down – into it. They leave a rope tied around his waist so when he gets knocked out, they can pull him back, revive him, then send him in again. Now that's what I call using your head!"

The company responded with guffaws. When it subsided, Flannan kept it going.

"We've been trying to understand the relationships involved with their marriage ceremonies for a long time now. In hundreds of years of study, we couldn't figure out how to tell betrothed from blood relation. As it turns out, neither can they!"

"The Chronicler recently told me how to keep track of orcish war dead. It seems there is a complex set of terms with very specific conditions for them to be used. He is very careful about what gets written down, you know. For instance, when you are marking a thousand dead orcs, one can simply write 'it was a good start'." The laughter rolled steadily now.

Dylaen, normally the quiet type, finally reached the threshold of intoxication that loosed his lips. "Did you hear about the orc who slew five elves in close combat? It seems he took their heads and arranged them into a basket to carry to the local warlord. What do you suppose he called it? A fruit basket!"

Marcel busied himself refilling tankards and keeping the food on the table stocked. Without thinking, he started to tell a joke that his grandfather had told, years ago. "Have you heard the one about the orc who defeated the dwarf in single combat?" He looked expectantly at the assembled dwarves. Their reaction started with quizzical looks, exchanged glances, and a simultaneous burst of uproarious laughter. Marcel did not try to disguise his confusion. "But I haven't told the joke yet," he protested.

"Nay, innkeeper," Angus said, "You've told the funniest joke all night – that a dwarf could ever fall to an orc!" The laughter rose anew, the dwarves clapping each other's backs and all wiping their eyes. Marcel pursed his lips, apparently thwarted by the dwarves' peculiar sense of humor. He took up some of the empty plates and scurried off to the kitchen with the very real excuse of keeping the table well provisioned.

As the night wore on, the human patrons headed off to their rooms or abodes. Carousing dwarves were not an everyday occurrence, worth watching at least - but even curious humans like their sleep in the wee hours. It was around four in the morning, the dwarves still going strong, when at last Marcel gave them leave to help themselves and staggered up to bed; cradling the heavy purse from the dwarven wager like an infant to his chest.

At first light, they stumbled out to the stables. And they did stumble because even a dwarven constitution eventually becomes overwhelmed with enough alcohol. Jean eagerly went over their mounts and possessions, showing that everything was as the dwarves intended. He was pleased to receive his coin. Angus said his good-byes to his old friends, heading southeast towards the forest. He squinted past the sunrise as the bright, cloudless morning mocked his painful hangover.

Chapter 6

A Branch in the Road

Pain, darkness and a pervasive ringing were all Angus perceived. The klaxon toll was deafening. It assumed a state of noise somehow *closer* than noise should be. Maybe it wasn't really noise, after all...

Opening his eyes wasn't much better. Everything swirled and swayed, blurred by tears. As the world gradually returned to something resembling focus, Angus assessed his situation. He lay on his back, spread-eagle. Looking up at a large, crooked tree branch, backed by sky and clouds; something shiny quivered there. It was his Dragonmaw helm. The stylized teeth that described the edges of the open visor impaled the wood, holding it there - a tenuous perch. He closed his eyes and shook his head, trying to clear the fog. He opened them again just in time to see his helmet bounce off his forehead with a heavy metallic 'donk', clanging off to roll up against the foot of the tree.

As the ringing in his ears subsided, Angus tried to sit up, and met unfamiliar resistance. Ah. He remembered he was wearing his new Holtgart armor, the type he had always hoped to own one day. "You'll be tougher than a cave tortoise in this, boy" the armor master Odhar Freeplate had said during the fitting. There simply was no better armor than Holtgart armor – made for substantial protection, reasonable freedom of movement, and ornately worked to befuddle the enemy - and look good doing it. Unfortunately, he had not been instructed in how to get back up quickly after being knocked on his arse while wearing heavy plate. He lifted his head to look in the direction of the cadent 'thud-crunch' that indicated his wagon. He could just make out the folded canopy stays over his boots, belly and braided red beard. The blasted pony was still walking. Away from him.

After several moments of rocking, flailing and cursing, Angus managed to prop himself up on an elbow. *I need to practice this – when I don't need to chase my kit down the road.* By the time he stood the cart passed out of sight around the next corner. The forest was rather dense here. He examined the branch that he had hit his head on. It must have knocked him clean off the bench, so he rolled over his gear and off the rear of his small wagon, landing on his head. *Surely that was too high to bump into. But a branch couldn't just move of its own volition. Could it?*

Retrieving his helmet from the base of the gnarled old tree, he vented a bit. "Lucky for you, my axe is still on that wagon, or by my beard, I'd have you down and hewn into planks inside the hour. My Da needs a new door back at the Holt, you know." As if in response, the ancient oak seemed to lean, as if blown by the wind, to arch over Angus. There was no wind.

Angus moved on. *Not because the tree was a threat – that would be ridiculous. It was only a tree. No, I just have to catch that pony and wagon if I want to eat anytime soon.*

As he walked, Angus pointedly tried to forget what he had been told about this forest and its inhabitants. Forget that this had once been the center for elven culture. Ignore what was said about trees walking and talking. Angus wouldn't even be here if he'd had his way. The message was supposed to be delivered to the elves here, yet no dwarf had even seen them for hundreds of years. *Maybe they're not here anymore.* His plan was to go straight through, sticking to the road. If nobody showed themselves while he was on the path, he would just fail to find the elves. *Who cares about treaties thousands of years old pertaining to sharing news, anyway? There was a problem, it was addressed, and it's done. No need to belabor the point.*

Angus took stock of the gear on his person. The full suit of Holtgart armor was painfully obvious. His hands ran over the stout belt knife, a small sack of gems, and one with gold and silver nuggets. He cracked a small smile when he found the wineskin still mostly filled with strong dwarven brandy which he had been quaffing vigorously when that damned tree bludgeoned him. Patting his beard, he located the lumpy mass of a leather pouch carrying some very unusual and - at least in this circumstance - un-useful relics. Even the silver-plated steel tube carrying his messages remained tied to his belt. Almost all of his useful gear resided on that bloody cart. He needed to catch up.

The cart left no clear tracks in the heavily rutted sandstone road. What he was hoping for was to find where it left the road. It certainly would, as that gravel-brained pony went for grass as often as it could. The gathering clouds enhanced his sense of urgency. Wet armor could get very, very cold. Rain would also mean that the rest of his possessions would be soaked, since he had lowered the wagon's canopy in order to have a better view on the road.

Angus walked for hours in that heavy armor. It moved well enough, but it still amounted to several dozen metal plates and some chainmail. His clothes had tripled in weight, padding absorbing the rain like a sponge. The fact that he had studiously avoided physical labor for years was showing in his heartbeat and ragged breath. Sweat matted his hair and beard. He was miserable. Then he caught his break – maybe.

Chapter 7

My Little Pony

Angus hoped that the pony would spot some grazing ground along the way and stop for a snack. That had been the extent of his plan. So, when he saw tracks move off the left side of the road, his heart leapt. He hurried near to see what the mud showed.

Angus wasn't really much of a tracker, but he knew the pattern of rivets from the wagon wheels – it was his for sure. The Argentine Holt coat of arms from the heavy hoof prints clinched it. Only dwarves took the time and effort to emboss detailed emblems on their animals' shoes, and very likely, Angus had been the only dwarf in this forest for some time. There was no question that this was the right way.

The tracks led into a long, meandering meadow; wide enough to be a road for several carts abreast and uniform as it went on. This should be a road, but the lush grass and soft mud stood witness that nothing else like his wagon had passed here since the previous winter, if not considerably longer. This would be an easy task. Follow the clear tracks until the stupid animal gets hung up on something, turn it around, and head to the next town. Angus' confidence was soaring.

His stomach, on the other hand, was empty. The angry rumbling came on suddenly, so loud he thought he might draw the local fauna out of curiosity. After his earlier experience with the flora, Angus wasn't keen on any more interaction than absolutely necessary. All he wanted at that moment was to find something to eat, retrieve his wagon, and get back to the road.

At first, he tried chewing some of the tall grass, which proved edible, but unpalatable. Dwarves, being meat-and-potatoes people, don't eat a lot of greens. For them a typical salad might consist of a large, well-sautéed mushroom with a sprig of parsley on top. Leafy green stuff doesn't sit well with most dwarves,

Angus being no exception. Along the way he found a couple of strange fruit, but how to tell what was safe to eat?

If not for Artemus' blasted orders, he could make a spear from a straight stick and his knife and try to hunt some of the rabbits he had spotted. Spit roasted rabbit sounded right tasty, and he suspected that a brandy marinade would add a heady depth of flavor. But he was a loyal King's dwarf, and the King had been very specific about that particular long point. No spear. The way Angus had been raised, an order was an order, even if it made no sense.

He started to daydream of hearty dwarven foodstuffs, like steaks and sausages, eggs and cheese. He could almost taste the dwarven breads that danced through his thoughts. Angus particularly enjoyed baked goods so thick they required soaking in oil for a day before they were edible. As his mind wandered, he thought of the puffed pastries that Bradley, the local human baker used to bring in occasionally in trade. Excellent work, every one a delicate explosion of culinary delight. Poor Bradley. After ruminating about the late pastry chef, he hit on pancakes and that syrup that the merchants would occasionally bring. He remembered asking where that syrup had come from, expecting to hear about a complex chemical process like one the alchemists used. Instead, he was told that they harvested it from certain trees by making spiral score marks along the trunk and collecting the syrup that oozed out. Now if he could only find the right tree...

He knew what came out of pine trees. That sap was used in a number of dwarven recipes for things like glue and varnish. That wouldn't taste good at all. So, he concentrated on the leafy trees, cutting coil-spring shaped grooves and waiting for a few minutes. After a few dozen trees were scored with no good result, he decided to chance some of the fruit.

They sat all right for a while, and he ate every one of the sweet, odd-shaped fruit he came across. Some seemed bitter – still green, and he spat them out on the ground. The more purple ones were juicy, sweet and filling, and before he knew it, he ate several pounds. Juice dripped from his beard, and the hunger subsided.

Picking up the pace, energized by the sugary meal, Angus moved on. The wagon track was still clear, right down the center of this vibrant green avenue. For a moment he wished he had his golf clubs – this seemed an ideal course for practicing long, level drives.[2]

A few miles further along the grassy lane, the first gas came; so violent and fumesome that Angus extinguished his pipe for fear of starting a forest fire. Not to say he would mind if this forest burned, he'd just rather not be there when it did. Pain racked his belly, and he sweat for two reasons now. Not wanting to stop, he clenched and moved on.

Marching until full dark, Angus never even caught sight of the wagon. As he cut some wood for a fire, he considered the scant evidence of the pony's grazing. It looked like the animal was on a mission; or being driven somewhere. Breaking branches that he notched with his knife, Angus got the feeling that something near was angry; and it wasn't him. He used some brandy and moss to start the green wood, and as soon as the fire was vigorously crackling, he dug a hole nearby. After filling it with that half-digested nasty fruit, he covered the hole and lay down next to the fragrant, smoky fire; shivering with cold sweats.

That pony would get a stern talking to when he caught up to it. There are certain things a pony should know; stopping to wait when your driver falls off being one of them. Angus intended to engrave that particular point deep into his pony's brain.

---

[2] Golf was, of course, invented by dwarves, as a battle art. Spherical balls would be fashioned from a variety of materials, from wood to metal or granite, depending on the purpose. These would be launched by smacking them smartly with a club, lofting the ball high above the target. When properly executed, this strike is known as 'death from above', which the very best players would accompany with a shout of, "forehead!", to call their shot.

An accurate golfer can cause havoc amongst milling troops, and from time immemorial dwarven golfsnipers have hidden in the rocky outcroppings overlooking the Holtgates to do just that. The alchemists often attempt recipes for exploding balls, but they haven't gotten it just right – yet.

Chapter 8

If a Dwarf Falls in the Woods

Angus woke, and immediately wished he hadn't. Grey morning light streamed through the eye slits in the lowered visor of his helmet, but not so much as the rain that found every chink in his armor. Rust wasn't an issue; Dwarvish metallurgy being the most advanced in the world, it was likely that this armor would last for generations. Indeed, this set already had. But Holtgart armor was not made for protection from the weather, and the padded under layer was soaked with heat-sapping moisture. Had Angus access to his wagon, he would have changed into a more weatherproof cloak; but then, if the wagon were present, he wouldn't have slept in the tall, wet grass without cover.

Reluctantly, he raised his visor and stood up. He'd recovered somewhat from the previous day, just a strong headache to stand witness to his concussion. Sleeping in his armor had left him with more than a few sore points, and his feet ached, but everything still worked. He took a swig of his brandy – hair of the boar, and all that – and looked around for the wagon's trail. Despite having camped right next to it, he couldn't seem to find any trace of it. The rain gave the soft grass new energy, and it sprang back almost instantly when he passed. Angus needed a high point to see a bit farther. He had to get out of this tall grass, which grew a lot overnight. Most of it stood taller than him now, making it hard to see where he was going.

Without any real navigational aid, Angus picked a direction and set off. Before too long, treetops rose above the grass; he hoped he would find a solid rock outcropping to climb. When he reached the trees however, there was no such thing – not a boulder in sight. No tracks, either. He followed the edge of the glade for a while, but the grasses faded out. He broke twigs and small branches to place makeshift arrows on the forest floor, marking the way he went in case he lost his way. As he did this, he noticed that this forest was just... *cleaner* than other forests. There were no fallen trees, no parasitic vines; even the ground seemed devoid of fallen leaves and twigs. It couldn't be this manicured without some evidence of people passing – a footprint, or wagon marks – but it was.

Eventually he decided that he wasn't going to get his desired vantage point from climbing boulders; there simply were none. A tree might do; Angus used to be a good climber - many years ago. True, all of his climbing had been in and around the Holt, and he had never climbed a tree – but Angus was convinced that climbing was climbing, whether a rock or a tree. As if to help solidify his convictions about the subject, he took several more gulps from his brandy-laden wineskin before selecting a proper tree.

He chose a grand pine with regularly spaced branches which started just several feet above the ground. Pushing past the needles at the wide base of the tree, he found easy foot and hand holds. The trunk here was more than two feet across and rose easily over a hundred feet. *I should be able to see something from up there.* Climbing in plate armor wasn't as hard as he would have suspected; the clever hinges and overlapped joints allowed him most of the movements he needed to climb. He only stopped a couple of times to reconsider his route, and soon he found himself at the limit of the branches that easily supported his weight.

Angus surveyed the scene, surrounded by trees. The grassland was beyond his field of view, admittedly reduced by the rain and morning mist. Not wanting to call this a waste of energy, he considered the risk of going higher. None of the branches creaked or cracked under the strain so far; surely he could push it another few yards? The tree's trunk was less than a foot wide here, and if he hugged the tree (not that he would) he could touch his fingers on the other side. He decided to risk it and climbed further.

He made it four more branches, stopping when they started to bend under his weight. The rain slowed, the mist subsided, and his line of sight improved. He could make out the glade to his left, could see it stretching far into the distance. The road must lay that way. If the cart had continued much further, it must have headed into the woods proper. *Creak.* With any luck, it would catch on something and be stuck nearby. *Crrreeak!* Now, he only needed to get his bearings; that tall redwood, *crack*, lined up with the sugar pine beyond should CRACK! SNAP!

Angus, engrossed with identifying landmarks, forgot his precarious position. He realized the gravity of his situation as the next level of branches came up to strike his codpiece. While he mentally thanked the smith that made this suit for his functional attention to detail, the second branch gave way. Clawing for handfuls of trunk, Angus watched the scene unfold in slow-motion. As the branch broke away where it connected to the trunk Angus tipped backwards, catching the next branch with his right pauldron. It held on as his body twirled to the left, bringing another branch within reach. Calling upon reflexes that had never been developed, he grasped a handful of needles, stripping them from the branch as it slid out of his grip. Now falling fully prone, the next chance was a thicker limb about ten feet down. He managed to turn his face to the side as he hit chest-on, arms and legs swinging forward as he hit. He hugged the limb with arms and legs, head faced away from the trunk, the wind knocked out of him from the impact. But the branch held fast.

His arboreal dismount paused forty feet above ground level, Angus contemplated his next move. He was in a difficult position; holding on to a round limb with no nearby branches, in metal armor that threatened to lose its tenuous grip on the smooth bark at any time. He figured he had fallen maybe twenty feet or so; Luck and the armor had kept him from major harm so far.

He swiveled only his head to look around, searching for a handhold, foothold, or any other reasonable exit strategy. As he searched, the heavy limb drooped and dipped outwards; slowly but inexorably. A few more moments, and Angus' grip slipped enough to allow his body to rotate around the limb so that he hung supine[3], slowly sliding downward. Downward equated to away from the trunk of the tree; and as he continued his dubious descent another branch came into reach. Angus flailed, reaching in desperation – and caught! This was exactly what he needed, since the rest of his body finished its slide. Now swinging in a downward spiral, he saw his chance – a large, full bush not too far

---

[3] Many people seem to believe that being prone means lying down. It doesn't. Well, it does, but specifically the face-down type. Supine, on the other hand, is the right good and proper way to say, "lying flat, face-up" - with a minimum of wordiness.

below. Letting go, everything rushed upwards. He just had time to drop his visor before he hit.

The bush did a good job of lessening Angus' impact, who lay still and panting thankfully for a moment before feeling the myriad pinpricks from the bush's thorns. They were small and irritating, and found every crack and cranny in his armor. Rolling out of the bush, he started off again. After a dozen shaky steps, he remembered to look for the redwood and the sugar pine. As he walked, he worked most of the thorny brambles out of his armor. This was not starting out as a good day.

The rain intensified, with a laden thunderhead darkening the sky. Visibility was so poor that he could only make a guess at his direction. Angus was truly lost. The manicured forest floor turned into a muddy mess as the rain increased to a deluge. More than once Angus had to stop and clear packed mud from his greaves and sollerets just to keep moving. The mud brought another unexpected problem; tree roots seemed to spring up randomly, tripping him. Bushes swatted his face and head. He was still very hungry and seeing several prize bucks cross near to his path only exacerbated his hunger pangs. Had he his wagon, he would've had his crossbow out and made an attempt or two.

Everything was cold, wet, and painful as well as increasingly hopeless. Angus continued on, drinking yet more brandy. The forest's abuse grew more and more severe. He fell several times, often feeling like he had been tripped or knocked down by something; but when he got up, there was never anything there. The clouds and canopy conspired to make a darkness like a moonless night. Angus was exhausted within a short time; how long he could not accurately tell. Then he tripped again, on a root concealed by the deep mud. This time, his head hit a rock. As consciousness slid away, Angus took comfort in knowing he had found the only rock in the forest.

Chapter 9

Too Good to be True

Covered in cold, clammy mud, Angus' head ached. His body ached. *It's not shaping up to be a good day, and I haven't even opened my eyes yet.* Eventually he summoned up the courage to do so, expecting yet another sour twist. Squinting past the bright morning light however, he saw a different story. His forehead rested on the moss-covered rock that knocked him out the night before, and the weather seemed perfect; if a bit bright.

He rose with effort. Great clods of the sticky mud from last nights' storm dried in the joints of his armor, effectively sticking him in an awkward pose. By the time he achieved a sit, he decided to take it all off to clean it thoroughly. Looking around, he found himself perched on a pile of boulders, well hidden in moss and ferns. A brook babbled nearby. As he stripped off his armor, he determined the source of the sound to be coming from above. Free of the priceless but encumbering plate, he scaled the stone stack.

Reaching the aquatic emanation, it took him a moment to absorb the scene before him. These boulders weren't random rocks; rather blocks from a ruined building. More importantly, the quality of the stonework told Angus it must have been built by dwarves. A pristine pool resided here, cut into the still-flat floor in the center of the room. *No one has been here in a long time. Years, certainly.* He fetched his armor in several trips and went to work cleaning.

Before stepping in, Angus closely studied the still, clear pool. Once confident it held no dark recesses for nasty creatures to hide, he entered the water. Piece by piece, he cleared the dried mud from his armor. *I must be diligent in this task; I feel bad about letting my equipment get into such a state in the first place.* He found handfuls of the ancient moss shined mithril nicely and used some of the fern stems to get into cracks and crannies. That task done, he carefully laid the armor out on one of the boulders.

This ghastly gunk is everywhere! He decided to wash it all, even his padded doublet and hose. Those he set to dry hanging on a tree fern. He found a stone crucible nearby, just the right dimensions to serve as a dwarven toilet. After relieving himself thoroughly, Angus dove into the pool. The water was cool; a great relief after days of hard travel and the various minor injuries recently sustained. The bath was exactly what he needed. He took his time to revel, having given up any real hope of recovering the rest of his gear. After this small respite, he intended to escape this dreadful, enchanted wood. He needed to find a town, rest, and re-supply.

Angus was scraping remnants of mud from his toenails with his knife when he felt eyes on him. He stopped humming and looked around. There was no one to be seen, no animals to be heard; nothing at all. Then it hit him – the absolute absence of normal forest noises. There must be a person or predator about. He sat on the edge of the pool in his small clothes. He looked over at his armor. Sitting on the far side of the pool, it would take too long to suit up for it to be useful. Still, he rose to be near it.

"Stay right there, dwarf!" The clarion, soprano voice filled the ruins with authority. Angus still could not see where it came from. "Put the knife down and lay on your belly!"

Angus considered the request. Issued as an order; but who was behind it? It might be a young human, maybe even a woman or a child. He wasn't about to surrender before he knew what he was up against.

In the boldest voice he could muster, he shouted, "Show yourself! And give me three good reasons why I should debase myself so!" There was laughter, from more than one direction; and then it all happened at once. A tall, slender, and unnaturally beautiful person stepped through an ancient archway; stopping casually but ending up in a pose that might have been the subject of one of the great tapestries. As she smiled, one, two and then three arrows stuck in the thick patch of moss Angus had been sitting on, all within an inch of his mostly bare skin. All from different directions; he was surrounded. Had he been in his armor, he might have tried to fight. This time, Angus stopped short. Like most dwarves, he was brave, but not suicidal.

"Ah. I see your reasons, and it appears that you have several good points. Well, schist." He slowly laid the knife on the ground next to him. "I've no intention of fighting; can you at least allow me my dignity?"

Her smile turned to a terribly wicked grimace. "You, filthy little dwarf, have done the unthinkable. You have desecrated the sacred, ancient pool of Sara-Tholah. No dwarf in recorded history has ever laid foot here, let alone bathed in and fouled the pool itself. Only once every decade do we come here to honor our ancestors and ask the spirits bound herein for their blessing. Little dwarf; can you guess what day this is?"

With the way his journey had gone so far, today must be that once-in-a-decade day. But he had no idea what they called it, and he still hoped to survive this encounter. "Thursday?" was all he managed.

Chapter 10

A Stolen Blessing

Angus' captors put a hood over his head, presumably to make sure he was good and lost. *Too late for that,* he thought. After binding him hand and foot, they led the stumbling dwarf through the forest. The occasional metallic clatter of the armor in its sack comforted him. Somehow, the thought that they had decided to bring his belongings instilled a sense of optimism. Still blind, barefoot, and in his small clothes, he saw little hope for a struggle at this point.

In so many stories about bandits, hoods are described as smelly and dirty. This cowl smelled of oranges and incense. Indeed, Angus' captivity yielded no truly unpleasant experiences. His captors were firm, but polite. Their fair voices and soft footfalls fit more with the stories about elves than men. He tried not to let his mind wander down that path.

About a half hour passed during their walk before the ground became much more even and easier on his bare soles. He heard voices as he walked, speaking in soft, low whispers. These included more than one gentle chuckle, and he envisioned small children gasping and giggling at him. Then more quiet feet assembled and followed behind. Angus feared what he would see when the hood was removed.

He felt stone under his bare feet. Smooth, well-worked stone, in a dwarvish style. His elation didn't last more than a few dozen steps before new bonds entwined his wrists and ankles, while the original ropes were removed. The fresh restraints were smooth and cool; not rope or leather, yet not metal like a chain or cable. The bonds raised him up like a marionette, and a solemn voice spoke in that soft, smooth language for a while.

No one interrupted the speaker. Whomever the audience, it was devoid of audible reaction. When the speaker finished, another voice began, this time in common, which Angus spoke fluently. "I think it only fair that the accused hear the charges in the common tongue. Yet I caution you, dwarf, not to utter that guttural language of yours in this hallowed place. Remove his shroud."

The bonds moved him to tilt forward, and the hood was snatched from his head in one smooth motion. He squinted for a few moments while his eyes adjusted to the light. The stone floor featured an intricate mosaic of a sunburst. Made up of more types of stone than Angus had seen in his lifetime, fitted together with invisible seams ground flat and polished to a perfect and glossy finish. It had to be dwarven stonework, and exceptional at that.

Gigantic, vibrant trees with a delicate red bark formed a circular colonnade; growing around and over boulders - effectively, walls and ceiling of a great hall. No roof stood here now, just well-groomed boughs that reminded him of the trees the dwarves shredded for the sweet-smelling wood to keep the boar sties from stinking too badly.

At one end of the clearing sat stone benches arranged in a semi-circle, set so that every seat faced the center of the design. On this, there were seven tall adults. None wore any facial hair, and every one was beautiful. Elves for sure. Others ringed the sunburst floor, standing somehow at ease while engrossed entirely.

He took in the details of his bonds for the first time; articulate, animated vines snaked around his extremities, lifting him off the ground. Plants that obeyed the will of the elves. The stories the longbeards told held true. Many of the events of the past couple of days made much more sense with this knowledge.

"I am Endaria lo Thenalah; Speaker for the High Council. Name yourself to the council, dwarf, and state your reason for entering our forest." The elven Speaker sat on the center of the bench. His voice held authority, confidence and grace. Angus got the impression that this elf had seen to the same years as the longbeards at the Holt. It was never a good plan to run afoul of a longbeard. He imagined the same wisdom held true for Endaria.

"My given name is Angus. I am a Holtgart of the Argentine Holt, which lies to the north and west of this place. My byname has of late changed, and in fact is the reason for my visit to your forest. I have come to fulfill the terms of the ancient treaties."

The members of the council exchanged glances, but no more. "What treaties do you speak of, Angus? They must be ancient in truth to escape our memory."

Angus wondered if the treaties actually existed in the first place. Knowing the elven forest would be his first stop, could this be just an elaborate execution by Artemus? "Mountain King Artemus instructed me to bring news of recent events that occurred at our Holt. My first stop is this forest, to meet with the council here. I carried on my person a silver tube with documents of these events. As you can see, I don't seem to have them on me at the moment; or much of anything for that matter." Was that a flicker of a smile on the lead elf's face?

One of the elves who initially bound Angus stepped forward with the tube, laying it on a small wooden table in front of the central elf. "We found this with his armor, Speaker." The council leader opened the tube and looked over the documents in silence. At first an eyebrow arched, and then as he read further, his head started to tilt to one side. One hand raised itself to cover his mouth, and he blinked rapidly as he finished reading. He passed the document along to the other council members; each had a similar reaction. Angus knew what they were reading. He rolled his eyes and sighed heavily.

When all had had the opportunity to read, the elves' leader spoke again. "This scroll says that a Dragon visited your home with the intention of murdering the lot of you. This I believe without hesitation. The animosity between dwarves and dragons has existed so long that it is now inborn; comically, it is your two peoples' similarly innate love of gold and other precious metals that drives this rivalry. Likewise, I believe you are correct in citing your right to be here to let us know. It has been a very long time since it has been exercised, a long time even by our standards; but you are in the right to be here. As to the rest," he looked around at the other elves. Those who had read were having a hard time concealing their amusement. "The scroll also says that you single-handedly defeated this Dragon with one blow. That you saved the Holt and are called Angus Dragonbane by those who know the truth. Forgive me for asking, but is this correct?" He gave a patronizing smile and cocked his head to the side again, waiting for an answer.

Angus braced himself. He inhaled deeply then let out an extended sigh. "It is, Speaker. I am embarrassed at the attention the deed garnered. I did what any other dwarf would do in my place, no more." He hoped that would be enough. The full truth still deeply upset him.

Endaria nodded with pursed lips. "Very well, then. The council will withdraw to discuss the matter. Please be patient with us, this should not take long." They filed out, each in perfect order. Every one of them oozed style and grace, while not seeming out of sync with the others. When they were out of sight, Angus looked again at his vine-like cuffs. He pulled against one, testing; but as he did a long thorn formed and extended from the runner near his wrist and threatened to pierce his skin if he pulled further. He stopped pulling.

A muffled set of sounds emanated from the direction the council had headed. Laughter? Most likely, he decided. They had just been presented with a lost, half-naked dwarf being held up by an enchanted vine and told he was a great hero; a Dragonbane. Even Angus understood his status as laughable. Even so, he might rather face certain death at the hands of angry elves than be the subject of elven humor for untold centuries to come. The elevated dwarf sighed. Nothing could be done about it now.

After a few minutes, the council returned, all grace and composure. A couple of them may have dabbed a tear from an eye, but Angus didn't know for sure what the verdict would be.

"Angus Dragonbane," the Speaker intoned, barely hiding the smile as the word 'Dragonbane' crossed his lips, "you have been found bathing in the sacred pool of Sara-Tholah, on the day we set aside for the coming-of-age ceremony for our young people. Once a decade this day comes along, and by desecrating the pool, you have put off that ceremony for another ten years. When you arrived, many elves thought you should be put to death immediately, including some of us on the council." A flash of anger passed over his face, but it was gone in an instant. "We believe the pool generates a form of energy, best described as a blessing. This blessing is transferred through a long bath in the pool, and our custom allows each elf to take his blessing after he has not only aged to adulthood but proved him or herself worthy to the Council. Over countless years, we found that it is most effective with ten years to steep in between visits; now that you have stolen this gift the pool will be useless to us until another decade has passed. For thousands of years, we have maintained the sacred purity of the pool; certainly, none but elves had been there in our long memory. And here you come, not only bathing, but soiling the premises thoroughly!" The anger was back, Endaria shouting; it took a moment for the Speaker to regain his composure.

"Yet you are here as a guest, under the terms of even more ancient treaties, which transcend our normal reasons for segregation; and had no knowledge of the sanctity of the site. Against all odds, you survived the natural defenses of the forest and by pure chance happened upon our sacred pool. As enlightened beings, we must resist our natural tendencies for vengeance and look at the whole situation. The Council has done just that, and we find you innocent of the intention to do wrong here. You are free," he gestured, and the vines released him gently. "And as for your gear, we collected not only what you had with you; but also, a certain pony that had found its way to us, with a crude wagon we can only assume to be yours."

Over the next few hours, the elves fed Angus what foodstuff they had that might seem palatable to a dwarf. By and large, the fare was not to Angus' liking. No meat, and even less beer. Angus retold the story to several different crowds, more uncomfortable with each telling.

When at last two dozen elves lined up on each side of his wagon to show him the way to the road, he smiled broadly. The young dwarf was ready to be out of this old and decidedly elven forest.

Chapter 11

The Mossy Knoll

Pulling at last onto the forest road, Angus turned to wave a farewell to his elven escort. Staring with right hand upraised, he found that not only were the Elves gone, but all traces of his wagon passing through the woods had vanished. If not for a surfeit of aches, pains, scrapes and bruises, the elves might have been nothing more than a bad dream.

Angus looked east along the road. He looked west. No travelers, nor any signs of anything other than a meandering forest road. Alone again, save the pony. He pulled his map from the pouch beside the seat and unrolled it. Tracing roads and marked settlements with a finger, he considered his next move.

He paused over the human empire to the south, known as Ivonia. He had to see the Ivon at some time, and the trip promised several days on the open road. Besides, a small mountain range lay in between, with an ancient trade route likely offering clear and easy travel at this time of the year. Getting out of these dank, elf–infested woods and into some proper mountain territory pulled his heart and brain.

Decided, Angus took the road eastward until it left the forest, at which point it forked to continue east or to a meandering southern route through the foothills. The southern road drew Angus, simple and unpopulated. He smoked his pipe while he rode, occasionally humming a happy dwarven tune.

After his experience with the elves he was wearing his armor. His demeanor vacillated between a vague denial and an acute awareness of how close he had just been to death. The incident had brought him a new perspective, and the best he could make of it was a new resolution to enjoy the small things.

This very line of thought ran through his head when he saw it. The sun slowly fell when he spotted a small knoll not far off the trail. Unnaturally thick, lush moss covered it, and an old bent tree sheltered it nicely. A perfect place for a dwarf to rest his weary bones. Angus hobbled his pony, retrieved some food and his flask from the wagon and leaned back into the moss. The extempore bed supported him such that he felt comfortable even in his armor; he ate his fill right there and drank just enough to feel sleepy. Soon he was snoring loudly, lost in an exhausted, dreamless sleep.

----- -----

An awful smell wafted into Black Zonka's hovel. The old orc crone had moved out here to be further away from the odors of the nearby orc clan who revered her for her special abilities. Whatever the source, it didn't mix well with her vegetable soup. She had just brought the spice combination to a crescendo; a study in culinary perfection. Over her long years she had developed an obsession with the experience of cooking and eating; indeed, the rituals she had set for herself took most of her time.

The world was quiet; wars were rare, and no great evil strove to take over, no unstoppable empire on an endless quest for expanding borders. In truth, the world expressed little need for an ancient wise one with the ability to see clearly what must be done. Visits to her home were only several times a year and not for reasons of great importance. These days left her largely alone for long periods, and she liked it that way.

Zonka set the copper pot aside and covered it with a large, waxy leaf. She grabbed her nastiest looking dagger, shrouded herself in her hoary rag cloak, and quietly stepped out the door. An observer would not see Zonka when she sat still; the multitude of rags tied into the weave broke up her profile, and she practiced silence. Slinking around toward the road – so many problems came from the road, after all – she saw Angus' hobbled pony. A flurry of recipes for young pony riffled through her brain; replaced quickly with cooking methods for the pony's likely owner. She almost hopped in anticipation.

There he lay, a portly young dwarf in a very shiny suit of plate armor, passed out on the backside of her house. Had he no armor, she would have slain him on the spot. But Zonka was not an impulsive orc; her exceedingly long years owed significantly to her very un-orcish tendency to think through a problem before acting. She pondered now, working out the best way to manage this dwarf.

She didn't want to kill him right away; as her best recipes for dwarf require extensive preparation. Some of the ingredients need to be gathered fresh, and that might take a few days. Better to incapacitate him for some time, marinating alive, inside and out.

She planned to start with a strong cocktail of inhaled medicines. Easy enough, with the dwarf's gaping mouth and his consistent snoring. Looking at his red beard, she reveled in the fact that this would be the youngest dwarf she had ever eaten. Tender and plump. She chuckled softly and returned to her abode to make things ready.

Zonka moved her largest cauldron over to the manacle mount, laying the crude but effective restraints open and ready for use. No need for a fire, yet. She thought one of those casks on his cart might have some booze in it – let him sit in that to properly pickle. Moving over to her 'special' cupboard, she selected several small, dried mushrooms and some powdered toad skins. To this she added two dried insects that carried a paralytic agent. She crushed them together in a mortar and pestle set made from a dwarven skull and thighbone – she enjoyed poetic justice as much as the next orc. Actually, quite a bit more.

She lay out a wide, waxy leaf from her skunk cabbage patch and arranged the powder in a rough line. She looked at it for a moment, frowning in consideration. Then half the frown turned up as she hit upon the missing ingredient; a healthy dash of red pepper powder. Not only a streak of color for presentation, but it might cause the dwarf to sweat a bit. Zonka held the belief that a little sweat went a long way to convey a sense of realism to a drug induced trance. She carefully curled the leaf for transport and headed back to the recumbent dwarf.

The evening turned out to be quite beautiful; she found herself pausing to take in the spider working away busily in the moonlight over her subject. It seemed to Zonka that she and the spider had a bit in common. Clucking herself to action, she slowly moved into position to blow the psychedelic cocktail into the dwarf's lungs. She took a few moments to synchronize her breathing with the opposite of his. It was a difficult feat, but one that Zonka had become quite good at over the years. Breathe in, breathe out… Breathe in, breathe out…

----- -----

The horsefly saw the bright glowing orb above and took flight with the intention of reaching it. When the light did not grow closer, it became distracted by something shiny down below. Flies are a distractible species, with really only two things on their minds: food, and sex. In an effort to conserve on brain cells, the two merge into the single thought 'foodsex'. In the absence of good light, they are apt to think that foodsex is shiny, rather like humans and taverns. In many cases, both are right.

But not tonight. Instead of foodsex, the horsefly found himself struggling in a web, almost within reach of the shiny thing. Keen on its goal, it continued to struggle.

----- -----

The spider had a good night catching small midges, several dozen so far. Flying insects were drawn to the new shiny thing below, a multitude of reflections from the full moon bouncing off it. She needed a few more good catches to bulk up before bearing her brood. She bundled up her last catch – a scrawny midge – having detached it from the web when a much larger fly became tangled nearby. It only took a moment for her to decide to leave one small midge for the chance at a large horsefly, and she let the web-wrapped midge drop.

----- -----

Breathe in, breathe out... breathe in, breathe out... as she inhaled deeply for the delivery, something tiny flashed in front of her eyes. The midge fell straight into Angus' throat, and he coughed reflexively – just as Zonka was inhaling. The too-strong medicine hit her square in the face, painting it in several colors. She breathed in most of the contents of her leaf in a fraction of a second, and staggered back, eyes stinging from the pepper powder.

"Oh no." She couldn't help letting that last out, and she stood rooted in terror, waiting for the dwarf to rise and slay her. He didn't. Her mind raced – she knew she faced a night of terrible hallucinations. She reached for her knife. Missing it, she saw a mental image of it sitting on her purple tablecloth. Trying again to open her eyes was useless. Everything was blurred by painful tears. She could make out the moon, however. If she kept it to her right, she reasoned, she would be traveling east, toward the clan.

Half stumbling, half running, seeing horrible things that weren't really there, she didn't scream. At least not for the first few minutes.

Chapter 12

The Scenic Route

Cool, crisp air beckoned to Angus' reclined psyche. He took several deep breaths of the verdant atmosphere before opening his eyes. The sun was just coming up, and he felt completely refreshed. Sitting up in his bed of soft greenery, he checked on his wagon and pony. Both were where they should be. Right. Next, he needed a specific item for his morning's business; as if bidden, he saw a large, waxy leaf[4] was right at his feet.

It didn't take him long to clear out of his kit. There was a spring a stone's throw away, and after he did his daily deed (using the leaf, of course) he went over to see if the water was suitable for a morning bath. Not only was it clean and fresh, an old ladle and bucket were set next to it. Angus looked around, half expecting to see a dozen elven bows pointing at him; he saw nothing – yet.

"Hello? Is anyone there? Please tell me if I'm about to defile a holy site..." He let a few moments pass in silence. Hearing no reply, he set about his morning wash. The water proved wonderful, and the ladle quite effective. He couldn't quite identify the material used in its manufacture; an off-white color, lightweight, and all of one piece. Vaguely reminiscent of bone, he supposed, but he thought it more likely another relic of elves long past. Leaving bucket and ladle behind, he dressed and packed his gear in the wagon.

Feeling secure and at ease, Angus considered how the greens seemed clear and intense, the sun brilliant yet not overpowering.

---

[4] Yes, it was that same leaf. And yes, it did hold some of Black Zonka's powdered medicine. Not much, but enough to help the normally well-grounded dwarf experience some elevated perceptions. If he'd been aware of the crone's order of operations, he would have been thankful that the pepper powder was applied last and had almost entirely left the frond before he used it to clean his backside.

Encountering no sign of people for a day now, he packed his armor on the wagon and went in plain clothes. Setting up a breakfast for the road – cold sausages, his pipe, and a flask – he hitched his pony to the wagon and climbed aboard.

Singing the old tune *A Dwarven Life is Anything but Short* he got rolling to the south. The old road meandered through the foothills, vibrant and viridescent. As the morning progressed, the birds he saw started to display aspects he had not seen before. Some trailed colors in their wake as they flew. One flew impossibly slowly; every wing beat clearly visible, each with its own slow, distinct 'whoosh' sound.

He watched a pair of jackrabbits scurry across the dirt of the road, multiplying as they ran. He had heard that rabbits were prolific, but this was ridiculous. The trees here were not tall or regular; the way was clear for the best part. Foothill grasses blew, flowing and moving like water. Watching this for a while, Angus spotted a wave of grass break over like a wind whipped lake. These foothills were a strange place indeed.

He regarded mountains drawing near – great, red rocky things. It would be good to be among the familiar again. Flicking his pony with the reins, he tried to get there a bit faster.

----- -----

Black Zonka had been enhancing people's consciousness for well over a thousand years. Very aware of the effects of the powder she had prepared for Angus – at least for a while. Ten hours later, she clung tenaciously to fading connections to her identity.

Covered in cuts and bruises, grass stains and smeared sap, she stumbled and weaved through the woods, desperately trying to evade the marauding Dwarven army that pursued her relentlessly. They had wrecked her home, spoiled her well and told her in no uncertain terms that all orcs were to be exterminated so that humans and elves and dwarves could establish their new world order.[5]

---

[5] This was, of course, all hallucination and conflation. In a different time, in a different reality, Zonka had experienced what could be called a 'bad trip' of truly epic proportions. This state, in general, is not recommended by the author. Consult your doctor, individual results may vary.

She would have been completely lost, but the orc wandered this territory since she was a child. She did find herself often off-course, but corrected time after time, inexorably drawing nearer the orcish hill fort. The sun rose before she finally saw it, her salvation in sight. She cried out for help as she drew near.

One of the sentries caught sight of her, rang a bell, and shouted for action. When she heard the orcish reaction, Zonka fell to her knees, wailing. She stayed in that state, even as they placed her on a litter and carried her into the fort. She sobbed as caring orc mothers treated her wounds. She advised many of these on their mating choices years earlier. They treated her with reverence.

No orc still lived that remembered the last time Zonka needed help. In fact, with orcish society being so based upon violence, average lifespan equated to something in the thirties. Rarely did an orc die of old age. No one knew the crone's age; even Zonka stopped counting long ago. She wasn't sure why she lived so long, but she suspected it might be something she ate or enjoyed near her hovel. At this point, she feared for her life; convinced that the marauders had destroyed her home and set the area aflame. Her secret of youth may be lost forever. She was afraid to go back to see what remained.

Soothing words and succor brought her out of her terror enough to start the flow of babbling. She recounted her various tormentors, the evil methods and devices they had used, and revealed the whole terrible plot to the assembled orcs. She went on for hours. Their chieftain, Ogrash, had sent out scouts as soon as he had heard of an invading army, but they came back with nothing untoward to report.

This put Ogrash in a tough spot. He had no evidence of what Black Zonka reported. War never left everyone whole and well. Yet common knowledge held that the crone could see what *would* happen as clearly as what *had* happened. Perhaps this was one of those times. He asked her "Black Zonka – what is the right path? How can we prevent our doom?"

"Kill them all! Gather the clans and destroy those that would destroy us! Start with the cursed ones that come from the mountains!" She shouted that last, then passed out cold. It seemed unlikely that she could be roused soon, and Ogrash figured that she needed the rest after her ordeal. He let her lie undisturbed.

Turning away from the unconscious crone, Ogrash spoke in authoritative tones. "Let those who have done this feel the wrath of all orcs. Send fast riders to the clans! Bear witness to Black Zonka's testimony. I will take our boys south, to the human settlement on the other side of the pass. They are the closest to us and came from those mountains when they attacked us in the past. Arm yourselves! We start out at noon!"

The orcs rushed to sort out who would do what. By noon they had sent riders and assembled several hundred orcs, each ready for battle. Those that would stay behind were busily camouflaging their fort and any other evidence of where the women and children were staying – very few of the orc males stayed behind. They started out, bypassing what may be left of Zonka's hovel with the intent of shortcutting cross country to the pass. The dire company made good time.

----- -----

Angus observed a number of oddities in the morning, but by lunch, the world began to normalize. He had taken to studying the rock formations on either side of the valley as the road wound slowly upward on the eastern slope. These hills looked different than the ones back home. Instead of granite and slate, these hills showed red sandstone that crumbled away. Small wonder that no dwarves called this range home.

Sometimes, an ancient boulder balanced atop a precarious spire of the sandstone, presumably worn away at a faster rate than the rock above. Sometime in the past, water ran freely along this valley, but not recently. *It must have been regular*, Angus supposed, *to have carved this valley*. He set a slow and steady pace for hours, stopping finally at a west-facing promontory. From this vantage point he could see most of the road ahead and behind; an awesome sight.

He stopped and retrieved a healthy serving of oats and water for his pony, then set about a leisurely dinner for himself. Dried salted pork, hard cheese, and dwarven way-bread would go nicely with a smoke and some brandy, he thought. Angus preferred the bread after soaking it in brandy to loosen it up and add some kick. When he finished assembling all of this, he set himself down at the edge of the road, feet dangling over the side; right at the furthest point west.

The magnificent view stretched more than three quarters the way around him. Chewing thoughtfully on a piece of cured pork, he executed a slow survey from the south to the north. Initially he observed a walled town about ten miles down the road, at the margin of the hills and mountains. Lazy wisps of smoke rose from chimneys, one of which billowed rhythmically. To Angus' dwarven eye, that meant a smith working hard. He would have to stop in and ask whether he needed a better silver supply. Angus did hail from the Argentine Holt, after all. The Holt produced mainly silver, but the local market had gone a bit soft of late. If silver wasn't plentiful here, maybe he could make a coin or twenty by trading shrewdly.

Far to the south, he could see more signs of human habitation. That was Ivonia proper; his next stop. Based on his experience at p'Eaux d'Ancre, it should be a much easier meeting than with the elves.

He spent a good deal of time considering the makeup of the mountains, and even came up with the idea for how to drop one of those precariously perched boulders on a passer-by. Dwarves were naturally good at booby-traps, and this seemed a good fit. Too bad there wasn't anything worth defending here.

He let his eye drift back to the north, wondering if he could see the elven forest, or even his own mountain range. What caught his gaze unsettled him. A small army marched up the same road he traveled, and there was only one possible destination: the Sliver. Here sat Angus, stuck in the middle, and he might not outrun them even if he abandoned his belongings.

I could ditch the wagon and gain speed; but there's a small fortune wrapped up there, he thought. *Especially that Argentine brandy. No, I need to get everything into the walled town, before they shut it up against the invaders. But how?* He took a long look down the valley to the north and considered his options.

He eventually spotted one of those erratic boulders that would fall naturally sometime in the next few centuries. Poised to roll down the steep slope, it would be very likely to damage the road heavily if not take it out entirely. He tried to estimate how much more of the sandstone would need to erode and where. In no immediate danger, Angus pondered the situation. While he could see the army, it was still a couple of miles away as the crow flies. Considering the way the road curved, and the ascent involved, he calculated he might have an hour or two before they caught him.

Angus took the time to draw a picture of the rock in the sand from his memory of the other side and reasoned out a weak point where it would likely fail given more time. He took the siege bow out and lashed the quiver to his belt. Taking nothing else, he walked back along the road until he had a good shot at the weak point. He took a long look again, considering his likelihood of success. The siege bow, powerful and accurate, should be enough. After a moment's reflection, he sighed and set about cocking the immense triple crossbow.

The strings, too heavy even for Angus to draw, were not pulled by hand. Instead, siege bows have clever ratcheting lever systems that pull all three bows back at once. The downside to this is the noise; a CRACKCRACKCRACKCRACK that echoed through the canyon. The orcs were certainly alerted to his presence. He loaded three bolts and set up the hard-sided quiver as a makeshift shooting stand. Kneeling beside it, he let all the weight of the crossbow rest on the quiver while he concentrated on making a straight shot.

Lining his target area up in his steel sights, he slowed his breathing. He inhaled, then let his breath half out, aimed carefully, and fired his first shot. The bolt smacked right into the erratic itself and careened off into the valley, dropping out of sight. Angus stretched his neck in a circular motion and lined up another shot. He sighted his target a bit lower this time, accounting for the extra power of Artemus' custom bow.

The second shot hit true, the head penetrating the sandstone and breaking off in splinters. It didn't drop the boulder, true; but one of Angus' two main concerns had been addressed: Yes, he could hit the target. His third shot bounced off the same area, knocking small chunks off the sandstone. Shooting a stationary target with a good crossbow isn't all that hard, even for a dwarf with only a couple hundred hours behind the stock. At this point, Angus had yet to figure out the vast advantage that dwarves gain from such a long lifespan; in human terms, he would be an accomplished shooter. As dwarves go, he was good enough to be allowed to use a bow unsupervised.

He poured shot after shot into the sandstone. Each time, he aimed carefully; no advantage in shooting too quickly. He was down to eleven bolts when he thought to step back up the road far enough to see where the army was. It would be close. Eleven thick, heavy crossbow bolts and a sketchy plan were all that stood between him and a gory death. For a moment he considered donning the armor but decided against it in favor of freedom of movement.

Reassuming his firing stance, he reloaded and fired again. And again. And again – this time followed by a small shower of red sandstone crumbling from the newly shifted balance point. Reloading, Angus considered whether the great spirit of the earth was with him. Inside of eight shots, he figured he would know.

As it turned out, it only took two. The wagon-sized boulder slipped off its perch and slid down the mountainside, just as the army came into view around a corner. Close enough to see clearly now – an orcish army! Several decades passed since Angus had even heard of such a thing, and he had been apprenticing in alchemy at the time and not sent to the fight. War would be a new experience for him.

The orcs saw him as well and would have charged if not for the impending boulder in the way. The sound and sight were fearsome and had everyone's full attention. It took about three seconds for it to reach the point that it hit the old road, which it blew right through. At that point it started tumbling, rocking the valley every time it made contact. It took another ten seconds for it all to stop when the rock had landed at the very bottom of the steep slope.

The gap that the careening monolith created was about twenty feet across. Angus stood up and laughed out loud, pointing at the orcs and holding his belly. "You dirty fools might as well pack it in – you'll never get across that!" He made a rude gesture, deliberately packed his bow and quiver, and made his way back to the pony. He made a show of walking slowly and proudly, even though he could hear and understand every epithet and threat that was called out behind him. He desperately hoped that they didn't have the brains and equipment to bridge the gap – it would not go well for that walled town by the looks of these orcs.

When he got to the wagon, he looked back once, just in time to see one of the orcs fall off the sheer wall where he had been trying to cross. They had the will, at least. He spurred his pony to the fastest walk that was safe towards the walled city below.

On this leg of the trip, he found himself musing about what it meant to have dropped that boulder. There had been a crisis that threatened him as well as a nearby town. He hatched a clever plan and succeeded, definitely saving his own skin and possibly a number of people at the town he was heading to. He thought that might just qualify as a heroic act.

On the other hand, no one witnessed Angus' deed. The orcs saw the result, and certainly heard the cracks and clatters from his siege bow, but it was less than likely that they could reason out how that boulder came to fall. The only thing they were sure of was that a short, stout, bearded person watched what happened, and chose to make fun at their expense. None present thought he was a hero.

He rode on as the sun started to set. He contemplated how it would go with Artemus, his Da, and the other dwarves of the Holt. He was sure that at least some would doubt his claim; so, he decided not to share. Angus needed to perform a witnessed event. He let out a long sigh as he approached the darkened gates.

Chapter 13

A Warm Bed

Richard pulled a punk out of the small fireplace to light the pipe weed he carefully tamped with his thumb. Puffing his carved nutwood pipe several times, the wiry, middle-aged man leaned back to enjoy the evening. Most of the watch saw the night shift as a punishment; but not Richard. Sitting up here in the north tower, he really only had one place he had to keep an eye on – the long narrow pass that wound its way up into the mountains. The pass was used heavily at certain times of the year, like after harvest, or when one of the monstrous trade caravans came through. Early summer was not the season for those activities, making the actual duty about as engaging as watching paint dry.

Instead, what often captured his interest were things happening inside the town walls. The sandstone tower stood four stories tall, the best vantage point for seeing many of the town's windows, streets and alleys. He couldn't usually hear what was going on, but in many cases the sight alone entertained Richard. On several occasions he made some extra cash by keeping quiet about what he had seen, other times making it public.

Tonight, there was a young couple whispering closely in the dark, an old drunk throwing up next to the tavern, and the sounds of an argument radiating from a nearby residence. Nothing with a real profit potential so far. He puffed at his pipe again and turned on a whim to look up the pass. In the filtered moonlight, he spied a small wagon rolling down the road towards the gate. Richard leaned casually over the parapet of the small tower, which rose roughly ten feet above the walls on either side. He puffed actively and considered his options.

As it drew closer, he determined that the small, two-wheeled wagon was pulled by a very stout pony; resembling a miniature draft horse. The wagon featured more metal than most; it looked heavier than it needed to be. The pilot was short and burly as well, with a braided beard. A dwarf might explain the heavy wagon; he could be selling ore. It didn't fit Richard's mold for dwarvish traders though – they usually came through at set times with massive convoys for safety. No one bothered a dwarven convoy; it would be like trying to attack a small army of very tough veterans.

Richard drew long on his pipe, red glow illuminating his eyes and nose in the darkened tower. He was intrigued. In eighteen years of standing this post, he could not remember seeing one dwarf alone. He always regarded dwarves as loud, obnoxious and crude, but Richard never dared express his feelings for fear of being kneecapped. A single, unarmored dwarf was a different story. Besides, with the gate closed, policy dictates that it stays closed until morning. Richard anticipated an evening of fun and profit after all.

----- -----

It took Angus a lot longer than he had expected to reach the walled town. The struggling twilight died as he approached the gate. Angus could see in the dark as well as the next dwarf, but it would have been better to arrive in the daylight. He cast an appreciative glance along the wall; the first time he could see it whole.

The town had been built in a strategic spot, nestled between two steep mountain walls. The perimeter wall spanned the gap entirely, providing an excellent place to defend Ivonia from this pass. Angus could see that parts of the wall had been rebuilt; see the scars where the sandstone of the mountains had been dug at by intruders to make a way in. It wasn't a dwarven wall, not even the oldest parts. Even so, it presented itself as effective – it would certainly keep him out.

Reflexively, he analyzed the wall for weak spots. There was a lone tower here on the eastern side of the valley where the road entered the town. The stout, crenelated walls and tower would make this a bad spot to attack. The valley dropped precipitously in the middle; but the bushes on the western slope might cloak a dwarven sapper; that would be the place for a small commando force to come in. It wouldn't matter here, of course; even if that orcish army managed to make it here, Angus doubted they would have that kind of strategic ability.

He was considering whether he should share his experience from the road with the gate guard as he came within earshot. There was a single guard visible, leaning on a halberd and smoking a crude pipe. The sentry looked intently and dispassionately at Angus. Angus raised his right hand in what he meant to be a friendly hail, opening his mouth to speak. The aloof guard beat him to the punch, however.

"Where do you think you're heading there, stunty?" The guard hadn't moved a muscle; even the pipe remained eerily motionless. But that didn't bother Angus as much as the remark. A wise man simply did not make fun of a dwarf's height. Such things often led to broken kneecaps. The guard seized upon Angus' stunned pause to add "out with it – unless you're short of breath? I know that wagon seat must be quite a climb for you."

Angus changed his gesture to a single raised forefinger, faced away to indicate he needed a moment. He took a deep breath and counted slowly towards ten. He stopped halfway when he realized he was only counting the ways he could set this lad straight. His honor wouldn't matter a whit if he didn't get inside before the orcs; he would bow and scrape if he must.

"I'm on my way to the city of Ivonal on pressing business. I plan to stop here for a night's rest, and I'll spend a fair amount of Argentine silver for food, drink and board. Could you see your way clear to let me in for the night?"

"Sorry, the gate has been closed for hours now. Policy dictates we cannot open up until daybreak for fear of brigands or thieves that might sneak in at night. I'm afraid you'll have to camp outside tonight."

Angus tilted his head, trying to understand what he was getting at. Turning in place, he looked all around. "I see no brigands or thieves. It's just me and my pony, and the vital supplies I am taking to Ivonal. Surely you can make an exception and watch closely – to guard against the incredibly stealthy thieves that camp outside your gates constantly."

"Don't get short with me, dwarf. Anyway, why should I break the rules to let you in? It's my job on the line, you know. You should have planned better and arrived during the day, when it's a normal toll road. No, spend your time breaking out your bedroll. Good evening."

Angus knew the game now, at least. The guard wanted 'justification' to break the rules; probably in the form of a 'toll'. He considered what he could let go of; he would be damned if this guard got one more cent than it would take. He pulled out the small purse from his waist; the one for the general public. It never contained more than he could lose entirely without concern. Most of the coin was hidden in several larger grain sacks on the wagon, or back at the Holt with his Da.

As he considered how much it would take, and how he would settle the score later, it hit him. He said, "Oy! You've a tankard or flagon up there, right? Filled with something acceptable for duty, and suitably boring?" He tossed a corner of the tarp behind him back, exposing one of the casks of brandy. "You let me in, and I'll fill whatever you've got up there with the best dwarven brandy you've ever tasted. Come now; it'll help you grow a proper beard!" He waited and hoped for the best.

The guard listened unmoving, holding for a moment after Angus stopped talking. Then, slowly, he twisted around to see who might be watching. Nobody near enough to hear. The street empty at the moment, the coast clear. He disappeared down the ladder after grabbing something from atop the crenellations.

The sounds of latches being thrown, and a chain pulled around a gear preceded the opening of the gate; a heavy wooden gate reinforced with thick bands of iron. The guard stepped out and tossed the contents of a large stein onto the flagstones.

"Make it quick – fill it up before you come in." The exchange was made; entry for enough stiff Argentine brandy to deaden Richard's senses. The man took a good slug as Angus entered.

"Welcome to the Sliver!" With that, Richard locked the gate and faded into his tower.

The Sliver consisted of about twenty blocks laid out on a north-south grid. The eastern and western margins were described by steep, sandstone mountainside, with several tunnels dug in. The main avenue ran between gates on the north and south end of town, mirror images of each other. After parting with more brandy than he cared to, Angus started southward.

Angus led the pony down the street towards one of several inns. The common room at the 'Posh Peddler' beckoned; bright and open, if somewhat empty. Only a few drinkers remained, most having retired to their rooms. Angus lashed the pony to the hitching post and stepped in the door, only to be met by a large man in a greasy apron. "The kitchen's closed, and we're full up. Sorry."

Angus nodded silently and walked out. As he grabbed the pony's bridle again, he noticed how empty the stables were. No matter, he thought, and went on toward the next inn. And passed it right by; the 'Elvish Respite' would not do for him. He had seen a third option back toward the wall on the west side of town and headed off to see what they had to offer. The 'Well-Turned Ankle' seemed to be more active, with a song and dance that Angus could hear, but not see; the house was "actually quite full", as the innkeeper soon informed him.

Angus stood in the street for a time, considering his options. There had been another gate at the south end of town, manned in a similar fashion. It might look worse trying to leave town in the middle of the night. What to do then? He went over what he knew about the town, remembering the smoke that suggested a smithy. He set about roaming the streets looking for a fellow metalworker that might take pity on him.

Angus spent a good fifteen minutes of leading the pony and wagon up and down streets before he found the smithy, nestled up against the west end of the north wall. Nothing was happening now, the coals cooling rapidly. He saw that the house next door displayed hammer and tongs over an anvil engraved on the sign and walked up to rap the heavy wrought-iron knocker. Three solid clacks, and he waited.

----- -----

When the smith opened the door, he looked right over Angus' head initially. A tall, broad man with a pugilist's nose, he looked down to see a dwarf standing on his porch. Drawing his head back a fraction in surprise, he stammered, "Y-Yes? What may I do for you master dwarf?"

"That's the best reception I've had all night. I am Angus... Redbeard, passing through town on business. All the acceptable inns seem to be full, so I thought I might ask if you would rent some space near your forge for me and my pony tonight. I'll pay whatever you think is fair."

The smith stuck his lower lip out a bit, chewing on his upper as he considered. "I guess I'm not surprised. The town's inns are not full, friend. Folks around here just don't hold with dwarves, is all. They think it's bad for business. I know better; your people make the best tools and weapons available; in fact, I use a dwarven cross-peen hammer in my smithing. It was a gift from a citizen of the Smaragdine Holt to the east; it draws metal with precise control." He smiled proudly and stood up a little straighter – he caught himself hunching to be closer to Angus' level.

"Suppose you stay there near the forge on a cot tonight. If you like it, you could leave a token of your appreciation. If not, no hard feelings. My wife may not let you in the house, but I don't feel right charging you for a simple cot in the shop."

"I'm grateful for the offer; and I'm sure you'll find something useful in the morning. What do I call you, master Smith?" Angus held out his right hand.

"You may call me Patrick, Patrick the Smith. It's always a pleasure to meet a fellow craftsman. Er, craftsdwarf. Please let me know if I can help at all. Otherwise, make yourself comfortable!" Patrick bobbed his head a couple of times as he backed into the house.

----- -----

As the door closed, Angus lead the pony into the shop proper. He unhitched the wagon and tied the beast to a supporting pole. He set out a serving of oats, then rolled out his blankets on the stone hearth, where the embers were giving the slab their last vestiges of warmth.

This, he thought, *is likely the best place in the entire Sliver for a dwarf.* With thoughts of home running through his head, he gave himself entirely to sleep's warm embrace.

Chapter 14

A Rude Awakening

Angus dreamt of being welcomed home as a hero when the adulations turned to cries of dismay and horror. People really were yelling; but not the cheers his dreams held. Opening his eyes, his senses cleared. He was in Patrick's shop at the Sliver. The still-dark sky yielded no evidence as to how long he'd slept. A dozen grim-faced men bearing torches and weapons ran toward him, filling the street that terminated at Patrick's place. As if bidden by the thought of his name, Patrick strode out of his house clad in chain mail head to toe; a great two-handed sword in his hands. He walked to meet the leader directly, had a brief talk, then they all started towards Angus again. If they came for him, they had him easily.

As he staggered, still half asleep, towards the front of the open shop, he thought of what to say to save his skin. He went to open his mouth just as the loose formation turned toward the northern gate where he had come in. He tried to get their attention, but none would talk with him. One big man shoved him down and said "What's a stubby little dwarf going to do against an orc raid, eh? Keep your head down and maybe you'll survive the night."

The orcs! In his hurry to get to bed, he had completely forgotten that they might come. The men passed out of sight and he ran to the wagon to get his armor. One of the biggest issues with full plate was the time needed to put it on. The very best could do it in about five minutes; Angus was not yet near the best. If it went well, he might be ready for action in a quarter hour.

The sounds of men and orcs taunting each other rose with more regularity. Angus thanked the deeper powers for the fact that the orcs could not have brought any substantial siege equipment over the pass. His armor halfway on, bows and crossbows fired back and forth with battle cries and agonizing screams indicating casualties on both sides. Then there were a series of resonant thuds that might be a battering ram; Angus worried that he should have warned the men, but would they have believed him?

It wasn't until his gauntlets and helm were on that he noticed the sound; an odd tinkle-scratch-crack originating inside the back wall of the smithy. He moved closer to hear; put his ear to the wall and recognized a hissing, fizzling noise as the stone under his nose melted inward. Orcish sappers must be in the bushes just outside, using some sort of acid on the sub-standard wall! These blocks here were sandstone and disintegrating under whatever vile mixture they applied.

The now-armored dwarf charged to the street and hollered for Patrick (or anyone) to come to his aid, but the battle raged at the gate; no one answered. *Time to try out this axe*, he thought. He snatched the stone-and-mithril weapon off the wagon and took a position right in front of the melting stone. As the hole dilated, he reconsidered and stood to the side, with the axe raised over his head. He tried to breathe normally, to keep himself from shaking; his first real hand-to-hand combat imminent.

Mere moments later, the hole became large enough for an orc to put his head through. Swiveling its head from right to left, the interloper checked to see if the nascent incursion had been detected. It caught sight of armor-clad feet and looked up to see the owner. The orc met Angus' eyes as the axe fell true. His body slumped as the severed head rolled along the ground, sporting a surprised stare.

Angus raised his axe for the next strike as low conversation in a language he did not know filtered through the hole. If only he had his spear, he could stab through the hole repeatedly, preventing the enemy from entering. This axe was great for severing parts, certainly, but he had voiced his concerns about its defensive potential for years. He was about to find the truth of the matter, one way or the other.

The hole grew still larger, with more of the fluid being used to dissolve the sandstone sloshed through. Angus smiled. The dolts were making the hole bigger, but more of the solution was working on the lower portion of the breach, meaning a dwarf might have the advantage of high ground. A scimitar was thrust through the opening and flailed about from side to side; Angus only took a half step back to avoid the weapon. After a few seconds without the feeling of blade on flesh, the orc tried to dive through, sword first. The black, blood onyx blade did not find the neck this time; instead it dug deep into the orc's left side, grinding to a stop, wedged inside the orc's ruined rib cage. The color of the blade changed as the orc's normally dark skin paled. The corpse sagged noiselessly to the ground, legs still on the other side.

Angus put a foot on the body to wrest the axe free from the wound. As he raised it this time, dribbles of blood ran down the surface of the axe then were absorbed into the reddening stone. It was still very black, but it had gained a crimson quality; as of a red ruby in a dark room. Angus slew two orcs in a bloody fashion, yet the axe did not radiate the brilliant blood red that he had heard stories about. How many would that take? He rather hoped he wouldn't find out today.

He did find out. As the sounds of the fight at the tower reached a climax and faded back, the ever-growing breach filled with orc corpses one after another. The orcs had to get in quickly, or their plan would fail; they just kept coming. Some had different tactics, like the one who jumped through, sliding on his back with a shield over him. Angus slammed the shield down heavily, breaking the orc's arm and stopping him right there. The second blow arrived, merciful and quick.

After what seemed an eternity, the orcs stopped coming. The last one had effectively plugged the hole again. He had lost count at twenty-two dead orcs, and they formed a pile in and around the breach. He moved around a bit to study the scene, and whether this was a momentary pause. After five quiet minutes, he was satisfied. Human cheers rose from the direction of the gates; the orcs must be retreating.

He considered joining the celebration that was, then decided against it. These people didn't really appreciate him. Instead, he set his helm on the forge's Holt and retrieved his pipe. No brandy now; he wanted to be sober until this breach was attended. He selected a couple of corpses that lay atop each other and took a seat. He sat there for a time, reflecting on whether this qualified as one of those heroic actions Artemus required. He thought maybe it was.

Angus continued reflecting an hour or so later. Running his fingers along the lustrous red axe blade, appreciating the vorpal gift for the first time. Still not a great defensive weapon, but perfect for that situation. Everything worked out remarkably – not one missed axe stroke, taking no hit strong enough to penetrate his armor – just flawless.

He did not bother to clean the spattered blood from his armor yet. It would dry on, and surely be a task in the morning. Angus, on his third load of pipe weed, considered breaking into the brandy when Patrick arrived home with a young friend in a bright red shirt and yellow vest. They were on the way to bypass the shop entirely when Patrick spotted something out of place on the stone wall behind his shop. He stepped closer, squinting to see in the still-dark, pre-dawn hours. He grabbed an unlit torch and set it in the forge fire pit, pumping the bellows once to get the embers hot enough for the wadding to catch. When the light sprang up, he cursed without thinking of it and approached Angus, who was now squinting from the sudden abundance of light.

"Did… Did you do all of this?" The smith indicated the orcs with his free hand. Angus noticed that Patrick's weapon and armor were as pristine as when he had left. If the gate had held, he suspected that none of the townsfolk had done more than fire arrows and throw rocks. The friend walked up to discover the source of Patrick's amazement.

"They were disturbing my sleep. I really value my sleep." Angus was bursting on the inside, trying not to laugh – the dwarf's stout beard hid a small smirk. "I do want to know who's responsible for using sandstone for these blocks. It's not right. If this were proper granite, they never would have breached the wall."

The friend hovered in the torchlight now, showing great interest. "These orcs all came through that hole?" Angus nodded. "And you slew them, all, in close combat, before they could take two steps in?" Another nod. "This is the stuff of legends! What's your name, good dwarf?"

"This is Angus Redbeard. He's on business that will take him to Ivonal." Patrick spoke absently, still absorbing the dwarf's impossible feat. "You are drenched in blood. I know at least some of it must be yours. Come, let's get you to the north tower – the doctor is there."

"I haven't a scratch. A couple of bumps, that's all. Now, if you had someone to clean this armor and launder the padding, that would be a treat." To show that he really was fine, Angus stood up. "But right now, I'd like to get cleaned up and back to sleep. Your Holt is calling me." He stretched his arms and yawned pointedly.

The brightly dressed fellow was mouthing words unspoken, surveying the whole scene. Patrick continued. "Stay right here. I need to talk to someone – I'll be right back." He left at a trot towards the tower. Angus shook his head.

"So, what's your story then?" Angus said when Patrick was gone.

"My story? Oh, well, haha, I have several stories. I am a storyteller; a bard. I collect stories, mostly handed down over many generations. A few, a very few, are my own. But now, well, with your permission, your story will be my story."

Angus blinked. *With his permission?* "You mean that my bringing a few orcs to their end is interesting enough to make a story from? I don't know that I can agree fully with that. Now, if it were a Dragon, that would be a different story." Angus allowed himself a snigger at that one. .

"I'm actually not sure about the name. Angus Redbeard is a young dwarf's name, if I'm not mistaken. I do have something that has come to mind, if you'd like to hear…" He seemed excited to share, but Angus was tired.

"Just do as you would. I'm tired, and with any luck, I'll be snoring in a few minutes. Tell me in the morning." With that, he made his way to the quenching barrel to clean some of the blood off. He was just beginning to splash some of the gore from his greaves when they came.

The bulk of the men of fighting age seemed to be approaching again, many with torches. Very much like earlier, except that Angus knew for certain that this time, they *were* coming for him. He washed with a measured pace, wondering about the next few moments. These men weren't all that welcoming earlier – now they approached him with weapons and torches. Not the way he wanted to start off with any town. He walked back toward the grisly pile and hefted his axe.

"Master Angus! These men are here to see what you have done. I tried to tell them about the attack that you drove back alone, but they wouldn't believe. So, I brought them here to see." Patrick walked up to the wall and looked closely.

Then the innkeeper from the 'Posh Peddler' stepped forward, speaking in that loud, clearly enunciated voice that merchants do when they are advertising, "Master Angus, in thanks for your defense of our little town, you are welcome anytime at the 'Posh Peddler', free of charge. Shall I make a room ready for you?"

Angus set the butt of his axe handle on the dirt floor and crossed his thick forearms, leaning them on the bright crimson blade. "A very fine offer, sir. But I am afraid that I will not be visiting the 'Posh Peddler', tonight or ever. Earlier tonight, you told me that you could not sell me food, drink or shelter even though you did have room and stores. You, sir, are a heightist. What I did here was not for you. Anyway, I am quite comfortable staying here with good master Patrick – his forge feels a bit like home."

The red-faced innkeeper turned and stormed back through the crowd, blustering as some of them booed him for his mistreatment of the dwarf. There was a general murmur, as they tried to decide what should come next. After a few seconds, the bard shouted from the edge of the crowd, "Three cheers for Grimbrow Bloodaxe! Hip hip…"

They cheered. A crowd of over a hundred men was cheering for Angus – using a new name. And not a bad name at that. He half frowned, half smiled, then nodded slowly. He held up a hand as their cheers subsided. "I am happy to be of service. I'll be leaving in the morning, but I would sleep better if I knew that you would be replacing these sandstone blocks with heartier stuff. If you don't feel you have someone up to the task, I'll write a letter to the Argentine Holt, asking for good stonemasons. They aren't cheap, but they could be here inside of a week and their stonework is unmatched.

"In the meantime, if someone would like to earn a little silver, I need these clothes cleaned, and I'd like to have someone polish my armor. Is anyone interested?" There were plenty of volunteers. The crowd dispersed, with a few men staying to clear the orcs and hastily patch the wall with dry-stacked rocks. Patrick stayed up to tend the armor himself, as much to study the quality and methods as to show his respect and thanks.

After he changed out of his bloody kit and into some fresh clothes, Angus laid back down on the stone hearth, sleeping deeply. This had turned out to be a good day after all.

Chapter 15

A Traveling Companion

A hearty, grease-infused aroma pulled Angus away from sleep in the morning. Breakfast! He sat up and swung his feet to dangle from the edge of the hearth. The sun, well into its daily ascent, illuminated the platter that lay next to him. A dozen or so eggs, a pile of fried and spiced potatoes and a separate pile of various sausages, with a couple pieces of fruit and a steaming dark drink that Angus didn't know – some sort of bitter tea, he decided after tasting it. He tore into the food happily.

The dwarf ate alone in the forge. He suspected that many were catching up on sleep missed in the night. His padded clothes that he wore under the plate armor were hanging dry from a line nearby, all the blood washed away. The armor, modeled by a crude wooden mannequin, exuded greatness; polished mithril gleaming in the morning light. Then Angus noticed a very light horse that was tied off to one of the posts. It bore saddlebags stuffed to overfull, but no bedroll. Craning his neck allowed him to see where the missing bedding lay, currently occupied by Mr. Brightshirt, still sleeping deeply.

As he finished his breakfast, he studied the repaired wall. It was a mess. If the orcs came back, they would make short work of reopening their new entry. He looked around the smithy for some paper, finding a small stack on a rough, dirty desk. He wrote a quick message on one sheet to the Mountain King Artemus requesting help with the wall.

The second sheet he used for instructions; addressed to Ylus in p'Eaux d'Ancre who would deliver it to the Holt from there, and an order for good stone. If they did as he suggested, the stone and masons should arrive at the same time.

He set about readying his rig. Stowing the armor with the rest of his gear, he only kept the siege bow and axe near enough for action. He left three argents, pure silver and the standard unit of currency for the Holt, lying under the head of Patrick's dwarven hammer, which he placed on the hearth where he'd slept. He grabbed his pipe, downed the last of that bitter drink – he'd have to find out what that was called – and climbed aboard the wagon.

He flicked the reins and was off. This place was rather pretty in the daytime. It was built into the mountainside, with short, stout bridges over the canyon creek at every block through the center of town. Looking over the edges, the drop into the canyon below was quite long – long enough to be potentially deadly. A creek trickled along the bottom, an iron grate far below completing the northern wall. The whole place had been forcefully carved into a strategic bottleneck at one end of the pass.

If the stonework were better, Angus might have supposed it the kind of work dwarves would do, but there was nothing here beyond the skill of a dwarven apprentice. Again, it was all-too apparent to Angus that there was a real difference in what could be accomplished in such a short life as humans had. And yet, they seemed happy; hopeful and determined. Humans, Angus decided, were a strange lot.

He kept at his slow pace through the sandstone streets. For a moment, he wondered who had brought him that wonderful breakfast. He might not have to stop for lunch today, except that the pony would need a break or three. Trying to recall how far the next town had been on his map, and what it was called, he came within sight of the southern gate. He pulled rein when he was even with the guard.

"You know, it's odd. I still don't know what this town is called. Could you enlighten me?" The guard looked puzzled for a moment.

"You mean to say you don't know of the Sliver? It's the oldest continually occupied fortress in Ivonia; the town is just support for that wall that you defended with us last night. I... I'm supposed to collect a toll, but I'm not sure that it would be right."

"Tell me what the toll is, and I'll pay. I can't see asking you not to do your job just because I helped a bit. It's only fair that I pay the same toll everyone else does."

Angus paid the toll, thanked the guard and rolled out of town. A few hours out, he stopped to rest his pony on a nice, grassy hill. While he was checking his load, he noticed movement from up the road he had just traveled. A single rider in red and yellow. He sighed. Mr. Brightshirt. Just the thing to spoil an otherwise perfect day. He would have left, but the pony was grazing on very good grass, the kind he might not see too often on a journey. By the time the bard caught up to him, he was leaned back catnapping in the sun.

"Master Bloodaxe!" Brightshirt called. "Master Bloodaxe, I'm so glad I caught up with you! I'm headed to Ivonal as well; do you mind if I travel with you?" His horse was wet with sweat; he had pushed hard to catch up so soon. His hair was a mess, and he hadn't shaved.

"You can travel quite well on that spindly legged thing you call a horse. Why would you want to slow yourself down to keep a dwarven pony's pace? It makes no sense."

"Oh, but it makes perfect sense, Master Bloodaxe! I'll be much safer near you, for one." Angus very much doubted that. His luck had held so far, but the problems seemed to be coming quite regularly, and this tyke might attract disaster. "Also, I *am* a storyteller. And you, sir, are worth telling stories about. I am here for the story more than anything. Do you see why I have to come with you?" The kid's plaintive stare made telling him no feel like slapping a puppy for wanting to tag along.

Angus made a big show of thinking this through. He had decided to let the kid come along before he had arrived, but why let him know? It might make a better story if he thought Angus was wise and thoughtful. "Well, I suppose you can ride nearby. But don't think you'll be getting any of my brandy! It's the good stuff, like you can't find anywhere but a dwarven Holt. I've a long way to go yet, and it needs to last." He had cocked an eyebrow when he talked about the hooch, in the way his father used to when making a point. The way that the young man squirmed was immensely entertaining. "Now, if you're going to be hanging around, you'll need to tell me what you are called. That is, unless Mr. Brightshirt sounds good to you."

The young man blinked. "You know, that might make a good stage name. I'll think about that. In the meantime, you can call me John. I'm from Ivonal originally, though I now consider myself to be more a citizen of the world and less an Ivonian." John pulled a sheaf of paper from a pocket inside his vest and started writing with a sharp charcoal pencil. "Mr. Brightshirt. Yes. I think that will be excellent for telling children's stories. Please, Master Bloodaxe, let me know if there are any other gems that pop to mind." He smiled and went back to his writing.

Angus started to wonder whether he made the right choice. He got up and moved a flask of brandy to the bench seat where he could get to it. When John's horse was rested, they mounted up and headed south. On the way, John alternated between providing useful information about Ivonia and asking inane questions like, "How many orcs have you killed?". By the afternoon, Angus was in a state past caring. He was glad of the open territory; it would be hard to get ambushed here. Farms and fields, ranches and domestic beasts were the most common sights. It was pretty, but Angus thought it was a place better suited for a visit than a life.

As they approached the next town, a small, open farming co-operative called the Greenway, John began to get antsy. When the houses started to get close, and people became plentiful, John took off at a gallop toward the busy inn. It took Angus another quarter hour to get there, dismount and pass control of the wagon to a groom. At first, the groom's eyes goggled at the promise of silver for keeping a simple wagon and animal; then they almost popped out of his face in fear of failure. Angus had apprenticed to masters who had used either the stick or the carrot; he preferred to use both.

When he finally walked around to the front of "The Hustled Bustle", there was a loud, clear voice speaking to a hushed and attentive audience. Not thinking anything of it, Angus opened the door and stepped inside.

"And here he is!" shouted the speaker, gesturing toward the door. Angus turned around to see who had followed him in. The door had swung shut behind him. His head tilted on its own as he turned to face the speaker again; he started to understand where this was going. It was indeed Mr. Brightshirt – who continued his presentation. "This good dwarf, ladies and gentlemen, is none other than Angus "Grimbrow Bloodaxe", who just last night turned the tide of battle at the Sliver. He slew easily thirty great orcs before any of the other defenders knew they were there." Angus eyed the bar wistfully, but dutifully endured the monologue.

"All orc attacks in memory had hit the gate with all their force; but Angus knew instinctively where they would breach the wall. He went to that point and laid in wait – beheading several with that terrible axe of his! We all owe him a deep debt. Without him, we might be swimming in orcs right here at the Greenway!" The crowd broke into applause, cheering the hero of the hour. Several men clapped him on the back smartly, shaking his hand and thanking him for his efforts. Angus nodded and smiled uncomfortably through it all.

At this point a man wearing greasy apron and several quivering chins approached Angus, wringing his hands. "Master Bloodaxe, can we serve you some local beer and roast beef, in honor of your good deeds? Come, sit here, and your food and drink will be right out." The man looked at the normal sized chair he had offered Angus, considering for a moment offering the boosting block they used for children. He wisely decided against that strategy, disappearing into the kitchen.

People resumed their conversations again, moving their eyes back to their own tables. Most were happy and excited about the story, and John was making the rounds answering questions. Round after round of local ale showed up at Angus' table, sent by this or that patron. But nobody wanted to stop and eat with him. After a while, he started to notice a second type of conversation with darker themes.

There was a group of mostly older men, with grey, white or no hair, sitting at a table in the corner. They had severe looks amongst them and kept their tones low. Angus caught phrases like, "need to be ready", "bloody savage orcs", and "they haven't attacked us for decades". There were sidelong glances from that table, and questioning looks; as if there was doubt as to Angus' potential.

He finished his meal and asked the chinny man if he minded if he tended his axe at table. The cook looked around, and seeing that most of the meals were finished, said, "There shouldn't be any problem with that. There's no – chunks, or gore – on it still, are there?" Angus assured him it would be fine and went to retrieve his armor and axe from the wagon.

He came back in with the axe held at his side, and the bundled armor over his shoulder. When he set the bundle down with a clatter at the side of the table, the bar went silent; anyone who knew what Mithril was knew that this represented half the wealth of the entire Greenway valley. But when he put the crimson axe on the table and started to clean it, the murmurs were rampant. He pulled out the special whetstone that had come with the axe and checked the blade edge with his thumb. When he realized that he was bleeding, adding a fresh, bright tinge to the crescent cutting surface, he put the whetstone away unused and started polishing. The axe didn't take long, but he took extra time to get into the seams and crannies of the priceless armor. He really wanted this gear to last, and he'd take pains to make it so.

When he had run over everything thoroughly, he made arrangements with the innkeeper for a room and adjourned. He made two trips, having exposed his fortune, bringing in everything of great value. He considered finding a bank. But for the moment, it was time for bed. He locked the door, setting noisemakers on both the door and window to announce unwanted visitors, and went to sleep.

Chapter 16

An Unwanted Visitor

Well past midnight the Greenway lay silent. The elders posted a couple of guards who were sleeping soundly at their posts. The Greenway was an exceedingly peaceful place, outside the realm of politics and strategy. The people here grew food and nothing else. There was no wall, no watch, and no one missed either.

This evening, however, something was up. A single dark figure slipped through the streets, sticking to the shadows as much as possible on the moonlit night. It moved with grace and agility; using all the best places to hide. Whatever it was up to had been done before.

It entered the inn by the back way, through the kitchen. The lock on the door eased just as if a key had turned in the tumbler; perhaps it was a key. Soft-soled leather slippers masked the mere hint of padding feet. Shrouded in a dark cloak or robe, the silhouette was impossible to make out. The thing might as well have been a shadow. Unseen and unheard, it entered the empty common room of the inn, and headed straight for the stairs. The shadow had been here before, too.

Halfway up the stairs, a single squeaky step lay in wait. The owner decided long ago not to fix it, as it seemed to him an excellent security device. Plus, it added a certain country charm to the place. But this phantom was not fooled; it simply bypassed the telltale board and moved on. It seemed to know every nuance; it was practiced and undetectable. And it moved with purpose.

Then Angus' door was right in front of it. An observer inside the room would have seen the bolt slide fractionally, a quarter inch at a time. Angus had set an open bag of loose coins on that bolt, but somehow, they stayed on their moving perch as the door opened slowly. Whatever this thing was, it had infinite patience. The hinges were somewhat squeaky but moving so slowly that only the individual clicks issued. The door was closed in a similar manner, and the bolt slid shut. All the while, Angus breathed at the deep, regular pace of sound slumber.

Now the figure approached, hovering over the recumbent dwarf. His face was up, and the newcomer bent close. A hint of parted lips showed themselves from under the drawn hood. It came closer, and closer, until their breath mixed. The dark lips met Angus'; their purpose achieved.

Angus' eyes opened fully, and he pushed frantically at the dark figure. He was being... being... kissed? He tore away from his assailant and sat up straight. The figure stood, and dropped the hood back, showing a beautiful young woman. Blonde, with freckles and flushed cheeks, she couldn't have been out of her twenties. Angus blinked. The girl smiled. And dropped her robe to the floor.

Angus was not an expert in human female anatomy, but a quick glance told him that everything corresponded with the works of art he had seen. The more popular works of art. He blinked for a moment, not able even to stammer. He closed his eyes when she giggled softly, then thought better of that – it could be a trap. Opening his eyes again, he locked his gaze with hers and got ready to ask for an explanation. "!" was all he got out.

Putting a slender finger to his lips, she whispered softly, "I came to thank you personally for saving us. I thought you might like...." Her playful smile said the rest.

"I most certainly do not want... I mean... what – why – how... how did you get in here?" Angus took note of the locked door, and his noisy trap still unsprung. The other was still on the windowsill. "What do you want?"

She persisted, with "I only want what you want; what all men want. Let's forget ourselves and enjoy the moment!" She leaned heavily over him, almost a tackle. Somehow, he evaded her, ending up standing where she had been a moment before. He grabbed her robe from the floor and tossed it to her.

"You seem to have mistaken me for a man – I am a dwarf, a proper dwarf, and this is not what we do." He started to grab his flask. "I appreciate the offer, but it's just not in me to..." flustered, he took a swig. "Um, if there's nothing else, I'd like to get back to sleep. Would you mind terribly?"

She pouted pointedly for a moment, then giggled again. "Maybe the next time you come through Greenway. I'm sure I'll be here!" She walked out quietly, robe in hand. Angus shut the door behind her, sliding the bolt closed and giving the door a couple of good tugs to make sure it was in. He realized that he was shaking; neither the battle at the Sliver, nor encountering the Dragon had been that stressful. He took a few more good swigs, then set about making the room as secure as it could be. After an hour of checks and double checks, he got back into bed. But sleep did not come again that night for Angus.

Chapter 17

An Early Start

After several hours of tossing and turning, Angus got up. He took everything out to the wagon and started before dawn, trying to avoid John among others. He cleared the town headed southeast without any conversation, apparently before anyone was up. He wasn't feeling great, but he just wanted to be a bit further down the road before he stopped.

A false dawn illuminated the countryside with a spooky grey-blue glow. No lights burned in the houses, the only noise beside those of his wagon an early cock crowing. By the time the true dawn broke, the Greenway was no longer in sight. He enjoyed this part of the journey; he was headed to a low-risk place, with no angry orcs, sneaky elves or eager young humans along the way to give him grief. And the land was pretty. Most of the farms were not fenced, and the buildings were set back from the road.

He was invited in for lunch by an old farmer and his wife who had been walking down the road, enjoying their retirement. It seemed that their whole life had been peaceful; never seeing an orc or Dragon or troll. The biggest problems they dealt with were droughts, pests and blight. Angus almost envied them. They were proud of what they felt was their advanced age, the old man having recently achieved sixty-five years. Angus declined to share his age.

A couple of fast riders passed south while they ate and talked, but Angus paid them no mind. After a long lunch, he parted ways with the old couple, having filled one of their jars with some of his brandy. They insisted that he stop in when he passed this way again.

He paused at a small town that was little more than a trading post and replenished some of his supplies. The pony went through oats like water before arriving in this grassy land, and Angus wanted to be ready. He noticed that the prices were far below what he would pay at the Holt. Again, he found himself considering becoming a trader when all this was over. After all, there were only nineteen years left on his first tour as a Holtgart.

He realized how much he had enjoyed this stop, and the couple who didn't know him. They treated him like he was normal; nothing exceptional except for being a traveler. He had never considered the downside to fame; the constant bombardment of attention, and the differing strong reactions people had to it. Artemus suffered only occasional light mockery back at the Holt, and he was always willing to admit an error. People loved him, and he was approachable. In fact, Artemus made a point of having a drink with each of his subjects at least once every few years. Angus wondered what it would take to get that kind of fame.

He had been deep in thought, letting the pony guide itself along the road, when he realized that he was coming up to another forest - a big forest. He stopped the wagon and consulted his map. According to the old parchment document, the open land should continue all the way to Ivonal, a city of perhaps a hundred thousand. But here there was a grand forest; not as tall and groomed as the elven forest certainly, but big enough to appear on the map. Checking the legend, he realized why.

Artemus had given him a map that was over 300 years old! If there was time for a forest like this to grow, what other surprises lay in wait for him? He decided that he would buy a newer map at the first opportunity. He rolled up the old one and tucked it back under the seat, and took a long, slow look at the woods. Angus wasn't about to let any more trouble befall him if he could avoid it.

Overcome by caution, he pulled off the road and put on the armor. Once suited up, he set up the axe, bow and quiver for easy access. Scanning the edge of the woods again, he continued along the well-worn track. When he reached the edge of the forest, he saw a sign with some sort of seal he didn't recognize; but the 'NO HUNTING' message was clear. He was well provisioned, and not a real hunter anyway; this shouldn't present a problem.

The forest road didn't twist or turn much at all; it seemed that it was raised up to avoid changing the route. It was fairly uniform, featuring only several kinds of leafy, gnarled trees and scattered brush. He didn't see any game near the trail, except for occasional deer crossings. The trees were mostly oaks, not much more than forty feet tall on average. Spreading limbs would make a great place for squirrels and birds, but they remained strangely absent as he traveled. It was like the forest knew there was a predator about and didn't want to draw attention.

After a few miles, he thought he could see an end to the trees, maybe another mile ahead. He started to hum a happy tune, sure that this would not be added to his list of bad places. It was about this time that he saw a young man sitting and leaning on a tree at the left side of the trail. He had a red shirt, and - yes, a yellow vest. John. Angus thought he must have been one of the fast riders from earlier, stopped to rest.

As he approached, John appeared to be sleeping, head sagging. "Wake up, youngster! There's plenty of time to rest once we're out of these woods!" But as John raised his head, Angus saw the gag and the rope tying him to the tree. He followed John's glance upwards, finding several men with longbows standing in the trees above. Then another man stepped out from behind one of the larger oaks to his right.

"You may have time later, dwarf, if you survive. But right now, I am in control." The man smiled, a wicked, scheming visage. "If you want that to happen, you will dismount, remove that armor, and start walking. Any other action means you and the kid both die."

Stalling, Angus tied the reins off to the wagon, making a show of shaking. He had heard stories of mithril armor shrugging off arrows, but he wasn't keen to learn the truth by becoming a pincushion. On the other hand, he doubted that he would have the chance to walk away from this encounter, as brazen as this thief was being. He slid over to the right side of the bench, holding on to the backrest with his right hand, just near the handle of the axe. He surveyed the ground as he moved slowly toward the edge, picking his landing spot. *This probably won't work*, he thought, *but it's something.*

In a blur he grabbed the axe and launched himself toward the leader – who was standing well out of range of a leaping attack. Angus hit the ground first, initiating a shoulder roll that would have earned him a nod from Bladin, his combat teacher. He came out of the roll with his axe sweeping overhead, making a terrible wound across his victim's side. As the shocked bandit fell, screaming and thrashing, Angus rose smoothly as arrows struck from several directions. Two of them hit solid plates and shattered, but one found a joint in his thigh and stuck fast.

Wincing in pain, Angus made himself walk upright back to the wagon. Three more arrows were loosed, two hitting; both glancing off without harm. Angus reached over the side of the wagon calmly and retrieved his siege bow. Leaning the axe up against the wagon wheel, he turned to face the bowmen who were drawing again. They loosed as he cranked the mighty bow, two hurried shots missing, and another hitting him true in the heart – but shattering as it struck.

He smiled broadly as he cocked the bow – the ratchet CRACKCRACKCRACK resonating through the forest. He turned his back to grab the bolts, but as he straightened, he realized that they were all dropping to horses they had nearby. He loaded anyway and took aim at the one that had wounded him. He fired, missing, but taking a thick branch off a tree ahead of the rider – who uttered a short scream and urged his steed faster.

Angus walked over to the fallen man, hoping for the chance to talk to him. He was dead by the time Angus reached him; eyes glazed and face ashen from blood loss. "A pity you didn't give me an option I could accept." He turned to John, releasing his hands before the gag. He really didn't want to hear it.

"Master Bloodaxe, I'm sorry for the trouble. They took me about an hour ago; it seems that people think your armor worth a small fortune. After seeing what it did to those arrows, I'm inclined to agree." Angus had forgotten the arrow embedded in his leg; he reached over and broke the end off.

"Is there a doctor nearby? I'd rather have a professional take care of this..." Angus was feeling the pain now. It really hurt! This was the first time he had been shot. He hoped it would be the last. "Also, I think you'll run the wagon the rest of the way in. I'm planning on a bit of drinking to kill the pain."

John did know a doctor in Ivonal, which was only a few hours away. They made a compress from a spare shirt and set off. Angus laid back in the cargo area of the wagon, leg elevated on a sack of oats. By the time they arrived, Angus had drunk more than he had bled, and John had to help with everything. The young man had been oddly quiet during the trip. Angus wasn't complaining.

Chapter 18

Ivonal

Unfamiliar faces hovered periodically above Angus. Sometimes they were feeding him, sometimes propping an eye open; using words he didn't recognize. A nasty liquid kept being dribbled into his mouth, sending him into another stage of dazed semi-consciousness. He was vaguely aware of being poked and prodded from time to time, but he just didn't care.

Then there was light. He was surrounded by a thin white curtain; translucent. He looked around, realizing he was wearing only a gauzy robe. The whole room was white; light streamed in from a big window. No one was here. He sat up. His leg had some pain, but not much. The bandage was clean and tight, no blood seeping through.

He pushed aside the veil as he swung his legs over the side of the bed. Testing it by putting some weight on it, he realized that it felt all right. Sore, but all right. He walked over to the window to see where he was - and gasped.

Ivonal was not a city of great dwarven stonework. It was not laid out on an efficient grid, nor was it well planned from the start. It was, however, bright. And big. It went on as far as he could see, dropping off in the distance into a blue horizon that must be the sea. Between there and here, every single vertical plane had been plastered and whitewashed. Smooth, alabaster surfaces and rounded archways were everywhere.

The roof tiles were equally as remarkable. A bright blue in an astonishingly consistent shade, their reflective glazed shells shimmered like waves on a lake. Every roof had a similar pitch, though at a multitude of heights. The whole place emitted a – lightness – that made one feel as if they were a part of something pure.

He couldn't close his eyes; for a quarter hour or more he stood and marveled at what these people had accomplished. True, it would need constant attention to stay this beautiful; not like good stone. The plaster would age and crack, and the smoke from winter fires would taint the surface. But in human terms, it meant continual employment for people who may not qualify for more skilled work.

Dwarves built things to last; a fortress may sit unchanged with little maintenance for centuries. Dwarven homes were often thousands of years old, little changed from their original form over the years. Furniture was made once and lasted for lifetimes. But then each of these items might take ten times as long to manufacture; and garner ten times the price. Humans, by and large, did not have time for the luxury of quality.

This city made a righteous attempt to look like it was entirely of a piece. Regardless of what lay underneath, the surface was admirable. It was impossible to tell whether a structure was sound or on the verge of collapse though all that plaster. Angus wasn't very comfortable with that.

He was interrupted by the sound of the door latch being opened behind him. He didn't turn his body, just looked over his shoulder and said, "Hello?" The door opened, and a young woman walked in. She was the picture of modesty; in a blue-fringed white dress cut for function. She was carrying a tray with food and water. She dropped her eyes to the floor when she saw Angus, keeping them there as her cheeks turned red.

"Master Bloodaxe," she stammered, "Your robe..." He looked down, realizing that the robe was open in the rear. He was uncovered, and not showing his best side. Now, it was his turn to blush. He faced her, took the tray, and politely shooed her out the door.

As it closed behind her, he set the tray down and looked for his clothes. He found them in a dresser at the far end of the room and put them on quickly. A cursory check of the room revealed more of his possessions, but no weapons. He stretched his wrists uneasily before heading out the door.

The hallway was white plaster as well. He followed a murmur down the hall. Wondering if John had stayed here waiting for him, he made himself walk straight. He rounded a corner and realized that the voices were coming from downstairs. He hoped that he really was healed enough for this; the last thing he wanted was another stint in that white bedroom. He descended the stairs with great care, taking each step on its own with both feet and holding the handrail fervently.

At the bottom he stepped into a large hall, brilliantly illuminated by rows of windows on high walls. Fine chandeliers hung at even intervals on the vaulted ceiling, plated in silver; they left Angus with the impression that this hall could be just as bright in the dead of night. Several men talked around a table at one end of the hall. They were all dressed in the same white and blue that the serving girl had been, but with more blue. It didn't seem that Mr. Brightshirt was here.

Angus was halfway to the men when they noticed him. Two of them were older, with full, styled beards. The third was a younger man, clean shaven and sporting a grand blue velvet tricorn hat. He looked familiar. It was John, who raised his hand in a quick wave.

"It seems you've come around all right, Master Bloodaxe. How are you feeling?" John asked, dripping with practiced eloquence. His normally eager demeanor had been replaced by an easy, aloof quality.

"I'm functional so far. How long was I out – and where are my things?"

"We arrived three days ago; the doctors kept you sedated to ensure you didn't damage yourself further. As for your things, we have your beast and wagon in the stable, and your weapons are secure in the armory. In Ivonal, only nobility can go about armed beyond a functional knife. Since I haven't established where you fall in that order, we thought it best to prevent you from causing problems without knowing it." As John was talking, Angus noticed that there was a thin, pointed saber at his waist. In fact, all three men were so armed. So Mr. Brightshirt was an affected identity, was he? They would talk about that, but later.

One of the older gentlemen spoke next. "Master Bloodaxe, I am Joseif C'Antrell. I am pleased to welcome you to my home. The room and stables are at your disposal for as long as you would like to stay. Johan told us about your deeds at the Sliver and how you saved him later in the woods; we are deeply in your debt."

"No, Master C'Antrell, I certainly owe you something for your care. Where can I go to settle my bill with the doctor?" Angus reached for his purse.

"Doctor Pheus has already been well compensated; he is here on staff for just such occasions. Indeed, I rather think he enjoyed the opportunity to treat a war wound. They are so rare these days."

Angus tried to imagine a large city where wounds from violence were a rarity. Even at the Holt, where there were many fewer people than here, fights broke out often – they just didn't turn out deadly. So many of the stories about the world outside started in a bar fight that he just assumed it to be a universal truth. So far, Ivonal was not what he had expected.

He decided to continue. "You gentlemen seem to be versed in local custom. How does one arrange a visit with the Ivon? I have news from the Argentine Holt to deliver." The older men looked at each other, then to Johan, who spoke.

"If you are referring to the battle at the Sliver, I have already conveyed that news to the Ivon myself. He is keen to meet you and thank you personally. I can arrange an audience this evening, if you like."

"Hmm. I do need to speak with him, and I would discuss anything he wishes, as long as I get to convey my news. First, I would like to access my wagon; I am missing several things that I feel naked without." He looked around pointedly, hoping for direction.

Johan was already taking a step away as he addressed the older men. "Father, General, I hope you won't mind if I show Ang – Master Bloodaxe the way. I shall return as soon as I have finished with him." Seeing their dismissive nods, he led Angus through grand hallways, open walkways and through groomed gardens. This place was beautiful, and if there were this many people tending it, it should last a good long time. They took the walk in silence, Angus following a step behind, taking it all in. When they reached the stables, Johan shut the door. They were alone.

"Thanks for not making a fuss. My father thinks I was out looking for business opportunities. If he knew what I was up to, he might cut me off!"

"Look, kid. It's not my business. My business is with the Ivon. The sooner I get him the news, the sooner I can finish my tasks and go home. Life was considerably easier back home…"

"News – excellent! Is it anything I could make a story from? Did the Orcs attack you first, then follow you to the Sliver; pursuing the last of your kind as you fled to Ivonal for help?"

Angus no longer had any doubt about whether Johan really was Mr. Brightshirt.

"Yeah. Sure. You've got it exact. Now help me get my axe and armor out of the wagon; if I'm the last of my kind, that must make me a noble by default, right?" He reached into the wagon and pulled his gear out. He did a little checking, to see what might have been lightened during his delirium. Everything he thought to check was accounted for. That was some comfort, at least.

The decision to don his armor had been made as soon as he saw the light swords at the men's waists. He may be safe in this house, from these people; but a society that allows some to have weapons and others none left the others at a distinct disadvantage. Besides; the gleaming armor and black-scarlet axe would do a better job of making the impression he desperately needed. John – or Johan – kept pushing for information about Angus' news. When he was acceptably equipped, Angus suggested that arranging the audience might be more likely to occur if Johan were to go arrange it. They left at the same time, Johan for the Ivon's palace, and Angus back to his room for his forgotten lunch.

Gasps and starts punctuated Angus' long walk back to his room. Once, a young lady dropped a glass she had been holding. It was very likely that none of these people had ever seen a dwarf before; much less in stylized full plate. When passing through sunny areas, light reflected off the armor and made shimmering patterns on the opposite walls. A smile came to Angus' lips, as he realized that here, in this city meant to impress, he was able to make an impression.

Back in his room, he braided his beard, tying in several of the Dragon's teeth. He took his time about it, taking large bites of food and chewing while he worked. He sat in front of the mirror for several hours, getting it just right. The food was solid, if a bit too subtle. It went down well, and they had thought to serve him some of his own brandy. When he was done with the food and beard, he sat up and took a long look. It had worked; for the first time in his life, Angus looked like a hero!

Chapter 19

The Ivon

It wasn't long before there was a knock at the door. Johan was on the other side, fancy hat and all. "The Ivon doesn't like to be kept waiting; we should go soon."

"Let's go now, then." Angus stood up, grabbing his blood red axe and taking a last swig of brandy. Together, they made their way through the vast complex that made up Johan's family home. They came out a gate that looked much like the others Angus had seen, stepping onto the rough, old cobblestones of Ivonal's streets. Heading toward the tallest buildings, the dwarf took note of the many reactions to his passing.

Often, people tried to act as if they hadn't seen the only person dressed in gleaming plate armor in the entire city. They might gasp, or let an eye linger for a half second too long, but for the most part they stepped into a doorway or changed directions just enough not to intersect his path. People here wore much more white than blue, and none were armed in any way. They went on for blocks, striding briskly with nothing to give them pause for most of the way.

Coming into a large, open-air marketplace, one little girl stayed right in their path when everyone else split like waves. She cocked her head as they drew near, transfixed by the silvery apparition unlike anything she had ever seen. Her freckled nose wrinkled as she considered the dwarf, her upper lip pulled back to reveal several missing front teeth.

"What are you?"

"Young lady, you may not speak to him so-" Johan started, but Angus cut him off with a gentle palm to the chest.

"Have you never seen a dwarf before, child?" She shook her head. "I am a dwarf. My name is Angus. Does that help?"

"I thought dwarves were only two feet tall. You're too tall for a dwarf, aren't you? And why are you all shiny?"

Angus chuckled. "Now that is an excellent question. I guess you might say that it's my way of getting dressed up. I'm on my way to see the Ivon, and I wanted to look my best. What do you think of it?" He puffed his chest out and smiled at her, posing.

"I don't see any blue. My daddy says that means you aren't important. You're not important, are you?"

"Hmm. Another good question. And one, I don't think right to answer for one's self. It seems to me that being important doesn't matter unless you are important to someone else. Perhaps Johan can tell us whether I am 'important'."

"Yes, child. Angus is not only important; he is a proper Hero. He used this shiny armor and that great axe to keep hordes of nasty orcs from invading Ivonal. Now what do you think about that?"

Her lower lip quivered for a moment, then she ran off crying for her mother. Angus and Johan exchanged glances, then continued on. Their pace was slightly abated after the encounter with the little girl. The rest of the city continued to avoid them, pointedly looking where they were headed. It seemed that most of the populace intended to ignore what did not fit into their daily molds.

The palace was immense. It rose well over a hundred feet in a stark white façade accented with that pearlescent blue tile used throughout the rest of the city. Johan moved through unfazed. It was obvious he had been here many times, the grandeur lost on him now. Angus missed a step on the approach taking it all in. The sheer mass was astonishing. The lines were straight and true, but he still wondered about what was underneath all that brilliant white plaster. He had always preferred structures that were so well built they needed no external finish.

There were guards here, half a dozen men with light halberds and leather jerkins. They bowed their heads in deference to Johan but moved to block Angus' entry. "No common man enters here armed or in armor. It is the law. You will have to lay aside your implements of war before facing the Ivon." Perfect diction and form flowed from the guard in practiced tones, deferential yet firm.

"I suppose it's a good thing that I'm a dwarf then. Got any laws about dwarves in that book of yours, youngster? No? I'll be on about my business then." Angus pushed past the guards to enter the gate, all rock-solid determination.

Johan gave the guards a calming gesture, saying only, "I'll be responsible for him." He followed Angus inside.

They passed through a long colonnade. From a distance, it looked like an immense amount of alabaster had been used in its manufacture. When Angus looked closely however, he discovered that it was a plaster surface treatment on hollow construction. The outside had been wet sanded for a perfectly smooth finish and painted with veins to look like real stone. Unimpressed, he moved on.

The colonnade led to a large courtyard. Its rectangular shape rose several stories and was ringed with galleries – more faux alabaster. The northern wall opposite their entry danced in color and light. This was not something Angus was familiar with. Shapes simple and complex danced or held. As he watched, he realized that someone was speaking from one of the galleries; several voices. The shapes resolved into people in a scene; some of the shapes seemed to depict a tower with men atop it. More voices started crying and shouting from the galleries; they were shouting battle cries, like those he had heard at the Sliver. He looked over at Johan who was beaming with pride. There was a tear at the corner of the man's eye! As Angus looked back, he saw that the scene had been shifted to the right and those voices, while constant, had quieted down.

On the left wall, a bright circle seemed to explode from the dark wall. Ugly, misshapen forms seemed to burst in, only to be chopped apart immediately by a short, stout figure. The dark forms piled up, with the smaller figure eventually climbing up to perch atop the pile. Angus heard the last line of the light-play clearly, and wished he hadn't – "Grimbrow Bloodaxe, savior of the Sliver, Hero from the North!" Well, it was official, at least in Ivonal.

There was a circular dais in the center of the courtyard, with several seats facing the wall where the lights were now fading. The whole thing now rotated slowly, bringing the seated figures to face Johan and himself. A quick glance showed him that Johan was kneeling, face downward, with one hand pressed to the floor. Angus quickly followed suit. His visor flipped down on its own – he really needed to adjust that – giving his face the semblance of a fierce dragon.

"Rise, gentlemen." The voice was melodious and fair, a good imitation of the elves. They stood. "Johan, it is a pleasure to see you. You have been absent for some while; it seems you have filled your time by finding a hero for us. That is a very interesting suit of armor you wear, Master Grimbrow. The dragon's visage is somewhat off-putting, however; would you mind removing your helm so we may talk face-to-face?"

Angus complied, tucking the helmet under his left arm. He rested the butt of his axe on the floor and draped his right arm over the blade in a proper dwarven 'at ease' stance. "As you wish, Ivon. You may call me Angus, if it pleases you. It is my given name."

"Given name, yes. But we have just been regaled by Johan's account of your heroic deeds at the Sliver. We owe you a debt, Angus. If it weren't for your actions, there would be far fewer men to guard our northern borders." The Ivon was a tall man, slender and graceful. His blond hair was cropped close with stylized designs shaved to his scalp in places; other designs were painted or dyed in blue; overlapping and producing a busy framework of geometric shapes. "I am curious about why a dwarf came to be in just the right place at exactly the right time. If I were a suspicious man, I might come up with several reasons. But I would like you to tell me yourself, Angus Grimbrow Bloodaxe. Why were you there on that night, and how was it that you were sitting, ready for a fight at just the point the invading orcs breached the wall?"

Angus looked over at Johan to see his young face regarding him with relaxed interest. He began to wonder if he would have to fight his way out of this hall if the Ivon didn't like his answer. But this was what he had come for, so he dove into telling the truth.

"I come from the Argentine Holt, hundreds of miles to the north, past the mountains where the Sliver lies. I suspect that some of the silver items that adorn your palace may have originated with ore from our mines, after passing through many traders' hands. We have lived in relative peace for decades but have always stayed ready for a day which we thought might come. Several weeks ago, we received the news that we had been right to train and secure ourselves; an old enemy had risen up.

"It has been well over a thousand years since this enemy has threatened our part of the world, but we dwarves live long and keep good records. We shared this enemy long ago, Dwarf and Elf and Man. When last we drove them out, there was an agreement - a treaty - that promised we would keep each other informed if and when they reappeared. One such enemy came to attack us, and he was slain. We have no word of others, but according to the treaty, I have come to warn you about what has happened, and what may happen."

"One, you say? Surely not one orc. Possibly a giant? Or a troll – an ogre, maybe. What could possibly have been worth such a fuss?" The Ivon suppressed a chuckle as he spoke.

"The treaties indicate that the person responsible for the fall of the enemy would be the one with the honor of relaying the story. This could be the King, if his strategy was followed. But in this case, it is the one who struck the killing blow. I have told you my given name, and Johan here has presented me with more; but my proper title will finish my story. I am now rightfully called Angus Dragonbane."

The slight titter that had been swirling through the room vanished, leaving a heavy vacuum of silence. The Ivon's expression hadn't changed, but something in his eyes was ever-so-slightly different. After a few moments passed, the Ivon spoke again.

"Remarkable. Yet you say there was only the one, and no word or sign of another?" Seeing Angus nod his head, he continued. "Well, then. A festival it is! Johan, I would like you to get the details from our Dragonbane and prepare a light-play for tomorrow; tonight, I invite you and Angus to a feast in his favor. The Angels will fly and sing tonight!" With that, the Ivon rose smartly, striding off with his attendants falling in behind him. The court applauded as the Ivon retreated.

Johan grabbed Angus by the elbow and led him back through the gate and all the way to his room before speaking. "This is the news you came to share? A Dragon? How is it you let me believe you were traveling on business, and would not share this?"

"My mission is to tell certain heads of state, not everyone. That is for the likes of you, bards and storytellers. How was it you let me believe you were a young upstart, and not a member of an affluent and influential family? Isn't that deceitful?"

Johan took a moment before answering. "I guess I am not the only one that can be more than meets the eye. I am a Gatherer. A Gatherer is one of the Angels who goes out and gathers."

"That sounds both odd and broad. What is it that you gather?"

"This and that. Information, mostly. We do everything from identify influentials and track their movements, to assess situations as they develop, to securing items that interest the Ivon. My training as a bard helps me to pass this information without raising suspicion that I might be a spy." He grabbed a cup and went to pour some of Angus' brandy.

Angus considered warning him of the potency difference between human and dwarven brandy, then decided to let him learn for himself. "I must say, I was taken in by your act. Does the whole of Ivonal work on this level?"

"Hardly. Ivonal is a well-greased machine dedicated solely to executing the Ivon's will. Speaking of which, I need to hear the story of this Dragon, and how you came to slay him. You can't tell me you managed to kill him with that axe…"

Angus told the story as it had been presented by Artemus to the dwarves. He colored it as if it were a spur-of-the-moment decision, which Johan seemed to like. Johan quizzed him on the size and color of the Dragon, and the angle at which it flew in, as well as a sense of the overall space involved. Twice during the conversation, he coughed; once in disbelief of the luck that set up the situation, and again when he tasted the brandy.

Angus, in turn, asked about the light plays and how that worked. Johan was coy, until Angus made this suggestion…

"I suppose it's similar to one of the defenses we drill on at the Holt. Dozens of dwarves will line the battlements in the sun, holding polished silver bowls to gather and concentrate sunlight, and send it into our enemies' eyes. Something like that?"

"Hmm. Yes, I would say it is very similar in concept; with some important variations. We use glass and cut out templates to make the shapes and colors. And forces against us are always depicted in silhouette, as shadows with little definition. Your Dragon will be such. I think it will take all night to build the templates, write the score and script, and block the puppeteers. I'm afraid I'll miss your party, Angus Dragonbane."

Johan took his leave, parting only after giving instructions about the timing of Angus' entrance, and a few topics that should just be avoided. He also said that Angus should avoid offending nobility, if he could, with little specific information. And then Angus was left alone with his thoughts and his brandy.

Chapter 20

Your Name in Lights

    Before leaving for dinner, Angus took a little time to touch up the shine on his armor. The city was very clean, but there were several coal-fired businesses on the way, and a thin patina of black dust coated everything he had worn earlier. It was another testament to their focus, he thought, that the city and people were always so clean. Appearances seemed to mean everything to these folk. Yet there was a substance to them; working towards a common goal of making a beautiful place to live was only the surface.
    The strategies and layers of nuance in this blue-and-white city were considerable. It went far beyond the proportion of blue that one wore; Angus just wasn't sure how. While they weren't making dwarven-style construction, they had shown ingenuity in the light-play. And Johan had taken him in with his alter ego. He had yet to see him use that short sword, however.
    Finishing his polishing, Angus put everything back on. Hopefully, there was some good beer tonight, with a roast beast of some sort. After telling his story, he had a hankering for a heavy meal. Taking one last look out the balcony window, he set out through the grand corridors to join the gathering dusk on the way to this feast.
    The walk was pleasant, with people scurrying away less often, and some even watching in slack-jawed awe. The story must have been spreading. People didn't see him with the respectful, silent terror they had when he first strode through the streets this morning. Angus took to wearing a smile, nodding and waving when folks made eye contact. In return, he received more than one curtsy or bow. Maybe these folks were friendly, after all.
    It was a nice evening. The sky had only a few high scattered clouds, none suggesting rain, and the heat was tempered by a

breeze that smelled faintly of salt. He walked with a hint of a proud strut, as easy of a lope as he could manage with his relatively short, and still healing, legs. Carrying his axe seemed appropriate now; he doubted that any of these folk had ever seen a Dragon, and his having slain one lent credibility to his right to bear arms.

At the palace, the guards parted before him with respect, falling into formation. They saluted Angus as he passed, fists over hearts. Angus tried to hide his sheepish grin with a nod as he stepped through, lifting his axe to return their salute. Repeating his steps from earlier brought him right past the masses of imitation alabaster. Passing through the colonnade was not distracting or impressive, until he *felt* one of them move.

That stopped him in his tracks. It wasn't anything he could see, per se; it was the same kind of feeling he might have when a rock fell unseen in one of the tunnels. Looking around to see that no one was taking an interest, he stepped up to the column that seemed wrong, laying a hand to its smooth surface. He couldn't swear to it, but he thought something might be moving inside the column. He gave it a long, appraising look before returning to his path.

As he approached the courtyard, he saw several long tables, lined with people wearing a lot of blue. Servants ringed the assembly, obvious by the preponderance of white. One intercepted Angus, guiding him to a seat near the head of the central table. Angus declined the man's polite offer to hold his axe while he ate, leaning it blade down against the table.

One of the servants stepped forward with a dainty pitcher, filling a small, blue cup in front of him with a clear liquid. Another stepped forward with a blue plate about the width of his outstretched hand. On it were several small doughy objects, a near translucent white-on-white, along with six drops of a sauce in a line. The first was red, the last white, with gradients of the two in between. Angus turned to thank the person who had served him, but they had already faded into the indiscriminable line of servants. Not at all like the service he had had at the Holt, p'Eaux d'Ancre or any place else – it was very crisp and formal.

Failing a quick tutorial, he observed the men and women around him. They were all in blue, crisp formal wear – silks, linens and even some sheer things that he could not describe without blushing. They laughed and talked, quietly, never looking directly at Angus while keeping him in their peripheral vision. Some of them had taken the two ivory sticks from the holder in front of them, holding them as if they were two styli. Held just so, they deftly lifted the small doughy balls and selected just one of the tiny dots of sauce, dipped and lifted to their mouths. Hands under the table, Angus surreptitiously removed his gauntlets and clipped them to his belt.

As he laid his hands on the sticks to determine how to use them, the lady sitting directly across from him made momentary eye contact. She smiled, tilted her head ever so slightly, and returned to her conversation. Her eyes twinkled with... amusement? Angus wasn't sure, but he decided to show that a dwarf could display just as much grace and style as a human. He arranged the sticks in his hands in imitation of those around him and made a few test movements. It took a few tries to get the ends of the sticks to intersect, but he did it. Smiling, he winked gratefully at the lady across from him and grabbed for the first ball. Much to his chagrin, it slipped right off the plate and onto the table.

His sticks were just closing around the errant ball when it disappeared in a flash – a servant had cleared the mess and wiped the table in an instant. Frowning, Angus tried again. The second ball kept trying to twist out of his light-pressure grip, so he waited until it was lined up properly and squeezed tighter. His sticks clattered together as his problematic morsel popped up in a high arc over the table, eight feet up at least. Angus was plotting its trajectory, determining that it might just land in the amused lady's cleavage when a white clad hand shot up and caught it in midair. As quickly as he had appeared, the servant faded away. The lady had never missed a beat; though a tightness to her eyes gave the impression of even more amusement.

This would not do. There was one bite-sized ball left on his plate, and Angus was hungry. He switched to a two-handed approach, preventing the foods escape with one while he stabbed it with the second stick. Bent on gaining every scrap of food value from this spare meal, he smeared the ball with all six of the sauce dots, coating it thoroughly. He popped it into his mouth, sucking the excess sauce from the stick as he pulled it out of his mouth. Several eyes were on him now, and Angus soon understood that it wasn't his manners that drew the attention.

The white sauce was some sort of strong horseradish, very strong. The red must have been pure red chili pepper oil; now he noticed that no one else had used the red spot at all. Tears welled up in force; he inhaled over the food to try to cool it, exhaling through his nose; another mistake. Now his sinuses burned, eyes and nose watering he reached for the meager cup. The hot alcohol was weak compared to his usual, but it did diminish the pain a bit. The cup came back to the table with a 'thock', silently filled again before a moment had passed.

The amused smiles and raised eyebrows were much more prevalent now, spreading even to some of the servants. A couple of hands covered mouths while shoulders shuddered in restrained laughter; not a good start, Angus decided. "Whoo! That's good stuff!" he said, a short wheezy cough punctuating his statement.

A polite chuckle ran through the table, relieving the pent-up feeling. These people were determined to be polite at all costs it seemed. After a few minutes, when almost all of the doughy balls had been consumed, the servants brought out the next course. Angus was relieved that one very spicy rice dough ball would not be the entire meal, but his hopes were dashed when there was no heavy red meat in front of him.

This second course seemed to be a salad, served in a small bowl not much larger than a teacup. Fine juliennes of a leaf he could not identify were mixed with seeds, oil, vinegar and a purple and white item that was also new to Angus. And again, the entire course could not be more than two or three bites. Angus' stomach rumbled as he attempted again to imitate the graceful movements of those around him. He had some success, making a three-bite salad into a dozen tiny bites as he got one piece into his mouth at a time. The leaf had a juicy crunch to it, and a flavor all its own; and the purple bits turned out to be a chewy meat with a very subtle flavor. *Not bad*, he thought, *and if I ever needed to lose a few pounds, this would be a great way to do it!*

Angus found great encouragement at the next course; a small fish apparently grilled and drizzled in sweet, salty sauce over white rice. It had been cleverly cut along diagonals to give the impression of everyone having an identical dish. Angus had never been a fish fan, but this stuff melted in his mouth, and the flavors mixed in a very pleasing way. He was also feeling much more confident with the sticks, taking his time and doing a decent job of mimicking the natives.

The final course of the evening was the most colorful plating Angus had ever seen. The food was arranged into bite-sized portions, with reds, oranges, translucent pinks and a pile of some mashed green vegetable. That last was rather dry, and it looked to him like a desiccated version of a pea soup he would have back at the Holt. Ready for something familiar, he dove into that first. The whole pile came up together, conforming easily to the styli. For once, he felt like he looked expert as he popped it into his mouth. It wasn't peas, he realized, with a strong mustard and horseradish flavor that got stronger as he worked it through. But he wasn't about to look the fool again; he fought back the tears, and emptied his little cup twice, letting out a sharp "Ahh!" after the second. Sniffling automatically, he smiled at the people near him, receiving smiles and nods in return.

The rest of the bites were each a flavor all their own, some sitting on small mounds of that sticky white rice, some wrapped in it, and some sitting alone. He savored the uniqueness and tried to take in the presentation; all so exquisite and clean. This was a high art, and something that might be worth sharing back at the Holt one day.

As he finished his last bite, attendants cleared the tables. The dusk had given way to dark, the courtyard lit seamlessly by increasing numbers of lamps; but looking up, the dark sky was obvious. The lights made the stars obscure. But something moved, black on black, just out of the lamplight.

"Ladies, Gentlemen and our esteemed guest Angus Dragonbane, please stay seated as the Angels fly for your enjoyment!" The booming voice was disembodied, emanating from somewhere in or above the galleries.

Angus saw someone appear at the opposite edge of the courtyard, standing on the roof. There was something not quite normal about the person's shape. A lone flute began playing, and the anomaly was revealed as the person's wings unfurled from behind it. This was new to Angus. The Angel scanned the crowd. Fixing on Angus' face, he jumped. He dipped straight down and out of view at first, appearing to fly at a great speed right over the amused lady, who watched unperturbed. As the blast from his wingbeat ruffled Angus' beard, the Angel rose straight up to fly right out of the courtyard and into the dark.

Angus realized he was holding his breath in awe. He tried to breathe and failed as the spectacle was repeated again and again. Four Angels had done a fly-by before he was able to inhale again; he was mesmerized and fascinated by the flying, amazed that Angels were real. Until he saw a face he recognized; a face that had been in servant's garb earlier in the day.

He started looking at the Angels outfits, working out the mechanics of the show. The movement he had seen earlier was some sort of rigging, and the Angels were flying suspended by a thin dark cord not visible when looking at the flyers. Putting this and that together, he wondered if the noise he heard in the hollow colonnade could have something to do with it; perhaps a counterweight dropping to raise them quickly out of the courtyard, giving the impression of flight?

Whatever the specifics, Angus had gained a new respect for these people and their ingenuity. Cords or no, there was certainly a high degree of skill displayed by these Angels. And the engineering behind it was remarkable. While their monuments would not last forever, tales of their greatness likely would.

Chapter 21

A Tale and A Ship

Angus made his way back to his bedroom, a pleasant buzz keeping him from feeling the performance fatigue that saturated his body. The streets were empty for the most part, and at no point did Angus feel threatened. Maybe Ivonal had some merits after all; when he was done with his tasks he may come for an extended visit.

Johan was waiting outside the house when Angus arrived. "Angus my friend, I'm guessing that the Ivon's idea of a feast doesn't quite match your appetite. I know a pub down by the docks that serves heavy meals and heavier beer – what do you say we get you fed properly?"

"I say that's a well-grounded plan. Now, when you say heavy beer, how heavy are we talking?"

The pair sauntered through the streets, southeast toward the docks. The further they descended, the less perfect everything appeared, leaving the impression that it wasn't just the amount of blue you wore, or the quality of the fabrics, but how high up the hill you lived that describes your place in society. By the time they reached the wharfs, walls might have large cracks and chunks of missing plaster, revealing the mud brick construction underneath.

The pub Johan had selected was just across from a dock with several tall ships, most of the crews having abandoned their work for fun or rest at this late hour. Only one of the ships was busy, crew quietly loading crates and sacks into the hold, using a counterweighted crane on the dock. Dismissing the activity, they went in and found a table in the corner.

It was a poorly lit place, which was a blessing considering it looked like it hadn't been over-cleaned for a while, if ever. The air was rich with the smells of grilled beef and corncobs, spilled beer and sweaty workers. This was the kind of place Angus felt more at home with. A plump young woman in a dress with entirely too many ruffles came over to their table.

"What are you boys drinking tonight?"

"I'll have some of the Bitterwood Pale," Johan began, "and a basket of fish and chips."

"And I'd like to get your darkest beer. Something that leaves a stain on your lips and grit in your teeth, if you've got it. And whatever flavor of roast beast I'm smelling in there." He put a large silver coin on the table, saying, "And whatever the kid tells you, I'm buying."

She winked at him and walked toward the kitchen, articulating her ample assets as she went. An argument erupted on the far side of the room, and Angus wondered for a moment if it might degrade into the kind of bar fight he had so often heard of, but never witnessed. A third man interceded, however, and soon the pub had returned to the cacophonous rumble that was typical of the place.

"I was beginning to get the impression that all of Ivonal was idyllic, clean and proper. It's nice to see that normal people live here, too."

"Well, you weren't really coherent when we came in through the north side, which isn't too different from the docks. But yes, you spent the last couple of days walking only the best parts of town. The Ivon is very concerned about looking his best at all times; much more than just his physical appearance. He feels that he is the city - the nation, really. And the Hill district is where he spends most of his time, so it is kept as close to perfect as can be." Johan stopped talking there, but it seemed like there might be more to that story.

The waitress came back with two beers, one pale pint in a glass with a neat head and a slice of lime over the edge, and a large unlidded tankard with a tight, foamy head spilling over the edges for Angus. He smiled and dipped his index finger through the foam and held it there a minute. The young woman waited, unsure what to do.

"Well, it's not dwarvish." Angus slurped the liquid from his finger. "There is no burning sensation, nor is there any debris. But it does have a nice flavor, and a good head. It'll do."

Johan laughed aloud as she walked away. "Angus, that's the stoutest brew in hundreds of miles. If it won't do, you'll have to carry your own libations from the Holt."

Deadpan, Angus replied, "You are right there. Did you notice the barrels of brandy on my wagon?" Johan was dumbstruck for a moment, then they both broke out laughing, louder than before.

The food was simple and rough, qualities that Angus felt at home with. This was turning out to be an excellent evening. Until there was a snorty neighing that drew his attention to the window; the ship's crew outside were winching a stout pony by use of a sling onto the ship. Normally, that would not be disturbing to Angus, but this pony looked familiar. Very familiar. He looked over at Johan, who was finishing his meal quickly.

"Angus, I'll level with you." His voice dropped to a whisper. "You have slain a Dragon, and we have no more to be defeated. In the Ivon's twisted way of looking at the world, you have a title that he can never have. And while that may be acceptable for a person from legend, he sees a real person with a grander title than his to be a threat, if only to his image."

"So you're going to dump me and my pony at sea?"

Johan laughed. "You don't get it. I was given specific instructions to change your story as I wrote it. The intention was to show that you were not only a fraud with your rather grand story, but also in league with the orcs that came to the Sliver. The Ivon wants to paint you as an infiltrator, coming ahead of the armies to soften us up."

Angus regarded Johan, devoid of expression. So much was wrong with the story, he didn't know where to begin processing it. "Johan – none of that is true. I have slain a Dragon, I am not in league with orcs, and I am here only to fulfill our part in ancient treaties. Dwarves are not, on the whole, devious people. We tend to say exactly what we mean, or not speak at all. I really am a typical dwarf; and everything I told you was true." That was true; he simply had not mentioned the fact that his spear had slipped from the pedal instead of being intentionally released.

"Angus, I believe you. But you must understand that I had to write the story as the Ivon wanted it and represent that I believed it. If I hadn't, I would likely disappear as so many others have done.

"I left the story outlines and plot points with my assistants, and they will complete the light play overnight. My father will find the note on my bed tomorrow, stating that I left in pursuit of you when I saw you booking passage on a boat, loaded down with what I could only assume was the loot you had tricked the people of Ivonal out of."

Angus opened his mouth, stammered for a second and closed it. He drained the dark brew that remained in the tankard, his fourth of the night. Not bothering to wipe the foam from his mustache, he spoke. "You must be very good with that pathetic excuse for a sword you carry. Otherwise, I'd say you were suicidal for not only betraying me so but boasting about it! Over dinner! That I paid for!"

Johan put both hands in front of him, palms outward in a calming gesture. "Angus, this was the only way I could think to save your life without losing mine! I went over it several ways first, and this is the best I could come up with. You see, I had all your belongings transferred to that ship over there, having spent a considerable sum to purchase the whole hold. I then had my horse Cutter and the items and provisions I would need put aboard as well. You see, if I had just sent you away alone, I would have been questioned at length, and likely flubbed my story, leading to a death sentence. If I fled with you, I would never be able to return, and some of the Angels would eventually find me wherever I fled. If we both stayed, one or both of us would have ended up dead. You, for sure. So, the only way was for me to 'chase' you as you fled on your own; it was the only way."

Angus wasn't sure which was worse – the rapid-fire explanations, or the fact that it made sense to him. "How long until they are loaded?"

"I think they are close," Johan said, leaning to see out the smallish window. "We could go now and see where they are at. Shall we?"

Chapter 22

We Didn't Ask for Room Service

After settling their bill, Angus and Johan slipped quietly across the street toward the ship. They tried to keep to the shadows as much as possible. There were very few people about, but the two refugees weren't taking any risks. As they neared the gangplank, a narrow, barefoot man with altogether too many tattoos met them, guiding them quietly aboard.

"I should like to check how everything is loaded before we cast off," Johan said in a low voice. "There may also be a thing or two Angus would like to have with him for the journey."

"Follow me, then," the scrawny man replied. They made their way down something that wasn't quite a stairway, but neither a ladder. Once below decks, they came to the hold where Angus' pony and wagon, Johan's horse and a few crates enjoyed plenty of room.

"I purchased the entire hold for the duration," Johan told Angus. "I wanted to be sure we would not be delayed. You should find everything loaded on your wagon, just as it was when we came to the city."

"I'm still not sure about this. I'm not comfortable on the water. But I do appreciate your efforts, Johan." Angus set about collecting his truly valuable possessions, filling his chest and a large duffle with various purses secreted about. He also brought in his siege bow and quarrels, responding to the seaman's objections by promising to take it apart for maintenance. "Owning a siege bow is like keeping your rigging and sails. They may appear to be in good repair, but you check them anyway, since your livelihood - and sometimes your life - depends on them. I need to disassemble it entirely, clean the parts, check the springs; it will take some time."

Their cabins were in the forward part of the ship, small bedrooms along either side of a longer room with a communal table. Even though there were several rooms on each side, Johan and Angus were the only two occupants.

"We'd like to not be disturbed, gentlemen. It's been a long couple of days." Johan took the curt nod as assent and closed the door to the dining room. That done, he turned back to Angus. "Take your pick of the rooms, Angus. I don't think there will be much difference. You can put your spare gear in one of the empty rooms if you would like more space."

"Johan, I've never been on the open water before. I've never even been on anything bigger than a ferry crossing the river."

"Don't worry. The Incande is a stout ship if not fast. She'll get us there safely in a few days. Keep your window open, and if you start to feel ill, pick a point on the horizon to focus on; that should help. If you think you would like to sleep in, I would pick a room on the larboard side since we are heading east. That should keep the sun from waking you."

Studying the wood walls around him, Angus asked "You'll have to forgive me; I'm not really up on the differences in wood. What does a 'lar' board look like?"

Johan smiled and pointed toward one side of the boat. "Larboard means the left side of the ship, if you are facing the prow." Seeing the blank look on the dwarf's face, he added, "The front. That way."

Angus didn't really think he would be sleeping in. The ship lurched as the men pushed it away from the docks with long poles. The rocking movements made Angus think he might not be able to sleep at all.

"There is one more thing I need from that wagon," Angus said, and walked out of the room. Johan chuckled. Maybe the stories about dwarves not being good swimmers were true after all.

A minute or so later, Angus returned. He was carrying a small, stout barrel under his arm. Setting the barrel on the table, Angus put his hands on his hips and looked around. Something was still not right. Then a memory struck him, of an unexpected visitor in the night. There was a chair at a small desk in the corner, and he took that to the single door that joined the deck with the common room; the natural bottleneck. Wedging the door shut with the chair, he turned back to Johan.

"There, that makes me feel better. I don't think I'm up for any more surprises tonight." He unhooked one of the low, wide mugs from the cupboard where they hung and filled it from the barrel. Draining half his drink in one swig, he refilled it, and picked a room on the left side of the boat. "I'll see you in the morning."

Johan picked a room to the larboard and turned down his bed. It wasn't as clean as he would have liked, but it would do. He opened the window and let the breeze and lapping sounds of the light chop against the hull lull him to sleep.

----- -----

A seagull's plaintive cry woke Angus the next day. A quick look over the items he had left beside his bed let him know that he hadn't missed anyone; no unexpected visitors. Sitting up, he smelled eggs and sausage from the next room. He pulled on his pants and stepped out into the common room, where Johan was enjoying a hot breakfast.

"Good morning! I didn't expect to see you up so soon."

"Laying about in bed does no one any good. Besides, I really do need to work on that bow." The floor tilted as the ship encountered a wave, and Angus decided that the bench at the table might be preferable to standing.

"Try these sausages, Angus. The cook just brought them a few minutes ago, and they are excellent! There is juice..."

They enjoyed a solid breakfast, followed by a detailed lesson in siege bow mechanics while Angus worked on it. He was surprised at how much interest Johan showed for being an entertainer. Then he made the connection.

"I know why you understand this."

"Really? Why is that do you think?"

"You said you create light plays, and you are one of the Angels. The lines and wires are well disguised, but a sharp eye will see them. But the way they climbed straight up as they swooped through the courtyard, now that takes some engineering."

"It is no great secret that we use rigging to accomplish our flights."

"I agree. The trick, I think, lies in those hollow columns. I think you must use counterweights on triggers. That makes more sense to me than men pulling on lines. And that would also explain your interest in dwarven precision trigger mechanisms."

"I hope I haven't betrayed your trust by observing. I didn't mean to simply copy your design, but rather apply some of the principles to a different cause."

"Oh, I wouldn't mind if you did copy our design. It is gratifying to have an influence. Besides, I am confident that humans would find it very difficult to replicate the quality of dwarven work."

The conversation stalled there for a while, while each considered what the other had said. Angus took the time to maintain each piece of equipment he had; he stayed busy until well after dark. They checked on their beasts a couple of times, found them to be well, and the day was relatively uneventful.

The crew spent most of their time on deck while Angus and Johan were inside. The dwarf was more comfortable with a ceiling and walls around him; being out on the deck with the world seeming to move around him was unsettling at best. So, he busied himself with shining, sharpening, greasing and tuning. When there was no more to be done, he detailed the heads of his crossbow bolts.

Johan was otherwise occupied. He would watch and talk with Angus for a while but would regress to scribble in a heavy sheaf of papers, sing low, pining songs about loves lost – there were many different loves and no mistake – or just sleep. Angus had never seen anyone sleep so much.

It was evening on the third day of the voyage. For the first time, they were out of sight of land. They had finished their unusually heavy meal, and both of them were feeling a bit drowsy. They had enjoyed the grog that came with it – its toxicity was almost at a dwarven level. Angus was getting up to climb into his bunk when he caught sight of Johan's face. He was squinting and tilting his head toward the door. Raising one hand as if to say, "wait," he raised his other hand to his ear, then pointed toward the stern.

The boat was very quiet. Normally at this time of night, there would be a song, the sound of men gambling and telling stories; but the sounds of lapping water, billowing sails and creaking oak were all they heard. After a moment, Johan said in carefree tones that did not match his expression, "well, Angus my short friend,

I'm off to bed. We'll break fast together late, I think; that food has made me quite tired." Letting the floorboards creak loudly, he stepped into the room. Instead of getting into bed, he slipped a sheathed knife into the back of his belt and drew his lightweight sword silently.

The dwarf was not an actor and took the safe route with a gruff grunt. He took his heavy crossbow and laid it on the table softly, setting the quiver on the low bench in easy reach. Propping his axe head down against the wall, Angus shuttered the lamps one by one. Johan interjected a loud, articulate yawn. There was still no noise on deck.

As they waited quietly, they could make out the faint sound of bare feet on wood. Angus had started to feel more secure lately and had stopped propping the chair against the door. He began to regret that decision as he saw the wooden latch start to rise in its slot. Johan moved to be closer to the door, and Angus set his hands on his siege bow, ready to cock and load. The latch cleared its catch, and the door was opened slowly.

Dark shapes clustered in the gathering night. The first took two steps in, stopping when it met resistance in the form of a slender sword resting at its voice box. Johan used his other hand to open the shuttered lamp, illuminating several members of the crew in the doorway, with more behind. They had their cutlasses ready.

"Pardon me for saying, gentlemen, but this does not appear to be a friendly visit." Johan managed to add authority to his voice that wasn't normally there. "What were you hoping for?"

The lead crew member was concentrating on not becoming one with the tip of Johan's sword; but one of the men behind said, "We're hoping for that armor, lad. Three days is too long to sit in arm's length of such wealth. You could make it easy on yourselves and jump out a window. Then we wouldn't have to kill you to get what we're after."

"A point of order, if I may," Johan started, "Your mate isn't in the best of positions. Why don't you back out peacefully and reconsider?"

The burly speaker did take one step back. He stopped there, a wide, sinister smile revealing years of poor dental hygiene. "I never liked him anyway." He delivered a hard thrust to the poor man's shoulders, Johan's sword running him halfway through.

"Get 'em, lads!" he shouted, and started towards Angus as Johan attempted to free his weapon from the dying man's thrashing body.

There was a reverberating CRACKCRACKCRACK as Angus worked the lever on his crossbow. He barely had time to drop the treble load of bolts into their slot when it was time to lean his head a foot back. The cutlass missed his neck but took a chunk out of his red beard. Snarling, he fired the first round into the pirate's chest. The quarrel went completely through him and pinned the pirate behind him to the wall, fletching coated in gore.

Angus pushed the first man down by smacking him in the face with the prod, then took aim at the man now assailing Johan. The Angel was deflecting blow after blow with the knife that was now in his off hand, still tugging at his sword with the other. When the man with the cutlass collapsed with a heavy bolt through his ribcage, Johan was able to put both hands into it and free his blade, just to impale another pirate. Angus' last round found its target, leaving one less pirate and the siege bow useless except as a club.

The crew were determined; when one of their number fell, cries arose like "One less for the split! Huzzah!" Angus almost felt bad for them; as it stood, he and Johan could hold them off well with the narrow door being the only way in. He was hefting his axe after discarding the bow when the gap in his logic hit him – there were windows, flung open in the comfortable evening weather. They had been flanked.

Spinning, he barely dodged the knife that had been aimed for his kidneys. It found his belt instead, dropping his pants around his ankles. He broke the small man's nose with the flat of his axe, then brought the butt end around to the side of his head. His opponent crumpled.

The attack had been well planned, if ill-advised. After a couple of minutes of brutal fighting, it was over. Crew-cum-pirates lay dead or unconscious everywhere. As the pair started to bind the living, they noticed several down that neither could account for. It was a great puzzlement, as there were no other ships in sight, with no one standing that wasn't bound.

Lining the living up on one side and the dead on the other, they took stock of the situation. A quick check of the stern showed the rudder strapped firmly in position, and the weather was mild with a soft wind pushing them along. The captain was among the dead. The rest of the night, they took turns watching the prisoners and letting the ship go where she would. Mysteries could be left for the morning.

Chapter 23

The Captain and The Cabin Boy

Mercifully, morning brought them in sight of land again. Or something like land; from a distance the Veyns seemed to be a city built right on the water. There was no land in sight – just buildings. As they drew closer, the captive crew murmured and tried to see over the side. It didn't take long to find out what they were interested in. The ship lurched as it dragged the keel over a sandbar, slowing considerably. A hundred paces further, and it lurched again, coming to a complete stop.

For the first time in days, the deck was still. They the ship stuck fast on the sandy bottom; captive seamen offered no help. It seemed a joke to them; a small victory among the humiliation of being beaten by just two landlubbers. Angus and Johan let them have their fun. They needed to plot the next few moves before heading out.

They determined that they would report the crew as mutinous, that they had slain the Captain and the crew loyal to him. Johan forged documents naming him as the new owner of the ship. When the Harbor Master came, Angus would go ashore while Johan freed the vessel. After repairs and a new crew, Johan would meet Angus at the wharves and drop off his pony and gear.

It was noon by the time the Harbor Master approached in a small rowboat. The pair didn't have a problem conveying their story, thanks to a series of rags stopping their captive's mouths. The heavy purse that "Captain John" passed to him for his assistance bolstered their credibility. It took several hours to secure a transport and transfer the prisoners to shore.

Angus, now clad in the Holtgart armor, carried his axe and a sea-bag duffle slung over one shoulder – stuffed to the brim. He tossed the bag onto the Harbor Master's boat and stepped down himself. Before he was settled, the slender cabin boy jumped aboard with him. Puzzled, Angus glanced at Johan, who shrugged unconcerned. Angus said nothing.

Forty minutes later they were climbing up a ladder to the wharf. "We'll work your friend's boat out of the sand by tomorrow. Don't you worry." The Harbor Master turned to the men working on the dock, barking orders. By the way they all leapt to action, the Master was not to be trifled with.

Angus turned to the cabin boy, who spoke first. "Let's get some food," he said in an affected low voice, "I know a place right down the street." He did need to eat, so he followed. Questions raced in his mind. He did not remember a cabin boy from the journey. True, he had kept to his quarters for most of the trip, but he thought he had seen each of the sixteen men aboard at least twice.

Why wasn't he part of the fighting? How did they miss him when they swept the boat? And why would a cabin boy feel the need to disguise his voice – poorly? Nothing made sense. There were other things that Angus noticed as they walked the narrow pathways. The kid didn't move the way Angus had seen boys move. There was an out-of-place gracefulness. His face structure was not in the normal range of human boys either. Close enough at a glance, but just not quite right.

Bawdy songs and laughter rolled out of the next doorway along with pipe smoke and the tell-tale odors of working people having fun. The boy ducked inside. Angus followed without hesitating. Immediately he wondered if he should have.

There were a lot of people inside, packing every square inch of the room. Some were sitting on top of each other – something that Angus had not yet seen in his travels. The floor was wet with spilled ale, the air cloudy with smoke. Everyone was happy and loud. Many of the men were visibly armed, and Angus suspected that more were secretly equipped. Their long-sleeved loose clothes and bright vests made hiding smaller weapons a cinch.

Not one man or woman wore a stitch of armor. He became very aware of the fact that the only dwarf here was wearing polished and detailed armor from head to toe. He took off his helmet and smiled his toothiest smile – anything less might not show through the beard – and followed the boy through the crowd. They made no obvious sign that they had noticed him, but he felt their eyes on his purse, his armor and his axe; weighing odds behind practiced smiles and raised tin cups.

He had to press people aside as he passed. Short as he was, he was just as broad shouldered, and wearing heavy pauldrons at that. He pulled his bag around to sit ahead of him and rested his axe atop that to try to make a more compact package. The boy was talking to a woman at the bottom of the stairs when he caught up. He saw them embrace briefly, then the youngster headed up the stairs. When Angus started up after him, he found himself restrained by an ear. The woman pulled him close.

"I don't know what you are about, but while you are in my house, there will be no funny business. Treat that child as a child and no more, you hear?" Her breath was in his face, the only one in the whole place who wasn't drinking. Besides Angus anyway, who decided to remedy his dry condition straight away. He nodded to indicate that there would indeed be no funny business, and she released him. "I'll have a meal up for you two in a few minutes. I hope you like fish."

He nodded again, managed a "Yes, ma'am. Thank you." and headed up the stairs. His earlobe hurt. Was it bleeding? He determined not to check if one was now longer than the other. It sure felt like it.

He knocked at the door the boy had entered. It opened, and a different voice said, "come in, we can talk in here." That must be the real voice. It held none of the artificial aspects he had heard at the wharf. He stepped inside and shut the door.

The room was well lit by several oil lamps. A pair of bunk beds and a small table and chairs were wedged inside; space appeared to be at a premium in the Veyns. As he unslung his gear and set it on the lower bunk, he took in the construction for the first time. Stone! The outer walls were well made, with sound, simple construction. Inside seemed to be more transient materials, as if the place had been re-worked over time to suit different needs. After being surrounded by wood for days, he took a moment to touch the stonework; feel the dressed joints. This was the kind of work dwarves might have done if they were in a hurry. He would have to investigate that later.

The small human had taken a seat at the table, head in hands. "I suppose I owe you an explanation. Sit down, please. Have a drink, if you wish."

"As a matter of fact, I do wish." As he spoke, he fished a large wineskin from his bag. "Dwarven brandy – would you like to try?" The kid shook his head without raising it. Angus filled one of the tin cups from the table and sat down. "I can see that you know your way around the Veyns. That you have friends – real friends – that look after you. And that you are not a cabin boy. I suppose you can fill in the blanks?"

"Well, you've got the easy parts. Let me help you a bit more." Removing the knit cap revealed curly gold tresses that fell past shoulders. "I was a stowaway. When I heard that the Incande was headed for the Veyns, I saw my way home. I'm very good at staying out of sight; I found a niche in the hold and stayed there while the crew were awake."

Angus forced his jaw shut. He had suspected something different; he was halfway convinced that the cabin boy was an elf. It had never entered his mind that she might be a girl! He drained his cup and started in on a second.

The girl continued. "I've stayed hidden for years; I needed to. I had to become ready before I could fulfill my destiny. And I do believe in destiny. My niche, as it happens, was directly under your rooms. I heard much of what you and Johan talked about. I was aware of Johan and his role in Ivonia for the past year. In fact, I had considered asking him for help. I still might. But when I had to decide which of you to stay with, you were the best choice. Angus, I need your help."

Angus was still taking it all in. He was here to deliver a message, then move on. He didn't really have the inclination to help a homeless stowaway. But this waif did not speak as a child. And here was a girl asking for help – he couldn't refuse before he heard what she needed. "I'm a dwarf. I'm only here on a quick errand – how could I possibly help you?"

Before she could answer, the door was opened and in strode the ear-puller. Her arms were laden with baskets of breaded fried fish and fried vegetables. "I see you've let your hair down already – is he with us?"

"Close the door, Beatrice, and come inside." The waif spoke with authority. "We were coming to that part. Angus, I want you to meet Beatrice Gardner. She owns the Hoot Owl and is loyal to the Queen."

"Queen? I was under the impression that the Veyns were ruled by Regent Villeuse. I am on my way to him with a message, in fact." Angus was in no mood for intrigue. "When I have delivered my message, I have to continue on to several other destinations. I can't see that there is much time for me to help."

The girl smiled. "I told you I was able to hear your conversations with Johan for the last few days. I know what your message is. I know you are the Dragonbane."

Beatrice gasped. "Dragons... but they don't exist! They were only stories told to keep the little ones in line. Traveler's tales, and no more. It's just not possible."

Angus reached for the pouch he kept hidden behind his beard and brought out one of the Dragon's teeth. "It's one of his smaller teeth." He placed it in Beatrice's hand and turned to the child. "What does this have to do with you?"

"I am called Alene, and I too am loyal to the Queen. It has been twenty years, but the time has come to set her name right with the people. I carry my own message for the Regent. But I do not have the notoriety to gain an audience. If I follow as your servant, I can have the chance to speak in court. All I ask is to follow you and allow me to speak when the time comes."

When she said no more, Angus looked to Beatrice. The middle-aged woman said nothing. "I'm sure I'm still missing something here. Let me make this plain: I will not be party to assassination. I have no problem with your declaring your loyalty to the Queen, but if you use my audience to attempt to kill the Regent, I will prevent it. Do we understand each other?" Angus tried to put a face on that said he was in control of the situation, even though he was pretty sure he wasn't the one in control.

Girl and woman smiled at each other and went to leave the room. "Enjoy your meal, Mr. Angus. This room will be yours at no charge as long as you need it. A token of our thanks," said Beatrice as she left. The door closed and Angus was left alone with his thoughts. And dinner! While he ate the breaded foods, he tried to get a handle on exactly what was going on. Why did humans like drama so much?

Chapter 24

Streets of Water

Waking after dreams that made no sense, Angus got up and into his regalia. It was not a fast process, putting on armor. There were no windows in his room, so it was difficult to tell the time. The noise from the common room was gone, so it must be early in the morning, he supposed. A walk before dawn would clear his head and give him a chance to survey the city.

Moving as quietly as possible, he descended the stairs and left the Hoot Owl. He had decided to leave his bag stuffed under the bed, but he did bring his axe. That he held leaned over his right shoulder. He wore his helmet with the visor up. He didn't really want to make a big statement but looking over the city was what he wanted to do more than watch his back.

The first thing he noticed was the marble. The crystalline stone, usually reserved for decorative bits, was used here for foundations. The white and grey stone was well worked; put together with tight joints and little slippage. The canal that was near the wharf extended through the city, with smaller canals branching off to either side. Indeed, he noted that the canals covered as much ground as the sidewalks. There were no roads.

Above the marble foundations the architecture varied. They were all masonry or stone with different levels of quality. Plaster came off the brick in sheets on some, while others were dwarven quality work to the roof. What interested him most was the age of the good work; none of it seemed recent. Perhaps a nearby Holt contracted with the builders, only to fall out of favor? While there were some fresh chisel marks, there were not many. His best estimate was a couple hundred years at least.

One of the buildings near the wharf – near enough to bring a mid-sized ship to – caught Angus' eye. It was one of the good stone buildings, to be sure. Straight lines and no ornamentation marked it as the most dwarven structure he had seen. This one was marble through and through; it looked as if it would be standing long after the rest of the city crumbled to dust.

The immense iron gates that led to its courtyard would have allowed a boat to dock inside – if they still worked. They too had not been maintained. Most of the glass had been blown out by storms or vandals. No one lived there at all currently, if Angus had the right of it. He noted the location and determined to ask the story after he had told his at court. He knew there would be something behind this.

He walked for several hours, covering as much of the place as he could without boarding a boat. What seemed to be an illusion at first was the reality; these people had built a city right upon the mud and sand. And overall, it was beautiful. The bridges were mostly of stone and marble, which did not wear as fast as sandstone or other choices here. He finally hit upon the reason as he came back to the Hoot Owl. The salty sea and salt air. The crystalline structures in the marble would be more stable in a salty environment.

The city was just beginning to rise when he stepped back in the door. Aside from a couple of watchmen who observed from their posts, he had seen very few people. It was a different schedule here apparently. With no animals to tend, people didn't need to rise as early.

Beatrice was scrubbing the floorboards when he walked in. She shot him a frustrated look and rose, the sudsy sponge still in her hand. "You had us worried sick, Mr. Angus. Where could you be going at this hour in the morning?" She was shaking the sponge with each syllable, water splashing to emphasize her words. "You'll have to deal with a cold breakfast, anyway. It's in your room."

Angus hurried up the stairs. That woman was very intimidating, and in ways he wasn't used to dealing with. Opening the doors to his room he found that his cold breakfast was not the only thing that awaited him. Alene had his bag open on the bed, going through its contents. "That's your food on the table, Angus. I've already eaten mine." She was putting things back in place now; and he had packed too much to see what she may have kept with just a quick glance.

He closed the door and sat down. What else was there to do? She was dressed as a girl today. Her golden curls had been done up properly for a middle-class young woman, and her dress was at once modest and attractive. It matched the base browns and whites with a red frill at the front that the women he had seen last night wore.

"I was going through your bag to see if I could figure out where you went. We'll want to get in line within the hour if we want to see the Regent today." She was insistent, but Angus doubted that was the case. People didn't seem to be in a hurry here so far. "There are always hundreds of people looking for an audience, and only a few dozen get to see him each day."

Angus swallowed the bite of bread with fish and sauce he had started. "No one was even awake yet when I came back. How do these people live, if they don't work hard to make food and goods?"

"Veyns product is trade. Aside from art, music and a free exchange of culture, we almost exclusively buy what is cheap in one port and sell it in another where it is scarcer. Even the fishing is done from the seaside towns; the Fish Market is famed but is just another exchange. It takes years to understand, really. Just because people don't rise at the crack of dawn does not mean they are lazy. It's just... a different way." She finished bundling his bag and stuffed it under the bed as he had left it. "Your things are as you left them. I'm sorry for disturbing them. Now finish up and meet me downstairs when you are ready. And remember, there will be a line. You might wish to bring your pipe to help pass the time." With that, she left.

The breakfast was odd but substantial. He didn't mind fish at all, and it was well prepared, but he had hoped for more variety. Somehow, he thought, a city based on trade alone should have a lot more choice in foodstuffs.

A short time later, they hit the marble pavement on the way to the Palace. "And it's not the Regent's palace. The Regent is only taking care of business while the Queen is away."

"It sounded to me like the Regent was the permanent ruler here; how long has the Queen been away?"

Alene looked down suddenly, her brow furrowing. "Two decades. But mark my words, the rightful Queen will sit on that throne, and very soon."

Angus had more questions, but he set them aside when he saw that Alene meant to get on one of the long, narrow boats in the canal. He wasn't a good swimmer under any circumstances, and here he was approaching a wobbly craft dressed in heavy armor. "Can we get there without the boat, Alene?"

She giggled, a small confirmation of her real age. "Don't worry. You won't fall off. The poleman moves to counterbalance your weight as you board. You see?" She stepped down onto the boat, which barely wiggled as the man at the rear adjusted his weight to compensate.

Angus raised an eyebrow doubtfully. The man couldn't weight even half what he did in his armor. "This seems like a very bad idea, Alene." But he held his breath and stepped down anyway. The boat was steadier than he had expected. What he did not see was the poleman frantically working behind him to make it so. Alene let out a snigger.

A wave of self-consciousness swept over him; how would it look, a Dragonbane afraid of a little boat? He puffed out his chest and swung his axe out, using it as a pointing device. "I've been looking at the stonework on this marble," he started, but it was too late. The sudden shift in weight was more than the poleman could keep up with, and the boat dipped in the direction of Angus' gesture. Momentum and tilt worked against him, and he went over the side.

He closed his eyes as he hit the water. Headfirst, the salty brine flooded his nostrils, stinging horribly. Thoughts about what was happening flooded through his head. *There's no chance of swimming, as heavy as my gear is. Oh! What will become of my armor? My axe? My brandy?* His feet finally felt the water. He tried to open his eyes but couldn't. All he had seen was darkness – he knew he had sunk far. *Too far. Maybe I could lighten myself, if I dropped the axe and the helm.* A desperate ploy, abandoning valuable – very valuable – gear to the bottom of the ocean; but he thought it might work. *It must work.*

The last hurried breath he had taken now burned his lungs. Forcing himself to action, he dropped both items, thoughts of how much of this city he could buy with the wealth they represented rushing through his head. But he jerked away from his treasures as soon as he let them loose. Overcome by vertigo, he clung desperately to the hope that he would float to the surface in time.

His head broke into the air and he gasped for breath. Flailing, he realized that something behind him was interfering with his movement. Was he caught on the boat? He tried again to open his eyes and realized that he was being held aloft by his back plate. He looked over his shoulder.

The poleman was standing there, holding him with both hands. "I can't keep you up – you'll have to put your feet down!" The man was shouting at him! Then the words the man had shouted sunk in. He unbent his knees and felt rocky sand underfoot. The poleman sighed heavily and sagged back against a marble foundation. "You... really need... to learn... how to swim!"

Sheepishly, Angus coughed a chuckle. "I, uh... thank you, sir. I'll look into that." He looked down and saw his gear. He made himself put his face in the water again while he retrieved it. He needed to get used to water, apparently.

The poleman led him past an unabashedly laughing Alene to a ladder carved into the stone – more dwarven work, he'd wager – and up onto the walk. Because of the location, they had to walk around a city block to come back to the place the boat was moored. Alene was still laughing.

"Thank you, Angus. That was priceless." She drew in a deep breath. "You really can't swim, can you?"

"As a rule, it's not something dwarves do. We are dense, you know." It didn't quiet her laughter. He decided to let it go and concentrate on their surroundings. "As I had been saying, this marble is very skilled work. I would say that whomever did this had dwarven training."

She tilted her head and took her time before answering. "So, you don't know, then? The marble was dwarven work, when there were dwarves here. It was long before my time. Most of the oldest buildings are less than two hundred years old, yet every block here is built on the original foundations. They have been in place for thousands of years. But for at least three hundred, there have been no new foundations laid, because the dwarves faded out."

"Faded out? I don't like the sound of that."

"Well, the story goes that the Veyns had a difficult century, and there was no money for expansion. Trade was faltering in a big way; and for decades the city shrank in population as many looked elsewhere. With no new construction, the only thing left for the dwarven stonemasons was maintenance work; but they had built the city too well. Their work needed very little upkeep.

"Many of the dwarves left in search of more work. They didn't need to leave for the money; they just felt unfulfilled with nothing to do. It took some time, but eventually it came down to just a few left. Then there were none. They even built a villa with shorter levels to fit more dwarves on a small lot. All of the other buildings were re-purposed over time, but that one sits abandoned. It's so strongly made, it wouldn't be profitable to knock it down and rebuild it for normal sized folk.

Now, centuries later, the Veyns is thriving. Every year we build higher and more densely, simply because we can't build a good foundation. We've tried, but the secrets belonged to those dwarves. It seems the Veyns will never be a larger city than it is today."

Angus realized that he had been stroking his beard, squeezing the water out of it unconsciously. He had taken on a lot of water. "Where did the dwarves go, do you think?"

"No one knows. And people search; but the dwarves we have found laugh when it's been brought up, saying no dwarf would live in a city surrounded by water." She watched as he pressed armor greaves against his arms, water dripping out the edges like squeezing a sponge. "Seeing how poorly you are doing with it, I begin to understand."

It was true, Angus thought. Dwarves in a city surrounded by water was a ridiculous idea. Every story he had heard in dwarven lore linking his people and water had been either comedy, object lesson in things to be avoided, or, more commonly, both.

Yet here was an opportunity for profit making lasting works; engineering feats in a format that would showcase the very talents that made dwarves different and valuable. If he'd taken another few decades apprenticing as a stonemason, he might have tried it himself. He filed the knowledge away for future reference and went back to studying the stonework as they passed. He could see the work quite clearly being level with it as they glided silently through the canals, the steady slorping noise of the pole moving in and out of the water rhythmically the only sound.

Chapter 25

Blood in the Veyns

The slim boat rounded a corner, revealing a part of the city Angus had not seen during his walk. He certainly would have remembered this. Standing up in the boat without thinking, he saw an open plaza surrounded on all sides by the canal. People clustered around in groups that made no sense, with one man in each standing elevated, waving something Angus could not make out. That man would speak for a bit, followed by what seemed to be chaotic yelling from the excited crowd. That kind of noise always meant a fight was brewing where Angus came from. He watched expectantly.

When the process repeated itself several times without incident, he went back to taking in the buildings. Those that surrounded the plaza were all of a height, three stories each. These builders knew their craft, and architectural lines were clean and sharp. At one end there was a taller building, but only by a single story. Four towers stood guard over what had to be the palace. For the first time since leaving the Holt, Angus was impressed.

They pulled up to a marble slab where more of the narrow boats stood moored. Angus stepped gingerly off. Turning, he asked the poleman what he owed; he felt the bill was too low and overpaid by ten times. "That's not only for saving my hide, but for the discretion that follows, young man. I thank you." The last thing Angus needed was this fellow getting drinks from that story in the years to come.

As they climbed the stairs to stand on the plaza, Angus saw the designs in the paving stones. There were some solid stones, and some aggregated and set together so as to become one. Yet the whole plaza was as flat as a windless pond. It took a little walking, but Angus came to understand that the designs were representations of different cities. "Which one represents Ivonia?"

Alene shot him a look, then directed his gaze to a rather dejected man sitting alone on a crate. "We're not exactly on the best of terms, you know. Ivonia imports more than she exports; and what has been shipped out lately has been shite." She shook her head. "That poor fellow might as well go home. The best outcome he can hope for today is to sell his goods at well below market price. Let's not worry about him though – we've lost enough time already. We need to get to the Palace for our audience, remember?"

Angus did of course remember. "I'm very interested to spend some time here later." Alene smiled at him appreciatively. After a moment, they started off again toward the bridge that connected the palace to the plaza. The palace was not immense; perhaps two hundred feet across the face. For Angus, it was the quality of the work; the complete lack of visible chisel marks, every stone perfectly in place. All of the seams were even. No moss grew. It was fabulous.

The guards here were armed but wore no armor. A non-military observer might mistake them for decoration; but Angus could see their training and discipline betrayed by subtle movements. These were not men to be taken lightly. Unlike Ivonia, they made no attempt to stop him, and no one barred their way in. The doors were sitting wide open. Angus could hear the low rumble of a crowd waiting inside. It seemed to come from upstairs, up the staircase that aimed right at the door.

They ascended and joined into a throng of perhaps five hundred people. They were merchants and good-wives, ship's captains and huddled poor. There was even a smattering of men and women of flexible morals. A full sampling of the city, it seemed; and very different from Ivonia.

"When the Queen was here, she never let a day end without everyone getting at least a minute to present themselves. But the Regent says there isn't enough time in the day. Most of these folks will not see the Regent today, so they will come back each day until they are seen, or they give up hope." She furrowed her brow. "I came with you selfishly; I would likely be one of the latter if I weren't offering something else..." Her eyes strayed to a scantily clad woman with an altogether-too-confident visage. Angus understood.

"Now that I know about the dwarf shortage, I see why you might think I'll be noticed. Would you rather speak first?"

"I would rather follow. I think that the court will be caught off-guard by you. Your story as well, of course, but let's do be honest; you don't fit any of our ordinary stereotypes."

They talked and waited for a little while, eventually seeing two men in loose fitting silk clothes descend the stairs. The stewards proceeded through the crowd, selecting some members and sending them up to the next level. Angus had his helmet off and was standing up on the slender stone base that supported one of the columns to get a better view. Maybe twenty percent of the petitioners were being chosen, and most of that seemed predicated on rank or attractiveness.

Those passed by did not complain openly; but bitterness and disappointment were written on their faces. The stewards almost passed Angus by, as well. But something caught one's eye, and he stepped through the crowd to stand in front of the elevated dwarf. "I cannot recall a more armored person in our midst. And one so unusually short, at that." Angus hopped down from the footing and drew up every bit of his four-foot-eight frame. He hoped he looked the part.

"In accordance with treaties from the early days of the Veyns, I bring news to the Queen from the Argentine Holt. I humbly request an audience." Angus worked at a shallow bow but couldn't bring himself to flourish as Johan had.

"I'm afraid that won't be possible. The Queen is absent these long years, but you may present your 'news' to the Lord Regent Villeuse." The man indicated the stairs at the far end of the room and moved on.

Angus shouldered his axe and started off, saying "Come, Alene. They are waiting for us." She followed, brushing past a steward who looked very much like he was going to object. They moved together, her just a half step behind, looking like a close but lower ranking associate. They made their way up the stairs, arriving at last onto the flat, open roof.

It was a square the size of the building, the four towers extending several stories above were the only real obstructions to the view. From this vantage, Angus could see most of the city. It seemed an excellent place to rule from. He wondered if the weather was always this nice.

The petitioners arranged themselves along the balustrade, seemingly in the order they had been sent up. Angus and Alene joined in order. They waited as several more people joined the surprisingly elegant queue. When everyone had arrived, there were possibly forty individuals who would have their moment with the Regent. Angus could hear Alene's irritated noises.

Eventually the Regent appeared, looking more the king in his fur-lined velvet cloak, with a dozen servants following him. Twenty men took their stations around the perimeter, each with an effective looking halberd held perfectly upright. One of the last petitioners in line caught Angus' eye; but he leaned back out of view before the dwarf could figure out what seemed familiar about him. His attention went back toward the Regent, as the first petitioner was announced.

"Hermes Dufont, Successful Merchant from the Pelican District. Regarding Port Business." That was spoken by the steward that Angus had met, and he had a way of making the capital letters audible. The man who approached was considerable; rotund enough that he swayed with each step. His backward lean left no doubt that the small chest he carried against his belly was heavy.

"Your Lordship, as you know, I run a small fleet of ships based in the Veyns." He panted as he talked – Angus didn't think he stood as much as he had today; he was obviously having difficulty. "I have two slips - where one ship can offload, taking the goods straight to the next – being counted and taxed, of course."

The Regent nodded. "Yes, Hermes, I am aware of your operation. I thought all was well. How may I assist you?"

"Sir, as it happens, my slips are located on different docks. I must move my goods a full quarter mile from one ship to the next. My crews aren't allowed to move the goods farther than two hundred feet without passing the work to an anointed dock worker, according to the current Trade Temple dogma. I have a neighbor who is willing to trade slips with me, and we have agreed upon terms, but the Temple has blocked that move, citing the latest canon which states that slips can only be assigned on the date of their yearly blessing. I respect the advancements for the workers that the Trade Temple has achieved, but I cannot move my products quickly as it stands, meaning less product moving through, and less tax dollars to the Veyns as a result. I have brought the amount of gold I could save in one month to present to you, so that you can fully understand the costs involved. Do you think you can help me?"

"The Trade Temple does not make canon lightly. I may be able to speak with the Elders about your situation, but I'm not sure that one month is enough to show a clear pattern. Perhaps you could return with a quarter year's savings, and I can see what I can do with that?"

The fat man turned bright red, but his tones stayed pleasant. "As you wish, my lord. I shall return on the morrow." He turned and staggered towards the stairs with his load. As he passed Angus the man muttered angrily about needing to hire help to carry the load, and guards to keep it in his possession.

And so it went, each person expressing something that they desired and offering subtle compensation – bribes, Angus would have called them. Not one person had arrived without something to offer, and most of those offerings were not up to the Regent's expectations. He tried to project how his news would go over. He hadn't come to offer anything, wasn't asking for anything, and this fellow likely didn't know or care about old treaties or slain dragons.

He was jarred from his thoughtful state by a sharp jab in his armpit. Alene had slipped a pin of some sort through one of the few chinks in his armor. Her eyes flicked towards the Regent, followed by a meaningful nod. When Angus still didn't understand, she said, "We've been announced. It's time." He rose and strode to the spot where the others had given their talks.

"Lord Villeuse, Regent for the Queen, I am Angus, a Holtgart of the Argentine Holt. Many years ago, at least fifty generations for you, there was a great treaty set up between our people and yours, among others. This treaty provided that when emergencies of unusual disposition occurred, we would share that news with each other, so as to be prepared should it happen again." He felt he might be getting better at this; he wasn't as nervous as the first few times he had related the story. His time on the ship with Johan may have helped that – he had told the story over and over again, cementing which details he would tell in public.

"One month ago, we were visited by a very large, very fierce Dragon. He terrorized the countryside, eating a large portion of the livestock as well as murdering a few humans. He coerced our neighbors into bringing us his threats of further violence if they did not disclose our location. We are very grateful to those people for their fortitude and character, for they came to us first. They related events, and being honest dwarves ourselves, we devised a way to lure the Dragon to our doorstep. That very night, we set the trap; and the Dragon obliged us with his presence."

Angus left a dramatic pause; Johan had suggested that. It was working so far – he had their attention. All he had to do was get through the embarrassing part and he could head for the next stop on his map. He pushed on.

"We had planned to bring him inside our Keep, set him off balance, then set our best warriors to work against him. Everything was in place, and we knew we would see him dead soon after he entered; the only question that remained was who would strike the killing blow, and how many would be injured or possibly killed.

"I had kin in the crowd, and friends, and mentors. My job was to spring the trap, closing the Dragon in by dropping the portcullis behind him. After that, I would follow the others in turn, until the Dragon was dead. But another opportunity presented itself to me, when the beast paused for a heartbeat when entering. His head was just beyond the portcullis, and I seized the moment to drop the heavy, spiked gate onto his neck. I took my chance, and it worked; the Dragon was slain. Nary a dwarf injured, and no rebuilding required. A flawless victory."

He paused again, and let that fact marinate. His audience was silent, stupefied. "My full name is Angus Dragonbane, and I have fulfilled my duty here, satisfied the old treaty. But before I take my leave, I have a friend here who would like to say something." He gestured to Alene who had been a step behind him and to his right. She stepped forward, standing taller than she had before.

"For many years, our Queen has been absent." Alene started right in with conviction. "She left just a few months more than two decades ago, in fact. While she has been away, business has thrived here in the Veyns, with some of our merchants becoming wildly rich. The streets and canals are clean, and the wharves are in excellent repair. Fifteen years ago, the Trade Temple was founded, with the announced intent of bringing order and predictability to the ebb and flow of trade, the very reason that the Veyns exist at all."

"We have been hearing rumors, in fact, from the Temple and those most successful merchants, that the Queen may never return. That the Veyns are better off, and do not need a monarch, as we have had for centuries. I have heard it said that some parts of the city just work better under the Regent than they did with the Queen."

There were hesitant yeas until that last, when Villeuse nodded his head, his entourage agreeing vigorously. The Regent went to speak, but Alene continued before he could get anything out. "That message sounds very well to those who are allowed to approach the court. But what of those who are sent away, day after day? The poor who need alms, the small merchants with only one ship, looking for a fair chance at success? Those people always had a voice with Queen Caroline, who made it a point to see each and every petitioner on the day they came. Those with nothing to offer today deserve just as much of a voice as those who come laden with chests of valuables. The Queen's people." Her young voice had grown ever-more-powerful as she spoke. She shouted that last, at the top of her lungs; managing an almost echoing reverberation.

Clamorous shouts and sounds of steel on steel rose from the square below, but none of the court paid any attention. They were fully in Alene's thrall. "I, too, come with news. News of Queen Caroline, and why she has not come back all these years. The Lord Regent knows about the failsafe built into the laws of the Veyns. If a Queen dies with no issue, no heir, then the Regent assumes control of the Veyns. The period for a person missing to be declared dead is twenty-five years; four more years, and Villeuse would likely become the first King in the history of the Veyns."

Villeuse broke the spell with a dismissive chuckle. "My dear, I like the way your mind works. I never would have arrived at your conclusion for myself, but it has merit. Perhaps you would be willing to stay on here, as a consultant? My personal and close... advisor?" Small noises came from most of the men in Villeuse's employ. None of them were polite - they knew the Regent's tastes all too well.

"I thank you, Regent Villeuse." Alene's face softened, a small-but-grateful smile playing at the corners of her mouth. She took a slow step, then another toward the Regent as he responded.

"But of course."

"Not," Alene went on, "for the reasons you expect. I thank you for removing any doubts I had about whether the rest of my message is good for the Veyns. Now that you have made it clear that you and your rule are hazardous to the people, I can continue." Her approach was gentle and safe; a mere waif with a chip on her shoulder. Certainly not a threat. She continued. "Regent Villeuse, you sent assassins after the Queen when she left – to ensure that she would not come back. They did succeed, finding her in her island retreat eighteen years ago. They slew her and her entire staff, everyone on the island, leaving no witnesses to his treason. Or so he thought!"

"This is preposterous!" Villeuse was on his feet. "Seize her and lock her up for her slander! You, my little pretty, will hang before dawn for your false words." The guards with their halberds moved a step in, hesitating a fraction when Angus donned his helmet and hefted his axe. He wouldn't see this girl executed without hearing her out.

Angus saw three guards to his right launch toward Alene. He tossed his flask - it just happened to be in his hand - at the furthest guard, striking him in the temple. He continued that movement into a roll, collapsing the middle guard at the knees with his bulk. As he rose, he maneuvered his axe to hook the feet of the third, pulling one foot up and overhead. Angus reset his axe and scanned the room - there were no more challengers. He saw the girl restraining the regent by an earlobe adjacent to the third-floor balcony.

She addressed both the court and the crown below with a clear shout. "My name is Alene, daughter of the late Queen Caroline! I come of age today and claim the throne that is rightfully mine! Look out at the Plaza, you traitorous dog, and see the real people of the Veyns!" She twisted his earlobe, pointing him at the plaza below. She couldn't possibly see anything from her vantage, but the ruckus had changed; it was rhythmic now. There were people chanting – a lot of people chanting.

"You have no proof. Why should we believe you?" Villeuse's face turned purple with rage and embarrassment. He followed some of his aide's gazes over the side; there thousands of armed people chanted "Queen Alene! Queen Alene!" The Royal guards had split; some still stood at their posts, but more had moved over to chant with the throng. Among the defectors Villeuse recognized his professional Tormentor. That man returned his gaze and started a new chant:

"Give us Villeuse! Give us Villeuse!" The cry was taken up by the whole crowd. Dark. Angry. Murderous.

"Does it matter if you believe me? They," She pointed towards the square, "They believe me. It's over, Villeuse. I have the right to rule the Veyns. My family reign stretches back to the treaties that this Dragonbane talks about. The worst choice here would be bloodshed. You will suffer less if you cede power quietly."

The former regent thought about that for a second. "You first." He pulled free of her earhold, blood spraying from his ruined earlobe. He grabbed the back of her head and shoved with all his strength, adding his body weight to ensure she went over the side. She folded so effortlessly, he followed her over the side, realizing too late his predicament.

Alene tumbled over the edge, helping them both over while searching for her next handhold. She found it in one of the many banner poles situated under the balcony. Grabbing it with one hand, she realized the Regent still had a death grip on the back of her head. Her grip slipped as the large man alternated between screaming and cursing. Her fingertips lost the tenuous hold and they both fell again. This time she found a purchase on the banner itself, burning her hands as she slid toward the bottom of the Veynsian standard. She knew she would fall again, this time with no further safety stop.

Her maid's bonnet, an essential part of her disguise, pulled free from its pins, falling away with the old man. Villeuse met the stone plaza headfirst, mid-scream. The sound let everyone know that Villeuse' reign was over. The Blood had returned to the Veyns.

Chapter 26

An Unexpected Turn

The afternoon had been rather different. Angus had never witnessed a coup before, and this one had been considerably more peaceful than those he had heard of. After the Regent had relinquished his life along with his power, co-conspirators had been rounded up quickly and easily and with no bloodshed. New offices were set up and officers installed at an astounding pace. It seemed to Angus that this had been planned all along, it had gone so well.

Alene had let him go, asking him to attend the celebration this evening. Since he didn't seem to be any use here, he decided to take the afternoon to see the city. Making his way down the stairs, Angus used his free hand to bring out his mariner-style scrimshaw pipe. It was the only piece of property he had looted from the ship; he was interested to see how it drew.

The Plaza had been cleared of traders and was now populated by several dozen people placing tables, chairs and decorations in a tremendous sunburst pattern. Angus found a large block of granite at the periphery to sit upon and watch. He tapped the open end of the pipe on his palm, freeing the dregs of burnt tobacco from its last use. Feeling with index and middle finger, he found the small nook behind his breastplate that hid several pouches. Each had a different drawstring so that he could tell them apart by feel. The dwarf selected the pouch that held his dwarven pipeweed and pulled it free.

Holding the ebony mouthpiece in his teeth, Angus used both hands to open the leather pouch. Water dripped from the seams. He knew it was useless, but he couldn't help himself. He felt the ruined leaf, held it up for close inspection. Shaking his head, he sighed deeply and turned the contents out onto the ground and replaced it and the pipe in their nooks.

Looking around, he saw people working steadily. One stood out, using two measured rods to ensure proper spacing between the tables. Any person who knew how to make the perfect seating arrangement must know a good tobacconist. He approached the slim man and asked for directions not only for tobacco, but several other merchants he needed. After leaving the steward with a generous tip, he left the plaza with what seemed to be excellent leads for a fletcher, baker and an importer of whale oil.

He filled the afternoon with walking, observing, and mundane errands; it was quite frankly relaxing to act 'normal' again. He managed to cover most of the city with only two more rides on the narrow pole boats, the last taking him back to the Hoot Owl. He took some time to put his purchases away, then took out his last siege bow bolt. He would head to the fletcher next, on the way to the celebration dinner. He hoped to have a full quiver for the next leg of his trip.

After a bit of rest and drying out, Angus suited up and hit the streets. It took a quarter hour to find the fletcher, a diminutive man with dark features. Bernard ran a business that he had inherited from his father several years ago. There was very little demand for fletching in the Veyns, really. If it weren't for the small standing army, Bernard wouldn't be in business. But what he did, he did well.

"Can you make these?" Angus presented his bolt. "I'm looking for several dozen."

Bernard tried to hide his surprise. "What kind of bow needs a projectile this thick? And this tip – is this armor grade steel? I can do it, but it will take time and it won't be cheap." He turned the bolt over in his hands again, admiring the work. "This seems like oak, is that right?"

Angus nodded. "The grain is supposed to be important somehow, but I don't know very much about wood. I was hoping you could help me re-supply. They've really come in quite handy in the past..."

"I could make them for you, but they are worth their weight in silver."

"Agreed. How long do you need?"

Bernard had been expecting a negotiation – he was caught out by Angus swift agreement. "I... You can have them in a week. Three dozen, you say?" The short man was hefting the bolt, trying to figure out how good that deal really was. When Angus left, he set the closed sign out and went to work with his calipers, measuring and sketching the subject. He supposed it would have to be done right, and he certainly wanted the chance at repeat business.

Angus made his way to the plaza in the afternoon light, dressed as he had been earlier. People still didn't treat him as if he were out of place. Veynsians were a diverse people, used to many different looks and cultures. Dwarves were rare, but the thing that really stood out was the mithril armor he wore; a vast display of functional wealth. Even so, the city wasn't as uncomfortable as Ivonia had been for him. He didn't feel like he belonged here, not yet, but he found that he wasn't really in a big hurry to leave, either.

As he came over the zenith of the narrow stone bridge to the plaza, he saw a very different scene than he had left a few hours ago. The whole place was alive with movement. There were thousands of people, talking, dancing, singing and shouting. Great copper cauldrons held bonfires spaced throughout the party, flickering flames enhancing the sensation of movement. Everyone seemed to be having a grand time.

There were armed men that might be soldiers, but they were enjoying the celebration too. One table was set just a few inches higher than the others, the only sign of rank or royalty. People milled about, mingling poor with rich; serving each other regardless of social standing. As he joined, a large, turned-wood goblet was shoved into his free hand, aromatic red wine sloshing over the rim. He poured some past his growing smile, laughing with the rest.

It wasn't long before Johan found him. "I've moored the *Hidden Queen* and put out a call for sailors. Seems there are many trained sailors jumping ship as some of the dirty merchants are being cleaned out; I should have a crew by the end of tomorrow. The hard part will be cargo and a destination."

"*Hidden Queen*, eh? I like that. As for your destination, I've a few ideas we can go over later – but not tonight. Have they given Alene her crown yet?"

"No – not yet. I hear she's looking for you – wants to mention you in the ceremonies. I've been hearing stories of how you faced down armed soldiers, giving her time to speak. Good work!"

Angus had a feeling he knew what was coming next, but he headed toward the dais anyway. It wouldn't do to have a queen looking for him. He drained the glass and stopped a girl who was dancing by with a large pitcher for a refill. If he kept up this pace, even he would be using his axe handle as a cane before the end of the night.

Just as he got near the dais, he found four men dancing in his way. They hadn't been in his path a moment before. Angus noticed that they were all armed and had to admire them. He'd never seen a security force that could carouse with the secured and still be effective. Unobtrusive bodyguards, essentially invisible in the throng until the need arose. Something was said behind them, and they moved aside as if the dance had called for it. There was the Queen.

Her clothes were finer, multi-colored silks. They were festive without pretense, and there was nary a mark of rank on her. She smiled as he approached, reaching her hands out towards his. Angus couldn't help himself and bowed as deeply as his armor allowed.

"Oh, get up! We don't stand on that kind of ceremony here. But your role was pivotal today, and I want to recognize it. Come with me!" She grabbed his hand and led him up onto the table, where she raised his hand over his head, like a victorious prize fighter. "Everyone, listen to me!" The din lessened remarkably, and most of the assembled populace turned to watch. "This morning, the late regent tried to have me silenced. The men who stepped forward were only following orders, and they shall enjoy full pardons for their part. But they might have caused this festive occasion to be somewhat less happy, had it not been for this good man – er – dwarf stepping forward. Angus Dragonbane is his right name and knowing that they were facing someone who had bested the most fearsome beast of legend gave me the time I needed to finish presenting myself. Three cheers for Angus, our first dwarven Protector!"

The cheers were remarkably cohesive for such a socially lubricated bunch. They stepped down from the table, and Alene continued her conversation with the dwarf. "As I told you earlier, dwarves played a large role in building the Veyns. It's been too long; the city needs to expand, and we can't do it without dwarven stonemasons. I'd like to deed you the dwarf villa here and ask that you oversee its restoration. Do you think you could get it going, so that we can start to grow as a city again? I can guarantee a very profitable business..."

Angus was taken aback. True, the business had seemed interesting when it was a vague concept; but here it was being handed to him on a silver platter. A few weeks ago, he was a simple dwarf, struggling to find his place in the Holt. Then everything suddenly started falling into place. He didn't understand what was happening, but he couldn't think of any other course but to go with it. "I would be honored, my lady."

"Then it is settled. I'll have the keys to your villa delivered to your room at the Hoot Owl. Enjoy the party, Angus, Lord Protector of the Veyns!"

Chapter 27

Pickled Marble

Angus awoke the next morning still foggy from the libations. After defeating several challengers at the ubiquitous "let's drink 'til one of us falls down" contest, Beatrice had stepped in and guided him back to his room at the inn. That had been a good thing; Angus wasn't at all sure he could have found his way home alone.

Home. It certainly wasn't the Hoot Owl, but he may have made the Veyns a home, if not his only home. The Argentine Holt would always be home, but a five-hundred-year career made up of mostly guard duty wasn't quite as appealing as it had been only a month ago. His eyes had been opened to the world, and it might take some time to see enough of it to settle down again.

This evening, however, he did settle down, into the modest-but-clean bedding. Sleep took him abruptly, and when he woke, he remembered no dreams. His head throbbed lightly from the previous evening's festivities, so he took his time before lighting the lamp. Instead, he looked around in the dark with dwarvish eyes.

It was a bit off-putting to see the key on his small table. Once again, someone had been able to invade his space without him noticing until after it had happened. Telling himself that everything would be in place, he reached for the key and turned it over. It was exceptional – dwarven work if he had ever seen it. Made up of several concentric tubes with flanges to activate the tumblers in the correct order, it was much more secure than every human lock he had ever seen. It was fashioned from brass and gilded to resist corrosion. He added it to the cord that held his dragon's teeth pouch and replaced it around his neck.

Once dressed and packed, he headed downstairs. Beatrice had a large breakfast ready for him and Johan, who had taken a room there as well.

"I hear you've a villa now." Johan's voice was so flat it had to have been forced.

"So I'm told. She sent me the key, so I'm off after breakfast to take a closer look."

"I'm terribly curious – mind if I tag along to see? You've given me material for several tales already, and this might be enough for another!" Johan winked at his fire-bearded friend.

"As if I could stop you. I'd be glad of the company. How is the *Incande*?"

"The *Hidden Queen*, you mean. Some sailors think it's bad luck to rename a ship – and I don't want to run into any associates that might think ill of the way ownership was transferred. She's quite a nice ship; and now that I have a few experienced seamen on board, she should be able to turn a profit. I'll stay on board for a month at least before returning to Ivonia to give report that you escaped. It's got to be believable, you know."

They enjoyed a very leisurely breakfast, laughing about how odd the last two weeks had been for both of them. Afterwards, they found their way to the dwarven villa in one of the *Queen's* launches, floating up to the door that opened right onto the water. Angus produced his special key and turned it over several times, each rotation engaging the next set of tumblers with a barely audible 'click'. The key pushed further inside the keyhole as well, as if it were on a spiral track. Johan was speechless.

Angus cracked a smile as he heard a sprung mechanism releasing multiple bolts along the heavy iron door. "Dwarven technology, that. Probably more secure than the royal vaults back in Ivonal. To still work after centuries of neglect..." He trailed off, pushing the door open with two fingers. It did not squeak.

Inside, the darkness was interrupted by windows that opened onto the courtyard. All of the outer ones were shuttered in the same iron, with no visible latch work. Those on the inside would be sheltered from both thieves and weather, needing no security. Not that Angus needed much light, of course. Dwarves had been tunnel-dwellers since the beginning, and the ability to see in the dark was inborn.

As he entered, Angus studied his surroundings. Except for the heavy layer of dust and a few well-developed cobwebs, things appeared to be in order. The heavy desk that sat just inside the door was clear, an inkwell with long-dry ink and a math board with sliding metal beads the only items on the surface. There were several offices behind it, and doors that opened on to the courtyard. They took only a brief look at the offices before heading out into the open air – the dust was a bit much.

It was a four-story building, shaped like a U, with a courtyard that included a boat slip. The open stairway at the back joined both sides of the building and each floor to the next. Balconies surrounded each level, covered by the one above. Angus was noting how the first level was tall enough to admit humans, but the next three were decidedly shorter; meant only for his folk. Angus gaze had headed up; but Johan was staring down into the slip.

The tide was in, and this building was closer to the outer edge and the main canal; they were dredged regularly to allow passage of barges and smaller boats, although none with masts could pass under the high, arched bridges. But just under the waterline lay shapes, rising in two places above the water, terminating in what Angus had taken at a glance to be ornate mooring posts. Obviously, he told himself, he was wrong.

Looking down into the somewhat murky water, it appeared as a small barge with a deep, wide hull for its short length. Humped sheets of metal were plated in gold on either side of the central cargo bay, an open area about twelve feet by twenty-four. "I doubt you could float a boat that has sat under water for generations, but I'd love to see it tried. I've never seen such an ornate barge." The man really did seem impressed.

"I don't think that's a barge. A cargo ship, certainly. But not a barge. This would have been made specifically to carry marble from the quarry to the building sites, unless I miss my mark."

"Angus, a barge is towed or pushed along with poles. A ship must be propelled, and this – boat – has no masts, no sail and no bench for rowing. It's a barge. Unless you have another way of getting a blunt-nosed, heavy and laden boat to move?" Johan waited for an answer, but Angus only set his finger alongside his nose and winked at him. And moved on.

The other side of the courtyard was a warehouse, replete with several stacks of marble block, lifting apparatus and dollies for moving stone around with little effort. The floors were very flat, which would aid in that movement. A secondary room had a large, metal trapdoor and nothing else, save the track in the ceiling that ran throughout this warehouse area. Angus nodded and moved back towards the staircase, trailing a very confused Johan. "Are you going to explain all of this to me, or not?" the man asked.

"Well, let's see. You, among other things, are most chiefly a storyteller. You gather information and share it with the world for fun and profit. Whatever it was that dwarves did to the marble to make it last so well hasn't been replicated by the residents of the Veyns for centuries. I'd say that constitutes a trade secret, wouldn't you? So, no. I won't explain how I think that boat moves, or what was done here all those years ago. You're welcome to look around, but as long as you are telling everyone about what you encounter, I'm afraid I'll have to keep mum – about a few things. There's just too much at risk, you see?"

Angus had been walking throughout his monologue, investigating the several dozen bedrooms, kitchen, dining room and common space. He didn't linger, merely took a quick look. He paused now, in a bedroom on the fourth floor, situated so that it had windows overlooking both the courtyard and the canal. He dropped his bag on the stone floor, raising a cloud of dust. They moved on up to the roof.

It was the only stone roof in the city, made of the same marble that lasted so long in the saltwater. Each piece was fitted so close you could not see the seam, looking like one solid slab. It was likely the only reason the place hadn't been looted; the departing dwarves hadn't left anything around to steal, and what they did leave was of little interest to the locals. It did provide a fabulous view, however.

"I think I'll employ some goodwives to clean the dust up, then lock up for a while. I still have my mission to accomplish, and I can't run this place on my own." He paused and stroked his beard, obviously thinking something through. "Johan, I think I have a good first cargo for you. Go into the plaza and pick up textiles; unfinished silks and fine fabrics. Then run the Cyfleus Afon upriver as far as you can, getting as close as you can to p'Eaux d'Ancre. I'll send some letters with you, and if you can be patient for a few days, I think you could find yourself with a hold full of silver at bargain prices, as well as a few dwarven passengers on their way back here."

Johan nodded as he listened. "Yes, I like that. If I can provision to bypass Ivonal proper, I might do all right."

Some hours later, letters written, Johan and Angus parted. One of the letters contained a pouch with something Angus called "Pickled Marble" with no other explanation. It was heavy, definitely some kind of stone or metal. The *Hidden Queen* was under sail within the hour.

Angus hired a woman that Beatrice recommended to oversee the housecleaning. She was stout and short, able to work comfortably on the upper, dwarf only floors. Her name was Gertrude. "This will take weeks to put right, Lord Angus. There is nothing in your kitchen, no linens, not even a mop or bucket! It can be done, but what about the pay?" she asked, after being introduced to the dust-encrusted villa.

She was very pleased with his offer, and immediately agreed to stay on as long as Angus liked. "My bedroom first, if you will. I'm off to retrieve my gear and arrange for transport to shore tomorrow. I'll return in a few weeks, and we'll see where we are."

As it turns out, there was a ferry running to the mainland in the morning, with room for Angus and the pony Johan had dropped off for him. He visited the Queen briefly, letting her know that he had put the recovery in motion, and was off to finish his mission.

"Angus, I can't thank you enough for what you are undertaking for us. Can I offer an escort to see you safely back?"

Angus laughed out loud. "I thank you for your kindness, your Majesty, but no. It's not a dangerous thing, for the most part, to be a messenger." That wasn't really true, he knew, but he did not want an escort. "I do have one favor to ask: my map seems to be outdated terribly. Could you spare an updated copy of the mainland?"

That evening, Angus took some time to study his new map. It wasn't just settlements that had moved, but forest boundaries, and in one case, the course of a river. The mountains to the north were in place, and that was where his next stop lay – the Smaragdine Holt. It would be a short journey, likely taking as much time to find the door as it had to travel to it. After a few hours, he went to settle in to his bed – his bed, for the first time in weeks. It had been designed by dwarves for dwarves, and with its new bedding laid carefully down by Gertrude it was the best rest he'd enjoyed since leaving the Holt.

Chapter 28

A Bounty-full Journey

Gate-guard-cum-Lord Angus was pleasantly surprised at how easily his pony and wagon were loaded on the ferry. It was a very wide boat, and long. Two heavy ropes ran along it, one on each side. A team of ten men would walk the ropes from the front of the boat to the back, three always pulling on each side while two cycled back to the beginning. It was a good system, if the ropes stayed in place.

There were several other wagons aboard, all larger cargo types, and a half dozen men with horses. The other score were people afoot, men and women and a few children. The ferry made its journey four times a day, the captain told him. Twice over and twice back, it was responsible for up to five hundred people in the course of the day. Angus quickly took his leave to sit quietly by his wagon, watching from a respectful distance the waves splashing against the hull. The Captain soon had two nobles cornered and was telling them proudly about his operation; their expressions were frozen in polite rictii that barely masked their horror.

The trip gave Angus time to savor what he considered to be a very mild tobacco; he had asked for the shopkeeper's most flavorful blend. Maybe the dwarves at the Smaragdine Holt would have something more potent to share. Smoking also gave him something to do other than fret over being on the water again. A light morning fog obscured everything farther than a few dozen yards and dampened all ambient sound; leaving the feeling that they were alone in the world. Lapping waves and an occasional sea bird were the only things audible outside the ferry. Angus concentrated on what was happening on board instead.

An hour later, sounds of people and carts came through the fog, which eventually parted to reveal a large village. There were a small fleet of fishing boats and a few barges being loaded with sacks of grain and other supplies from land. Angus was eager to stand on solid ground again.

Within minutes, he was off the ferry, orienting himself with landmarks he had memorized on the maps. Several roads converged on Veynsport, bringing goods by land from all directions. He chose the one to the north-west and started inland. As he was passing through the suburbs, he watched the people. They were watching him.

There was no single reaction, but it was definitely reaction. The folk were more of a homogeneous group here, mostly sun-tanned bodies working hard. Their expressions ranged from awestruck to suspicious to a few whose eyes were measuring his value in a hundred currencies. He decided not to stop here for lunch, in case there was something to that look. He could still make twenty miles or better today, if he stayed underway.

The town melted away into more agrarian surroundings, split rail fencing, haystacks and manure piles. In and around one particularly large pile, there were several young boys playing. As the cart swaggered past only a dozen feet away, Angus saw that they had dug tunnels in the filth, and were singing simple, repetitive songs about gold. He flicked the reins irritably after a fight broke out between two dung-smeared lads over who got to play "Andar the Protector of the Veyns".

He spent the next few hours in his own dark cloud, trying to convince himself that there must really be an 'Andar the filthy', but to no avail. He was sure they were mocking dwarves in general and him in particular, at best playing out what they had been raised to believe. At first blush, it seemed trivial. These were children, horribly dirty children, playing their version of 'Orcs and Heroes'. He should think nothing of it.

But the more he brooded, the darker his thoughts became. Sure, these were kids, but kids work from models provided by adults. It was almost a certainty that Dwarves were portrayed as dirty, gold-hoarding pipsqueaks. Was that just Veynsport, or were the people of the Veyns proper just better at hiding their prejudice?

He got his answer a few hours down the road. Having spotted a piece of paper nailed to the railing of a short bridge, he dismounted to take care of some business. He took a moment to read the page whilst relieving himself (he hadn't seen a soul for a long while now). It was a good likeness of a very menacing dwarf in armor; with a great red axe. The words read "Angus, A Traitor and Friend of Orcs; Wanted Dead Or Alive! Reward: 500 Acres of Prime Farm Land with Plentiful Water!" No wonder the townspeople had been acting odd around him; to be announced Lord Protector in the Veyns and wanted as a nefarious criminal in Ivonia did offer a reasonable doubt.

On the bright side, the weather seemed to be holding, pleasant warm air with a healthy dose of humidity. These lowlands were marked as swamp on Artemus' map; they must have been drained to make arable farmland. The small levees here and there held up that postulation. He passed through the occasional human settlements without pausing – he would sleep under the stars tonight.

To that end, Angus rolled along until the sun was going down, only stopping to let the beast graze. He found a meandering creek with a few trees and followed it off the road and upstream for a quarter mile. An ancient briar provided enough cover for him to be comfortable building a fire and setting up a simple stew. While that cooked, he decided to have a bath. After checking carefully for any signs of this being a holy site, of course.

Another two days of easy travel, avoiding humans, brought him to the low mountains that housed the dwarves of the Smaragdine Holt. They were attractive, sharp and still green from the spring rains. There were no roads towards them, only the rare trail splitting off the highway. Angus decided that it would be one with wagon tracks, for the supplies the dwarves almost certainly traded for with the locals. He found some high ground and enjoyed a lunch while he consulted Artemus' map again.

After finding a few local landmarks that he knew would get him close, Angus camped for the night. In the morning he would dress up in his armor and ride up the valley cross country, hoping to be spotted by lookouts. In the meantime, he set about re-constituting more jerky and scones in another simple stew and enjoyed a pipe full of the weak – er – *mild* Veynsian tobacco. The sunset was amber and blue, layers upon layers. A nice evening.

He awoke with a start in the middle of the night. The fire had died down to embers, and there were two groups of wolves howling to each other from opposite sides of the valley. The sound echoed eerily down the slopes, making for an unsettling night.

Sleep was fitful and elusive until dawn broke, but he remained unmolested save a few biting insects.

When he set off in the morning, he had donned the Holtgart armor and had the Blood Onyx axe laid across his knees. The canopy stays were laid flat, with Artemus' siege bow laying atop his other gear. Angus wanted to be noticed. To finish the effect, he began to sing loudly as he passed into the valley, hoping to use some of the same acoustic properties he had heard the wolves using the night before.

Some of the songs were loud and bawdy. Others were deep, sonorous dirges. But all of them were in dwarvish, and aside from his outright sobriety, properly sung. He resisted singing the songs that Johan had taught him; too many of them involved Angus. And it would not do to start singing about yourself. Not while you were still sober, anyway.

The landscape became more picturesque the further he went. There were some trees, but not enough to cover an unwanted visitor's entry. There would be a half-dozen or more lookouts if this Holt were anything like his. He knew from personal experience; most of the dwarves at those posts would be young, and who had not found another talent to call their own. Angus had spent many hours sitting in a somewhat awkward position, leaning on an outcropping that gave a pretty good view of the foothills that led up toward the fortified gate. The shifts were long and lonely.

It was a little before noon when Angus saw what he was hoping for. Not a path or a door, but a moving crescent on the ground in front of him; it looked a bit like light reflecting off a wave. Without moving his head, he marked where the sun was and where the reflection was and took a guess. Turning over his left shoulder, he saw the sunlight glint against what he knew would be a gemstone lens. He stopped his pony and looked right at the glint and waved.

Immediately, the shiny object was covered. *Rookie*. That meant all was well in the area – not expecting trouble, younger, more inexperienced dwarves would be on guard duty. It was incredibly boring duty, but his father had always told him that it built character. That was one of the best parts of becoming a Holtgart; he would only get that type of work when it really mattered.

He was very glad that a rookie had spotted him; while there would be no great recognition from his elders or supervisors, being the first to see the Dragonbane would carry weight with the young one's peers. Were their places reversed, Angus would have enjoyed it.

With no immediate sign of the right path, Angus continued on. It would make the lad look better to seem as if he had remained hidden. Besides, it was a splendid day for a casual ride. He knew that soon he would be surrounded by warriors and led inside. Inside! He was very excited to see another Holt. Angus had not traveled before this, not beyond p'Eaux d'Ancre anyway. This would be the first time he would see how other dwarves lived.

He was another mile up before it happened. One moment he was alone on the trail, then within the space of a breath four stern Greybeards stood around him, well-armed and armored. They weren't threatening him, but there was no doubt about which way the fight would go if Angus was bringing trouble.

"That's a fine suit of armor for such a red beard. I don't believe we've met – I'm Thannon Clearstone, Captain of the Smaragdine Holtgart. We aren't expecting anyone; I'd like to hear what brings you around." The dwarf was grizzled, the tales of countless battles and presumed victories carved into his face and hands.

"I come with news, of the sort that needs to be told to the King directly. I can assure you there is no immediate threat, but the rest will be reserved for him. Trust me; you'll like what I have to say. I've also got a bit of brandy from the Argentine Holt here in the cart..."

The rest of the conversation became much more jovial. Dwarves were not immune to the human trait of relaxing in the presence of potent libations. In fact, it might be more properly said that humans weren't immune to the dwarven trait. Dwarvish liquors were more potent by far than those that men made, and even more flavorful. Time was the secret there; a ten-year-old bottle would be mature to men, but just laid up by a dwarf. Brandy was often over five hundred years old at the Argentine Holt – unheard of in places like Ivonia or the Veyns.

The group was laughing together like lifelong friends by the time they arrived at the gates, which opened wide as they approached with no obvious signal. While very different in style, the general concept was traditional – a perfectly worked and maintained stone wall blocking a natural cavern mouth. The gates were beyond stout, likely impenetrable by any means including Dragons. Angus story was an old one; Dragons and dwarves have fought for prime real estate seemingly forever. The only unusual detail was the actual method of Szicthys' death. That, and the fact that the Holt survived a Dragon getting past the gates at all. That never ended well. Well, almost never.

The inside of the Holt was impressive. Here, the real strengths of this community were displayed. The most obvious difference lay in the materials. The Argentine Holt was surrounded by massive silver deposits, hence a preponderance of silver in everyday objects. Here, the abundance of gemstones was obvious. Thousands of gemstones were on display, used as lenses on lanterns and inset into doors and windows. His new companions had gems worked into their armor, too. It was beautiful.

"I've got to warn you," Thannon began as they approached the King's offices, "The king has been in a foul state for two days now. He received three letters from the surrounding human communities, borne by men with faces pale with fear. Since then he's cloistered himself, cursing and yelling; but he won't say what's going on. If your news is as good as you say, perhaps it will bring him out of it."

The king's apartment was set up in stages, from public to private. The outer public meeting room was empty and orderly, a long, low oval table with benches at the right height for dwarves dominating the room. Here is where meetings would be held, announcements made, and treaties signed. Like most dwarven things, it was supremely functional and exuded quality. Despite the room's age, there were no signs of wear; it could have been built yesterday.

A gem-encrusted steel door lay on the far side of the meeting room, and that is what they made for. Thannon knocked three times and waited. After a short while with no answer, he opened the door a notch.

"Sire pardon the intrusion," he began, but was cut off by a gruff voice.

"I said no interruptions! It is imperative that I get this right, and I need to concentrate!"

"Yes, sire, but if I may-"

"Are there enemies at the gates, Thannon?"

"No, sire, but-"
"Are you carrying a platter of sausage and beer?"
"No, sire, rather-"
"Then my order stands! No interruptions! Now shut the door and be off before you raise my ire!"

Thannon shut the door and faced Angus. "It's worse than before. I'm not even sure that he would have let me in if I had brought beer. For the first time, I'm worried."

"I've something better than beer. Stay here, I'll be right back." Angus headed back to the stables where they had left the wagon, still loaded. He fetched a small cask of brandy and brought it up to the meeting room. Opening the door, he set the cask on its side and rolled it along the floor. It bumped into the desk next to the King's chair, where the leader sat in a dressing robe. His hair was tousled, his beard un-braided. In short, the King was a mess.

The slight thump against his desk got him to look up from the maps and letters arrayed in front of him, but he did not rise. Then he looked at what had caused the noise; a small oaken cask with a silvered seal. Picking it up, he turned the thing so he could read the seal, which he did slowly.

"Artemus? Is that you?"

Angus stepped inside and closed the door. "No, sir, but Artemus asked me to show you something. The brandy was just to get your attention."

"Five-hundred-year-old Argentine brandy – you have my attention. What can old Bedwyn do for you?"

Angus' heart skipped a beat. Bedwyn! This was one of his favorite heroes from the stories, standing here in front of him! Bedwyn had engineered several victories when facing terrible odds – impossible odds, as the stories said. This was the dwarf responsible for ending the last of the orc wars! Angus found himself unable to speak; so, he just stepped forward and laid the tube of papers Artemus had given him on the table.

Bedwyn nodded and read the papers quietly. After a moment, he turned to look Angus in the eye for the first time. "Dragonbane, eh? Well, except for the beard, you look the part. And well-timed, I'd say, with the new trouble brewing. Yes, I can use this; your arrival will catalyze my people and put the desire to do great deeds back in their hearts. An inspired army always does better than one that is merely pressed." He stood up and took the cask to a cabinet where he kept an assortment of plates and glasses. Selecting two wide, gilded goblets, he filled each with a generous portion. "Angus Dragonbane – let us drink to inspiration."

Chapter 29

How to Win Hearts

Two hours later, Bedwyn and Angus stumbled out of the chamber. It was obvious that they had been enjoying the brandy. "Take this young dwarf downstairs and get him something to eat before he caves in. Thannon – come in here; we've arrangements to make!"

Angus was brought to a dining room, not unlike a human tavern except for the stout, low tables that were wide enough for some dwarves to be dancing on them while others ate and drank. A large lamb shank was brought down to him, with some mashed tubers and a pint of beer. When he held the glass up to the light and raised his eyebrows, the younger dwarf serving him took the hint and brought out a pitcher. They shared a laugh over that.

Half an hour later, preparations began in earnest. All hands were set to cooking, decorating and getting ready for a significant event. Hearts were light and curious. Expectant looks were aimed at the dwarf in the Dragon-themed suit of armor more than once.

When Bedwyn emerged, he was no longer the frazzled old dwarf that Angus had met this afternoon, but rather resplendent in his own mithril suit of armor. This was more than a dwarven King before him now; this was Bedwyn Foresight, General of the Combined Dwarven Armies. His armor was themed with sextants, maps and representations of his numerous glorious victories. It had been made and re-made as his deeds grew, and today it sported a shine that enhanced the overall effect suitably.

The dwarves of the Holt quickly assembled, seating themselves and readying glasses to be raised in what surely would be one of the King's famous toasts. They were not about to be disappointed.

"Good Dwarves of the Smaragdine Holt, I greet you!" There was a greeting returned as a shout, and Bedwyn continued without losing any tempo. "It is three hundred years since our army left the field after vanquishing the orcs, scattering their remnants to the four winds. That is an accomplishment that still bears celebrating, centuries later. Since then, our military actions have been simple in comparison; mountain trolls, mining disputes with our goblin neighbors; all nearly flawless victories. We have a lot to be proud of.

"With so much success, one begins to wonder if there ever will be a challenge again. Will we have need of great deeds? I had been pondering this question for a few decades now, with no clear answer. Despite the name, I can't really tell the future, after all." Laughter.

"But now, we have some answers. The first I would like to present to you tonight is this young dwarf – stand up, Angus – who brought me some news today. Angus hails from the Argentine Holt where my old friend Artemus rules. A bit over a month ago, they had a visitor, but not the kind you bring home to mother. No, friends, they were visited by a Dragon!"

He let that sink in. "Artemus had set a plan in motion that included luring the Dragon into the Holt and killing it where it could not fly away; a solid plan, if risky. But the young gate-guard had an inspired moment. Angus attacked the dragon with the portcullis, even as it took the bait and was entering. One of the big spikes severed the beast's spine just below the skull, and that was that; so this dwarf, Angus, has not only the distinction of being a Dragonbane, but doing it faster than any Dragonbane in history! Such a blow cannot be planned as much as inspired. Let's all raise our glasses to Angus, Dragonbane from the Argentine Holt!"

The cheering and toasting lasted for minutes, while many of the dwarves moved in to clap Angus on the back, shake his hand or fill his glass. Now this was a reception worthy of the title. What Angus, indeed all the dwarves, failed to notice was what Bedwyn was doing during the commotion. He had pulled a chest onto the dais, as well as a tripod map holder. He did take the time to drain a mug, leaving the frothy head on his beard. It was important to maintain the appearance that this was a celebration for him as much as the others. There he stood, waiting for the ruckus to die down. When it did, he took the reins of this emotional crowd and whipped them to a frenzy.

"Angus is here as part of the old treaties. To get here he has endured the company of Elves and befriended men. There is still one stop to make for him, although he does not yet know his full mission. As you all know, we keep in contact with local men, to keep in touch with what is happening outside the Holt as much as for provisions. The goblins that inhabit the caves on the northern slopes of our mountains have had little to say to us recently, having found trading partners of their own. Now I am ready to give you the full story."

"A week ago, I received a package from one of our friends that contained this poster." He handed it down to the dwarf closest to him, who then passed it to his neighbor. Astonished gasps could be heard as the message spread; the Ivonians had made a wanted poster that featured Angus, or a poor likeness of the noble dwarf they had just met. "The man who brought me that also gave me this sword, which concerns me even more." He held up a boxy sword that had several more points than it needed, layers of folded steel revealed by an acid etch. This time, there were cries of anger. "Yes, it is orcish in form. But more concerning is the quality of steel; it is most like the metal we used to source from our one-time trading partners, the goblins!" More cries, and fists pounding on tables. "Now, now – for us, the ones who saved them from extinction at the orcs' hands hundreds of years ago, that is offensive. But remember; they have lives more like men, and their memories fade as fast as their technology grows. We must deal with the problem instead of our anger.

"Which leads me to the problem. The orcs are active again. Something woke their warlike nature, and they are forming larger and larger groups. They are better armed than the last time we met them in force; and their main army is north of the mountains. After studying their placement, I see only one good course of action for them; they need to eliminate the Aureate Holt first, then either the Argentine, or us. After that, the humans south of the mountains will be easy prey. Unfortunately, those to the north are near enough to defenseless as to make no difference. The path around the mountains to the east is the fastest way for us to arrive at the Aureate Holt, but we will come too late to warn them. Those longbeards and greybeards will need extra time to prepare, and we must give that to them. The old goblin trade tunnel would work for a messenger, but not an army. The goblins would see that as an attack, and even if – when – we won, we would still be too late.

"So, here is what we will do. Angus, being the only dwarf not of the Smaragdine Holt, will run the trade route alone and on foot. He will warn the Aureate Holt when he brings his message and give them time to prepare for a siege as we come in from behind to rescue them. The orcs are better at open field battle than we are, so we will hit them in the morning when most are in their beds."

There was a pause while the ramifications of Bedwyn's words hit home. If they did nothing, it would only be a matter of time before the orcs came after them, or Ivonia turned on the dwarves as a nation, or both. Action was needed, and it was terribly obvious.

"Angus, you leave in the morning. You will need to run as much as possible – every hour will count. It will take nine days for our army to reach the Aureate. You need to warn them and help them last until then. Are there any objections?" Dead silence. "Then go and prepare for war!"

Chapter 30

A Walk in the Dark

Paring down his rig was problematic. The Dragonbane needed speed for the journey, but he also needed to be ready for battle along the way. He found himself wishing for his spear again; it really was the best weapon for tunnel fighting. He put that thought out of his mind and went down the list of things to bring.

The Armor was a difficult decision. It was built of very light and strong materials, but there was still a lot of mass to carry. It would slow him down, but in the end, Angus decided to wear it – better late than never, he thought. The axe, of course. The color was starting to fade slowly toward black, but that would change again soon. He took some dried foods - thick, hard bread and thicker, harder cheese. One healthy bag of mixed silver, gold and gems would probably not be used, but currency often made things easier. His large knife, a flint and a coil of rope rounded out his kit; he'd leave the siege bow behind with the pony, wagon and his beloved brandy.

So off he went, into a tunnel that hadn't been used for decades. The floor was heavily rutted from the wagons that used to carry ore and goods back and forth between the two mountain communities. Angus found that walking on the higher hump in the center of the tunnel the easiest route. He had mounted the small tin full of fluorescent fungus on his helmet. The dwarven lantern produced just enough light to let him see in the dark with his very sensitive eyes. The axe worked well at clearing the occasional cobweb and helped him keep his balance when things got slippery.

The going was easy for the first leg. Angus kept up a cadence that was more than a jog but less than a run. It helped that here, the tunnel led slightly downward. He tried not to think about how much harder it would be ascending again. A couple of hours in, he stopped to take a rest and drink some water. This tunnel would be guarded, but there was no war between the dwarves and goblins - just some animosity because of their trade dispute – so Angus didn't expect any trouble when he emerged. With any luck, he could pass by the goblins entirely without being stopped.

About four hours in Angus started to feel as if he were being watched or followed. He stopped several times, listening and looking – but there was nothing around. He started isolating each clink and squeak of his getup, and one by one found ways to silence the noises he was making. Another two hours, and he was certain that no one would hear him coming.

The going got slower when the tunnel started its slow climb back up. The air changed; stale, dead air that hadn't circulated in years. It became increasingly tinged with smells of goblin activity – grease, burned metal and leather were prevalent. They were a very mechanical people, making machines often just because they could. Their stated philosophy was that machines were to make life easier; but goblins would make a machine even if it made life more difficult. They tended not to get involved in politics outside their circle and were very concerned with outsiders stealing their secrets. A good thing, too, or some king or other would always be after them to make a better killing machine. That was a slippery slope Angus didn't want to start down.

He hefted the axe as he trudged on. *It is an honest weapon. Better at taking life than a woodsman's axe - no crude tool this. But somehow being face to face with an enemy, to look in their eyes as you try to darken them makes the whole thing seem – well, honest.* He chuckled as he caught his mistake. *I certainly hadn't looked into the eyes of that Dragon, had I? Perhaps, but that was never going to be a fair fight. Maybe alternative strategies are all right if the match isn't even*, he thought. Then he thought of his armor, and how there really was no finer in the world; how that gave him an immediate advantage, then tossed the whole line of thought out of his head.

It was fortunate that he chose that moment to pay attention to where he was, for there was light ahead in the tunnel. He reached up quickly and closed the tin on his helmet, and advanced slowly until he could see what was happening. There was nowhere to hide, so he just kept advancing slowly, visor up and his axe over one shoulder. There was something large and round blocking the tunnel almost completely, flickering shadows showing some movement behind it. There was nothing menacing about what he was seeing, so he strode right up, fearlessly if quietly.

He didn't even need to be very quiet; the goblins hadn't expected to encounter anyone here at all. There were six of the scrawny creatures, heads larger than they should be and a notable lack of hygiene their trademark physical features. The large round thing turned out to be a heavy black-iron boiler, apparently just coming up to full steam. Two goblins fed shovelfuls of coal into a furnace while two worked with some large contraption further back. The last seemed to be checking dials and adjusting levers. The machine almost filled the tunnel. Now that he could see the whole thing, it seemed to be some sort of self-propelled wagon with a trailer. Angus stepped close to the boiler and observed from the shadows.

"Keep shoveling! We need more pressure for it to get all the way!" Howled one of the goblins. Waves of heat coming from the boiler warped the air in the tunnel.

"32...33...33.5... we're almost there, just a bit more pressure and we'll be ready, Steam Master!"

"Is the payload ready?" shouted the first to the two on the trailer.

"We're ready to arm the device on your command, sir!"

"Do it, and head back to the High Engineer. Tell him that the attack is underway."

Attack? Angus tried to think about what was happening here. He hadn't passed a single branch or side passage along the way, and the large spike on the front of the boiler gave him the strong impression that this machine was headed for the Smaragdine Holt. The army would be away by now, leaving just the Holtgart; they could repel an attack from without, but this – whatever the device was – would hit from within. He had to try to stop it. But how?

"34.8...34.9...There! 35, and we're ready to go. Everyone off the machine – I'll set it and jump off once its underway!"

Angus stepped around the right side of the boiler, looking for the way to the controls. A platform where the boiler and furnace came together held several dials and smaller levers, and one large one that the goblin apparently in charge was pulling towards himself, in the direction of the Holt. Angus tapped him on the shoulder. The goblin turned his oversized head to look over his left shoulder, only to see Angus' right gauntlet crack hard against his chin. He crumpled, leaning heavily on the lever, which changed direction towards the goblin city. The platform lurched in that direction, accelerating slowly. Angus hung on.

The other goblins were shouting, obviously alarmed at the direction of the machine. It was moving at a slow walk now, with a couple of the cunning little nasties coming alongside to step onto the platform. One spotted Angus and screamed in horror, howling curses that the dwarves were attacking, just like the orcs had said they would. Another climbed up at the same time, brandishing a heavy wrench in one hand and a long screwdriver in the other. Angus waited for the lunge and let the screwdriver slide right off the Armor. This wasn't fair. Angus reared his head back and delivered a solid head-butt to the goblin, who dropped his tools and fell backward off the platform – which was now moving at running speed, and still accelerating.

Another goblin had climbed aboard and jumped onto Angus' back. He thumped wildly with his small brass hammer on Angus' helmet – aside from the noise, Angus really wasn't feeling any pain. The goblin's war cries turned into screams of agony as Angus stepped backward to lean the creature against the red-hot iron of the furnace door. The machine moved as fast as a horse now and still accelerating. Angus started to think about how to get off the machine. What he wanted was an exit.

What he saw, fast approaching, was a staircase set into the side of the tunnel. Without thinking, Angus jumped and rolled right past, clattering to a stop a dozen yards too far. He didn't know why, but he felt an urgency about getting into that staircase. As he made the opening several seconds later, he glanced over his shoulder as he ducked in. The machine had encountered a slight turn in the tunnel and had climbed the wall on one side. Disaster was impending, and Angus had seen enough. He ran up the stairs as fast as he could, hoping they led somewhere that he wouldn't have to fight his way out of.

There was a single percussive blast that knocked Angus off his feet, two flights up. Then the rumbling began. Air pushed up the stairs with enough force to lift his pauldrons, growing hotter and hotter until flames shot up, coming just shy of enveloping Angus before retreating with just as much alacrity. Angus held on to the steps until the storm died down, then continued up the stairs. Whatever that 'device' had been would have devastated the Holt.

He hoped it hadn't been too bad for the goblins. This is something that he would talk over with all the Holts in the next few months – next time, they would be ready.

The stair rose for hundreds of feet; after a while Angus sat down for a break. There had been no noise from above or below. Despite Angus having left those goblins alive, he doubted they were still breathing now. He took a bite of the hard cheese and chewed slowly. Goblins had never been aggressive before. Not ever. Something must have them fearing for their way of life. He took a drink and headed up the stairs again. This time he didn't stop until he saw daylight.

Chapter 31

By Any Means Available

As he staggered to the opening at the top of the stair, Angus knew he was spent. He had jogged all night, fought a short battle around dawn and climbed for more than an hour – all in full armor. If there was another fight waiting for him at the top, he wasn't sure he could even raise his axe. His breath was ragged and labored, a little frothed spittle ringing his mouth on beard and mustache.

There were people up here, two goblins working together in assembly line fashion. They had glass jugs with several fins at the top, where a smaller glass globe sat. One was filling the larger container with a thick liquid almost like molasses. They were being very careful and methodical, until one took note of Angus.

His eyes swiveled up from his task to see the dwarf, all in shining armor with a great stone axe in his hands. Angus' shoulders rose and fell from the effort of his climb, but that wasn't how this chemist took the action. In his oversized, overactive brain Angus was filled with a murderous rage, and would shortly slay him. He said 'EEP!' and took off around the corner, leaving his companion holding a large jug steady. The second watched the first run away, then looked around to see what the problem was. When he saw Angus there, he fell over backwards, scrambling to follow his friend like a crab on its back.

Angus couldn't stop himself from uttering a maniacal laugh and started to follow the fleeing pair. They had disappeared into a large tin shed that was built into the side of the mountain, opposite a steep drop-off. Smiling, Angus stepped around to stand in the doorway. He did not find more goblins as he had expected. Instead, there was a – wagon? - with spars and horizontal sails, tubes and several seats. The two goblins were in those seats, one pulling a lever frantically.

There was a sizzling noise from behind the contraption. Angus stepped onto the structure at the front, looking for a way to get closer to the goblins. Their eyes were as wide as saucers, and they had no weapons in sight. He was only several feet away from them when the popping noises began. He slipped, and one hand went grasping for the horizontal pole above him. He missed his mark as the whole contraption lurched forward, and he went down, headfirst into one of the seats. The goblins screamed.

Angus could not get up for several seconds. He was held with his head in the sling-style chair he had fallen into, as if ten stout dwarves were keeping him there. There was so much sound – a staccato roar from the rear, creaks and rattles – that Angus feared for his life. Goblin machines either worked very well or exploded with deadly effect. He hoped desperately that the former was the case here. The goblins were still screaming but seemed to be running out of breath.

Some time on – seconds, not minutes, Angus would wager – the intense pressure keeping Angus in place let up. He pushed his head up and was blasted by cold air coming up through the chinks in his armor. He looked at the goblin on his right who smiled sheepishly and shrugged. The other was looking away from Angus, at the landscape far below. FAR BELOW! Angus was in a flying machine, in the air! This was not good. Slowly he tried to turn himself to sit properly in the seat; it was not designed for his girth, and certainly not for armor. He caught his breath and realized that the roaring noise had stopped. He started to laugh.

The goblins laughed, too. They all realized that with the noise done, they had passed that point that most failed projects would have failed. The chemistry had worked, and here they were, flying. Angus tried to get his bearings as the goblins started chattering back and forth in their consonant-heavy language. They were headed north, or near enough. The mountains in front of him were where he was headed, roughly.

"Well, this is a surprise, isn't it?" Angus stated in common tongue. "Have either of you boys ever been flying before?"

They chattered a moment before the one on his left responded. "We've watched flights take off before, but we haven't talked with anyone who has landed successfully. We have always assumed that they flew into enemy hands or took the technology to sell on the black market." The goblin on his right nodded sagely.

Angus considered that logic. He had always thought goblins who tried flying to be suicidal, but perhaps they were just paranoid. They didn't seem to be concerned at any rate. "So I guess we are in a bit of a position here, then. You couldn't possibly drop me over the edge, and I can't harm you if I want any chance of a safe landing." He thought about a way out of that for a moment, then continued. "You can't land near the other goblins, or they will think you a traitor for giving a dwarf a tour of your technology."

"But that's not true!" the one on his right shouted.

"I know that, and you know that, but will they believe you? And what if they don't? Much better if you appear as being taken against your will."

The goblins talked with each other again in their nattering manner. "What do you want, then?"

Angus pointed at the mountains to the north. "Take me as close to those mountains as you can. When we land, I'll head north, and you head south. We each make our own stories for our people, and everyone goes home safely. That's fair, isn't it?"

They nattered again for a while. "We accept."

And so, they flew on, gliding north. The view was transcendent. Angus wouldn't say he was over his fears so much as ready to accept his end if it was coming. So, he got as comfortable as possible and enjoyed the ride. Scary as it was, this opportunity would not come again for him. He was enjoying the view of the world, as if looking at a map, when he saw the columns. Several groups of orcs, converging toward a common path to the Aureate Holt. They were drifting low enough that he could tell that they were orcs, and even hear the edges of their cries when the unlikely trio passed overhead. The nattering was rising to a fevered pitch as a landing site was selected; rolling, grassy foothills with only scattered boulders popping up out of the grass. Angus wasn't too worried until the goblins started to scream again. He put his visor down and held the flat of his axe blade across his chest.

The sled skis at the front of the vehicle dug right into the grass almost immediately, throwing it upside down, and launching Angus ahead. He had no better plan than to curl up into a ball, hugging his axe tight. He hit the ground at the base of one of the grassy foothills with enough speed to skip several times like a stone on a still lake. Except that Angus was tumbling now, rolling end over end and twisting slowly, too. He was still rolling when he stopped skipping, rolling right up the hill and catching some more air at the crest. He rolled to the bottom of that hill before coming to rest.

He lay there, spread-eagle, just breathing for some time. Then he started moving, limb by limb, testing for breaks or damage. Amazingly, he was only bruised and not broken. He did wish he had brought some of his brandy. Check that, he wished he had brought a lot of his brandy.

Chapter 32

No Time to Waste

It was difficult even getting up. Without the armor, he doubted that even his stout build would have survived that landing. He still had his axe, though the rope and small pack that held his food and water was shredded and splayed over the hillside behind him. He was already leaning toward not checking on the goblins when he heard them.

No, not the goblins. Howls of orcs on the hunt. They had seen the flyer go down and were interested – very interested by the hooting and hollering – to meet the occupants. It was a motivating sound for Angus, and he rose with alacrity. No time even to collect his belongings. He lurched into motion.

It was a halting cadence at first, before the adrenaline kicked in. He hadn't slept, had run thirty miles in armor, and now had fallen from the sky. Everything hurt. He was exhausted. Untold droves of angry orcs were shortly on his trail. And he didn't know exactly where the entrance to the Holt was. The situation was hopeless.

And so, Angus found himself, at what must soon be the end of his story, going over in his head the different ways that he might be killed. For that part, he hoped to make a good account of himself as he had at the Sliver, but in truth, he wasn't sure he could convince his arms to raise his axe even once. Some story that would make, he thought, a Dragonbane dying simply because he's too tired. As these scenarios played out in his head, he forced one foot continually in front of the other, making progress. He was sure it would not be enough.

A nearby stream babbled happily around a peaceful pool ringed by granite boulders. *These would have been dropped off by the great glaciers of the far past,* he thought. Then a slight movement atop one of the boulders caught his eye. A lone dwarf with a long, white beard that dangled between his knees was sitting down and

– fishing! How he could have missed the clamor, Angus didn't know. He suspected that hearing loss from advanced age might have something to do with it. He made a beeline for the longbeard, to warn him quietly of the danger.

"Psst!" No reaction. He tried again louder. "Hey!" Still nothing. Desperate, he let his frustration through. "Can't you hear, you old codger? There's orcs coming for us both!" Angus knew he had given up their position as he came up to the base of the boulder.

"Eh?" said the longbeard, cupping a hand to his ear. "What's that?"

"We've got to get to safety but quick! There's a fair horde of orcs coming to give you and I what for, and if we are here in a minute, I'll wager that'll be an end to us. Which way to the Holt?" The exhausted Angus panted breathlessly.

"Oh! I see! Well, then! I suppose we can make the mineshaft ere they get to us, if we hurry!" The elder dwarf tossed his beard over one shoulder and reached for his things. "Hold my catch for me, would you? There's a good boy!" With that he thrust a line with several rainbow trout still flapping into the younger dwarf's arms.

He led Angus between two of the low hills to where an old – very old – mine shaft was set. It was supported with stone instead of the wood beams men use, and had not seen use for centuries, other than the one well-worn footpath that ran from it to the boulders. *This fellow must fish a lot*, Angus thought. Orcs came over the rise as the dwarves were entering the shaft and howled as they gave chase. It seemed the whole army was right behind them.

"Stand here, young feller, and hold the gap while I run for help. We're all counting on you!" With that the elder shuffled deeper into the mine.

Angus turned to face the open doorway, about a hundred feet in. He tried to heft his axe and made the most determined face he could muster. As the orcs piled in, he managed to raise the killing tool over his head for one solid strike and yelled at the top of his lungs a wordless battle cry - full of pain, loss and meaning, and a final determination. The orcs hooted in answer as at least fifty piled in. There was no hope for Angus or his new cohort, who had continued down the tunnel.

The heavy dust along the line where floor met wall *shifted*, as if a snake was moving quickly just beneath the surface. Angus saw this movement but paid no attention; this was going to be combat at its toughest. He focused only on the orcs. The orcish invaders didn't give any sign that they saw what was happening either, just lined up three wide and so many deep that Angus could not count them. It was clear to him that they wanted to make the shiny dwarf go away more than anything.

And who could blame them? What sounds more threatening, an armored dwarf holding a large red axe over his head screaming at you, or a cord being pulled by the helpless old dwarf behind him? If you listen to dwarven tales, you already know the answer. Never discount the elders; they often know things that come in very useful at times. This was one of those times.

The cord was connected to a small rock, barely larger than a pebble. It pulled free from the point where it was wedged in between the ancient granite post and beam. Without this tiny but critical bridge, the mouth of the mineshaft caved in behind, and on top of, the rear-most orcs. A second, and a third cord were yanked, and the rest of the orcs were crushed in an instant. Angus had been about to swing at the closest when the beam directly above him flattened the orc so completely he may as well have never existed.

It took a moment for the full reality to register in Angus' overwhelmed brain. This was just too perfect; but this time, his involvement amounted to being the bait. This trap was lain ages ago, and the long, low belly laugh the longbeard let out gave proof.

"I just can't imagine how that happened! These tunnels were supposed to be quite solid! I'll have to have a word with the Elders about that."

Chapter 33

A Dwarf Shortage

If ever there was a more inglorious entrance, Angus had not heard of it. He was staggering and using his axe as an awkward cane. If that was the whole picture, he might appear grand as a hero returning from a battle. But the string of fish over his shoulder kind of killed that effect. The fish, and the large chunks of sod sticking out from just about every crack and cranny of his armor. Angus was not yet aware of the chunk in his helmet that sat rather upright with a single, sad daisy waving like a feather in his cap.

The longbeard had noticed but decided to save the laugh for his friends. This kind of comedy didn't come around very often to any Holt, let alone one with such a small and aging population. Dwarves, like elves, have incredibly long lifespans. Their activities carry a certain amount of risk, and they do get into the business of outsiders from time to time; but the deaths that occur during work and war are only the majority. Dwarves do not often become sick; rather those that live on eventually die of boredom. The remaining dwarves of the Aureate were very, very bored. A laugh could only do them good.

And so, they walked – well, the elder dwarf walked, Angus was shambling like a zombie – through the mine shaft for a solid half-hour before things started to look like a proper Holt. There were some notable differences that struck Angus. The floors were not polished – not even swept. They were walking in a trail on the clear floor; the shortest distance to their destination. Everything else was covered in a thick layer of dust. And the lights weren't up. Some lamps were lit right next to the path, in even intervals, but spaced at the maximum distance to allow safe walking. This was very odd.

As they entered areas that would normally have seen scads of traffic, everything was empty – and silent. Angus could see the marketplace, everything tightly shuttered, and tables and furniture bundled up, often covered with old tarps. So old, Angus realized, that many were falling to pieces even here, where the temperature was constant and there was no wind or rain to work on them. He began to worry.

The longbeard led on. They passed through the main hall, ceiling so high it could not be seen in the dim light, save for the occasional glint of gold. The entire hall seemed to have been gilded at some point. Other worn paths had started to cross the one they were on, all arrow straight. It was hard to get his bearings, but Angus thought they might be headed toward the dining hall. He considered asking his host what the plan was but thought better of it. They were making the best possible speed – the longbeard was shortening his stride to stay with Angus – and interrupting wouldn't get him there any faster.

They entered a low, wide, arched doorway where several trails converged and came into the dining hall. This room had an abundance of tables and benches, much like the Smaragdine Holt, but they too were dreadfully dusty. The old dwarf kept to his trail, headed toward what should be the kitchen. It was – and it held the first dwarves Angus had seen here aside from his escort. They were all old; past the age where it was easy to tell. Angus would have put them all as peers to the oldest Elders of his Holt.

He leaned his axe on the wall and started toward the large sink. Seven sets of eyes were on him, appraising. Their expressions were very hard for Angus to read. He set the string of fish in the sink and took off his helmet. He saw the flower as he set it on the counter. The other dwarves burst into deep, uproarious belly laughs when they saw his reaction – the utter dismay of a dwarf just about to go over the edge.

The dwarf that had acted as his escort had been pouring a large tankard of soupy, dark beer with a head so tight it would have supported a large coin. Still laughing, he handed it to Angus, whose face matched his beard for hue. "Son, you look like you could use a drink!" The dwarves continued to laugh as Angus drained the proffered liquid.

When he finally set the tankard down, he sucked the froth from his mustache and made eye contact with each of the dwarves. They settled down, but most still had tears in their eyes from laughter. To a dwarf, each was exceedingly casual. If one had authority over another, Angus could not see it. There were no weapons, no armor in sight. "I need to talk to the King. My business is urgent."

The shortest of them spoke up. "Di ye commune wi'the deed there, feller? I'no, ye'll've a touf time o'it!"

Seeing Angus' confusion, another jumped in with a more current dialect. "What he's trying to say is that when the good king passed on, we didn't feel the need for another. We've a good system here, and it hasn't been a problem for these many years."

"So, you might as well spill it, kid. We're as close to a king as you'll get around here!" His escort was as cheeky as the others. The Elders just didn't get this kind of entertainment often!

"Well. This isn't what I expected, but I won't argue a ruling council. As you saw, sir, there is a large army of orcs headed this way. You saw dozens; from my previous vantage, I saw thousands. I came by way of a shortcut, faster than I thought possible, to warn you and to let you know that help is on the way. King Bedwyn is bringing a small army of dwarves from the Smaragdine Holt; but it will still be close to a week before they are here. I really think we should gather the rest of the dwarves and prepare your defenses!"

The older dwarves traded looks. Eyebrows rose along with the corners of their mouths, and soon they were all laughing again. The one who had caught the fish was re-filling Angus' tankard, spilling a little as he laughed.

"What's that for?" said Angus as he took the drink. He looked over his shoulders, and down his front. "There aren't any more of those ridiculous flowers, are there?"

"No, my boy, there are no more flowers sticking out from your armor. But neither are there more dwarves."

Shocked, Angus plopped down on a nearby stool.

"The Aureate is a very old place; we believe the oldest Holt still inhabited by dwarves. There are others, to be sure, that were founded earlier but abandoned long ago. There are simple economics at work; when the ore, stones or other resources that brought dwarves and caused the founding of the Holt run out, it is only a matter of time before other opportunities call." Angus' escort stopped his speech and went to pour his own beer.

The most rotund of the elders continued. "Our mines haven't produced a significant amount of ore for hundreds of years. They were diminishing for a long time before that. So, our people have moved on to more promising futures, joining other Holts or scouting for locations for new ones."

"So, you see," said the one who had been chopping tubers, "we are all that is left of the Aureate Holt. We have stayed here to keep a portion of our history alive, and because we are pretty happy here as things are. We've all lived full lives, accomplished a lot and find that a few close friendships are very worthwhile. We have no reason to leave."

The first dwarf Angus had met piped in again, having slaked his thirst. "Solitude has apparently not improved our manners. We haven't had any introductions! You can call me Leod."

The fat dwarf spoke next. "Agluin. A pleasure." They went through their names, oddly using only those their parents had given them. Duibni, Maitian, Drailin, Coenor and Cainnech, they were called, with some pleasantries thrown in; but absolutely no titles. Angus knew that it was impossible to gain the years these dwarves had between them without titles. He was pretty sure that some of them were in the older stories if you just pronounced the name differently.

"Angus. At your service." That was the best he could come up with. "I suppose," he continued, "that we should leave via a back way. Even the tallest tales don't have our kind winning against such inconceivable odds."

"Leave?" Drailin was incredulous. "Abandon the Aureate? It is our home!"

"And center to our gathered history!"

"What's inconceivable is not defending the Holt!"

As the objections cascaded over him, Angus drained his second beer. "Leod," he asked, "Based on where they were at the mineshaft, how long do we have until they reach the gates?"

"There is only one approach, and the switchbacks take hours even after you find the trail. If they have thousands as you say, we have at least three hours, maybe four. You need some rest; we'll see to the fortifications. One of us will wake you when it's time."

Angus would not have been much use at that moment given his weakened state. He had a sandwich and set himself up on one of the tables; he was tired enough to sleep anywhere. It was a deep, dreamless sleep.

Chapter 34

The Aureate's Last Stand

Angus awoke with a snort. He sat up, wiping drool from his beard. The lamps had been dimmed, and no one was in sight. How long had he slept? Long enough for the moist sod to dry out completely, falling from his armor as he stood. Still bruised, but most of the pain was a dull ache. Strength and mobility seemed to have returned during his nap.

There was a platter with a lid on it nearby, and a lidded tankard. Fried fish and chips, now cold, and a warm beer. Smiling, Angus rushed the meal, but chewed each bite. No sense in going to battle with a sour stomach. Refreshed by sleep and food, Angus took up his axe and stepped out to find the others.

The hall was still dim, but a constant clattering came from off to his left. One of the clear paths led that way, and he followed it. The floor was perfectly smooth, with a myriad of colors and curves. Angus wished he could see it when it was clean. The design must be stunning. His pace was brisk and purposeful. He was ready for anything.

Ready, yes. But he did not expect to see what came into view at the gatehouse. A pair of donkeys walking in a treadmill powered a large flywheel, with spinning metal shafts leading off in a dozen directions. A taunt echoed through the chamber, followed by another, then another. He couldn't yet make out the words, but he thought they were coming from the defensive tunnels that ran through the wall.

He stepped to the stairway and started up. Several of the shafts ran into the wall directly above the stairway; he noted the location with the intention of picking up the trail when he arrived. At the first landing, he recognized the symbol for the gate controls. It seemed as good a place as any to check first, and certainly where he had the most experience.

The layout was familiar, with levers to start and stop the flow of water to the gate and portcullis. Interestingly, there was no safety on this portcullis; the dead dwarf's pedal must have been an innovation between when this gate was installed, and the Argentine system put in place. He thought he could operate it, if the need arose.

"Angus!" Angus nearly jumped out of his armor when Drailin called from down the hall. "Don't touch that – you don't know what those levers can do!"

Chuckling, the younger dwarf trotted along the tunnel to join Drailin. "Sorry, my first post was as the gate guard at the Argentine Holt. I'm surprised at how similar the controls are from gate to gate."

"Well, we designed them that way, so you shouldn't be surprised. But come here. Follow me and I'll show you something you haven't seen before!"

Angus followed. They ascended another flight of stone stair and came to a second level, where light streamed in from outside. It was still daylight but fading. The descending sun illuminated the source of the clattering: a suit of plate armor at each arrow slit, swaying gently back and forth in a good imitation of a dwarf on guard. The movement was introduced by eccentric cam lobes running along one of those rotating shafts. They had made the appearance of an army!

"None shall take this Holt while I stand!" Drailin had shouted toward the arrow slit from behind the suit. He then hurried over to another and issued a taunt again. He then turned to Angus and said, quietly, "This is what old dwarves do when we are bored. With so much endless time on our hands, we devised a way to defend the Holt while allowing the younger dwarves to go seek their fortunes elsewhere. Bedwyn knows about our situation, as does Artemus; but this is a secret you must not take beyond these walls. The ruse loses its potency when it is discovered."

"It's brilliant! With the gate closed and stout, and the appearance of an army, they won't come close! We can sit and wait for the Smaragdine army, and all will be well!" Angus' spirits were lifted greatly by this revelation. But not for long.

"About that. The gate, you see, was made from the finest Ivonian Oak, and plated in gold to last a thousand years."

"More brilliance. We plated ours with silver, so it tarnishes, but there are enough young dwarves at the Argentine Holt to keep it polished." He was still impressed but could see that Drailin knew something he hadn't said.

"Yes, it was a brilliant design; but the gate is very old, much more than a thousand years. Closer to two thousand. The gold is in excellent shape, but the wood inside has long since rotted. We use the dwarf gate for trade, and we haven't opened the main gate in ages, for fear that it would fold in upon itself. Even the portcullis is useless; if not for the gilding, there would be nothing but a pile of rust. We cannot allow them to reach the gate."

No wonder he had been so touchy when Angus had been near the controls. Dwarven defenses were almost always based on real strength; lasting stonework and strong weapons. But this place was a mess, in real need of restoration. He promised himself that if they survived, he would see to these defenses himself.

"Well, Master Illusionist, what exactly is the plan, and how can I help?" Angus was hoping for something a lot better than what he had seen so far.

"Well, we have other defenses. Look out onto the field and notice the patterns on the floor. Do you see the gold 'coins' set into the stonework? Know that if you stand on one of those, you are safe. Anywhere else, and I cannot guarantee anything."

"You mean me to attack them on foot? You must be kidding!"

"Angus, we are old. We've set up many defenses here, active and passive, but we really are not up to open field battle. You, on the other hand, are obviously young, in your prime; and already you wear dragon themed Holtgart armor. Your axe is most interesting – something I will ask you about soon enough. What is clear is that you must be a capable warrior to merit this equipment. Certainly, more capable than all of us old has-beens. Leod was having a bit of fun with you earlier in the mine shaft. But what he learned was that you are willing to face certain death without hesitating. So, yes, you are the one; our Champion. The one dwarf that will face the orcs outside the gate. Drawing attention will allow our deception to continue, and our other plans to succeed. Remember the coins, Angus. They will save you."

"I'd like to know more about these other defenses..." Angus was cut off by an angry cry in a guttural language – orcs!

"My boy, I'm afraid you'll have to trust me. There is no time left." With that, he steered Angus down the stairs and pointed out the smaller dwarf door. "I'm sure you'll make us all proud. May your axe strike true, Angus!" He ran back up the stairs, and Angus heard the taunting resume. Angus wished again that he had found the room for a flask.

He checked his armor, loosening a few more chunks of dried dirt. Looking first to ensure no one was watching, he did some stretching, moving in every direction he could think of. Then he took up the axe and ran through a short set of moves designed to practice transitioning from one strike to the next with the unbalanced weapon. He closed his eyes and listened to memories of Bladin and his lectures on fighting with axes.

"Never target the front of your opponent; aim for his back and follow through."

"The axe is a weapon of power; nobody expects to see power combined with finesse. Keep one circular strike flowing into the next and you can attack constantly while expending little energy. Out, down, back, up, out, down, back, up..."

"Trust your armor. It is difficult to parry with the axe; you must both trust the armor and turn to deflect most of the blow. Dwarven plate is very strong, and with strategic positioning can withstand terrible punishment."

"Tumbling is an excellent way to close with an enemy. You present a smaller target, and if you time it properly, you can rise while striking, converting the circle from the tumble into power for a circular strike."

"Use the pick sparingly. It is to penetrate heavy armor, or to move or pin your opponent. If you do use the pick, have a good knife handy; you may need it when the pick becomes stuck!"

Angus opened his eyes as he exited the routine in a proper salute. He took a deep breath, held it a second, and exhaled a prayer. He had never been so focused, so ready, in his life. "For the Holt!" he shouted and opened the dwarf gate.

Orcs swarmed over the rise in the switchback trail that led to this plateau at the mouth of the Holt. They formed up along the edge, passing out torches. So far, there were only orcs, no siege engines. Angus had seen none approaching, but he also knew now that none were needed. He stepped through the gate and closed it loosely behind him.

Dwarven taunts sounded regularly, and if Angus didn't know better, he might believe that hundreds of dwarves sat inside ready for battle. These codgers seemed to know what they were doing. He chased thoughts about whether any of them were names he recognized, and what stories they were in, out of his head. He needed to maintain his focus for what would happen in a moment.

Angus looked around and located several nearby golden coin plaques and stepped onto the nearest. A "Thank you, now we can begin" rang out among the taunts. There were now several clusters of orcs arrayed against him. They formed loose lines, with a single group of archers at the rear. There was still a distance of maybe a hundred yards that separated the dwarf from the attackers.

He stood his ground, axe in hands, ready. His visor was raised for a good view. What he saw next struck him as rather odd. Four orcs carried a palanquin on their shoulders. The figure that rode on the platform was cloaked entirely in what looked like rags, blurring its outline. The deep hood lifted enough for Angus to see darkness inside. The figure pointed straight at Angus and screamed – truly screamed – something that the dwarf could not understand.

The orcs understood, shouting convincing battle cries and charging as one. Angus lowered his visor. And realized, as they drew closer, that they were not charging the gate, but him personally! The taunting from above stopped altogether, and sounds of machinery clicking, gears whirring and triggers clicking became more pronounced. Angus shut the noises out and set himself. He changed his grip on the axe, holding it behind him and to one side, ready for an overhead strike. A volley of arrows came over the heads of the charging orcs, all coming for Angus. Trusting his armor, he leaned forward so that they should hit his helmet and pauldrons.

It sounded and felt like being out in a heavy hailstorm that lasted only two seconds. When it was over, he reset himself and saw that a few of the orcs would reach him a second or two before the whole group hit. They were close enough that he could discriminate a repeated word - "Zonka!" - although he did not understand it.

Then the entire plateau started to rumble as if a heavy cavalry charge was underway. Angus saw only the orcs in front of him. The first closed the gap. He was slender, likely a prime example of a young warrior. He charged with a long spear held in both hands, overhead with the point aimed right at Angus, who laughed and waited for the strike. The youth was committed with that stance, and as he thrust downward with all his might, Angus spun around, letting his momentum carry him past. The axe came around, sending the orc flying in two pieces to land against the wall.

The axe came back, up, out and down to take the arm off the next orc, sending blocky sword and the arm holding it flying high to clatter off the gatehouse. That orc fell clutching at the missing chunk of chest that went with the rest, and Angus didn't have to look to know that life would end soon for that creature. One more before the main group hit, when he would be overwhelmed.

Back, up, out and down to strike another sword, smashing it into his opponent's chest with brute force. His continuous circle was broken, and he had to reset his axe. There were a dozen who would hit him at once now. It was only a matter of time. Or so he thought. The first of the dwarves' traps had been sprung.

A large stone wheel – as tall as four dwarves, and half as wide – rolled from his left to right, smashing the orcs who were coming at him. It came only inches from his face. He looked down and saw that he was right on the edge of one of the coins. A quick glance around showed several more wheels causing havoc; hundreds of orcs had been smashed into oblivion. The survivors were looking around for more traps. One was standing near a coin plaque, and Angus ran to it, killing another orc on the way. He turned a bit to let this one's spear slide off his breastplate, coming down with his own killing blow. More orcs turned back to attack Angus, convinced the trap was through.

A wicked mace clanged off Angus' left pauldron, leaving a good dent and a stinging bruise. Back, up, out and down, and another orc lay gurgling in its own blood. A sword came in from Angus' right, catching him in the bicep and loosening his grip with that hand. He spun clockwise, sweeping the attacker's foot as he worked to regain his grasp on the axe. Putting the axe horizontal as he completed his circle the attackers were driven back, giving him the moment he needed to get ready again.

Then the rumbling started, and Angus checked his position on the coin. A quick adjustment took place as he struck out again and again and again. Re-formed orcs were smashed, and those that managed to escape were confused. Some were running back down the road. Angus finished his last opponent and watched as the rest followed in retreat. A quick estimate said they had done a lot of damage, but it likely wasn't enough. He stepped back inside the fortress to check in with the other dwarves.

Chapter 35

Zonked Out

Black Zonka screamed all the way down the mountain as her palanquin was carried by the four burly bodyguards. She was furious at the cowardice of her army. But Ogrash was the real power here, and he had seen a quarter of his forces dropped in seconds. He already had an idea of how to stop the rollers on their next attack, and now that he had seen the gate, he knew what else he needed: a battering ram. He had passed a pine grove a few miles back, so he sent a group off to bring in several long tree trunks. One would act as a battering ram; the others should help to trip up the rollers.

Ogrash had also done some counting during the skirmish, and he was sure they outnumbered the dwarves by at least ten to one. He would talk to Zonka tomorrow, when she had calmed down. Ogrash suspected she could help with some specific motivation. For now, he would rest his troops, and let the few wounded tend to their injuries.

----- -----

Duibni was just coming down the stairs when Angus entered. "Nai tha'was a ba'aul, ee'eye e'er di see'oon! Ye d'serve a grand bit o food 'n drink ah'ter that werk!" This time, Angus caught that Duibni was impressed, and thought he needed a meal during the break. His stomach grumbled in agreement, and he followed the small, aged dwarf back toward the kitchen.

There were more cheers and extended laughter from within the wall. Angus knew about the ebb and flow of many battles and expected that there would be a break as the orcs re-grouped and came back with adjustments. While charged up from his success, he wasn't looking forward to those adjustments. The orcs knew now that there was one champion and would doubtless have a strategy to counteract him.

"Master Duibni, I have a question," Angus began, but Duibni cut him off.

"Ye dinnah nee' ti call me master, youngster. Ye've pruv'd yerself mah thin worthy tidday. Duibni will be fine." The stories that Angus had heard of a 'Dubni' were very impressive and very old; but still he resisted asking if they were one and the same. There would be time for that later, if any of them survived.

"Duibni, then. What's the next part of the plan? I mean, I see that we killed hundreds, and drove them away, but they'll expect more of those rolling stones. That was a great idea, and effective. But there are only so many you could have; please tell me what you have in mind next."

"All rye, here's the next par'. We've soom hooney-baked ham in 'ere, and a tall beer or two; I fair say you'll eat tha' and have a wee repose. Th'other boys'll tay car'o'threst." As Duibni spoke, he became more convinced that he was the Dubni from the stories. A heavy accent from the old country was part of each of those stories. He got a chill.

He also took Duibni's advice and rested for a few hours after eating. He was still not over the other activities of the last couple days, and intense battle takes a lot out of you, even if it only lasts a short while. He drank a good amount of water as well as the beer and puffed thoughtfully on a pipe Duibni had left for him as he went over the fight in his mind.

Bladin would have approved of Angus' performance, he decided. He had used his training well and thoroughly. Moreover, it had worked! He probably only had a full year practicing the axe, if you added it all up, much less than his time with the spear; but it had worked marvelously against the lightly armored and comparatively unskilled orcish warriors.

Duibni returned with his pauldron some time later, repaired quite well. Angus was ready again, but the ancient suggested – strongly – that he take another nap. Battle would come soon enough. But this time he was given a cot in the gatehouse. It didn't take long to drift off to sleep amid the noises of working dwarves.

When Drailin woke him, the sun was again going down. "They do better in the dark," Drailin said, "but we'll do what we can to keep things lit for you. It's time."

Angus had slept through an entire day, and most of the night! But he did feel rested, if dreadfully sore. He arose and located his helmet, stopping off at the privy before going to the door again. The orcs had set up some light fortifications at the top of the road, essentially blinds where they could observe from and likely issue commands.

"Today, I'd like you to walk along that red crescent in front of the gate. Like yesterday, that is your solid ground. Anywhere else, and you won't do as well. Please try not to let them past that line; you see that it describes an area just beyond both the main gate and the dwarf gate. That is all we ask of you today."

"It sounds easy enough, but let's see what they'll bring to the party. They are orcs, but they've had some time to prepare..."

----- -----

"Black Zonka, we are ready." Ogrash felt much more prepared this time, with his battering ram, 'roller blocker' logs and a team of oversized orc toughs to clear a path through that one troublesome dwarf.

"Bring me the body of the evil one. I will prepare a special treat for your soldiers. After I eat his flesh, I will prepare a magical broth from his bones. His formidable power will flow into your warriors and make them very strong." Zonka did not know exactly why she hated this particular dwarf so much, but he haunted her dreams. For the last few weeks, he had appeared every night, clearly, to attack her with his breath. The other dwarves that tormented her were faceless, without personality. It was this one dwarf that needed to end more than all the others combined.

Her palanquin was lifted, and she and Ogrash ascended the path at the same time. This time, they stayed on the path when they neared the top, where they could both see and retreat to safety quickly. The warriors were arrayed before them, their plan solid. Ogrash barked the command to attack, and the orcs moved as one.

----- -----

Angus was still closing the gate behind him when he heard the barked order. He didn't know what they said, but he could guess close enough. A team of orcs charged over the lip of the plateau, carrying a long, thick log on their shoulders. They veered off to his left and tossed the thing so that it rolled up near the edge of the wall where the rolling stones had come from. A second team did the same to his right almost immediately. Both groups then ran back down the trail; apparently their commander knew they were tired and should not fight right away.

The next group was a half-dozen large – unnaturally large – orcs in heavy armor. They carried large flails and maces, and only had eyes for Angus. They split into two groups of three and set about moving around to each side where they could flank him. Angus stepped forward to the apex of the red crescent, centering himself in front of the door.

Next up the hill was a larger tree trunk, formed into a very functional battering ram. The orcs had studded the business end with stones; a measure that looked menacing, but Angus knew to be overkill against the weakened gate. *How am I supposed to stop that?* He set himself, readied his axe, and shouted, "Come on, you pansies! Let's be done with it!"

The lead orc barked an order again, and all three groups came at him as one. They started slow and accelerated, to try to hit him all at once. Off to his right, one of the bigger orcs flew backwards, a siege bow bolt through his chest. One dropped to his left in a similar fashion. They were halfway to Angus now, only a moment away. All of them were shouting wordlessly.

Duibni's voice rang out with a "Fooreed!" and a dozen yards away, another large orc fell to its side, a dimpled, round marble ball buried between heavy eyebrows. Another called shot brought another big one down in a similar fashion. The elders were not targeting the battering ram at all! It was hurtling at him now, with a few dozen orcs sprinting underneath. So far, he didn't like this plan.

Then the big orcs slipped, each sliding as if they were suddenly running on marbles. One went down, then the other, still sliding toward Angus. The front runners under the ram also slipped at about the same time, tossing the leading edge of the log high above their heads. Some of them were under it when it came back down, the rest of the team also losing their footing. Their battle cries became dismayed shouts and more than a few screams as everything skidded to a halt.

The larger orcs' momentum carried them closer to Angus, right up to his feet. The closest one had ended up headfirst, and Angus buried his pick into the orc's helmet. The remaining bulkster struggled to get up as Angus wrestled to free the pick, which only came loose after he pushed with a foot and pulled with both hands.

But not soon enough! The last gigantic orc was standing now, a dreadful mace just about to thump down onto Angus' head. He would have been doomed if Coenor hadn't been taking aim with his mounted siege bow. The momentum of the heavy shaft hitting the orc's head toppled the creature and weapon backwards and away from Angus, who took that chance to get ready again.

He saw what was happening now. The elders had greased some of the plateau with a clear film. The other orcs were having a tough time of rising, too. The ram slid to stop just a few feet away from Angus, and one of the lead orcs had been crushed under the stone-studded end. Inspiration hit, and Angus used that orc's torso as a step to get up and onto the log, running along its length, attacking all the orcs he could reach. He heard the snap of the siege bows and the sw-thwack of golf clubs several more times before he was done. He looked over at the orcs that stood just over the edge and shouted, "Ha HA!" As they raised bows, he turned and sprinted along the log, leaping down onto the ungreased red crescent amidst a hail of arrows. He ducked into the dwarf-gate, hearing jeers and laughter from the elders over the frustrated yells of the orcs.

Chapter 36

Pride Before the Fall

Ogrash was furious. His troops had been fooled into stepping into something slippery and paid for the mistake with their lives. The loss of his six brutes was especially painful; their bulk and temper were particularly difficult to produce. But the dwarves had left the ram in place; his archers had stayed behind to ensure there were no more tricks in his absence. They needed traction to proceed, and he thought he had a pretty solid plan. It would take a few hours to go over the specifics, and his remaining warriors needed a rest after carrying the logs up the hill. They would succeed this time, he was confident.

----- -----

"They'll feel the sting from that beating long into the night, I'll warrant!" Drailin was really enjoying this.

"They left archers this time. We'll have to keep to the plans already in motion." Coenor was a bit more serious, but none of the dwarves appeared worried. "I think we should be all right, if everything goes to plan, and Angus can keep up this schedule."

"Well, everything has ended well so far, but I've no doubt I would be flat as a pancake if it weren't for someone's fancy shooting. I'd like to buy that dwarf a drink!"

"Tha'ud be me, youngster. I coo'na haive ye leuk li'a pincooshin, nai coo I?"

They laughed together and went over the day's events, looking for a while out one of the arrow slits and counting dead. Duibni brought out a tower shield for Angus to hold as a first line of defense against the archers. They set that just inside the dwarf gate. When Angus pressed for more details about their defenses, Coenor insisted that the best thing would be for him to just keep presenting himself and fighting. If Angus knew what was coming, he might give away the surprise. And surprise was what let each of the strategies work.

They still had several days before the other dwarves would arrive; each day's planning needed to be executed perfectly just to survive to the next. So, they set up their meal just inside the portcullis and ate heartily. Angus cleaned his armor and sharpened his axe after the meal, always with one of the dwarves on watch in case the orcs decided to try something.

They sang the old songs, songs that Angus thought he knew. But the elders used slightly different harmonies, and a few of the words were different; and in one case, the hero was the butt of the joke! He planned on spending a few years here with the elders, learning their stories and history, songs and jokes. Most dwarves worked for many centuries before they took that kind of time to experience life outside their Holts, but Angus had fallen into this opportunity early. He wasn't going to let the fact that it was truly an accident stop him from enjoying life now that he knew how.

Eventually they started to take turns at sleeping. Angus felt much closer to normal now and took his shifts at watch with the rest. He was sleeping when Coenor raised the alarm.

"They're here! And running a relay of some sort!" Coenor punctuated his sentence with the 'THUNG!' of a siege bow firing. A half second later, two of the orcs could be heard screaming in pain outside.

Angus threw his helmet on, grabbed his axe and hit the dwarf gate sprinting. He saw orcs running right alongside the battering ram, each with a bundle in his arms. One orc would advance partway, drop the bundle with a 'pshh' sound, then turn and run back to allow the next to repeat. Each cycle brought the orcs closer by a foot or two. They were silent and consistent with their work, obviously running a plan. By the time Angus caught on, they were more than halfway along the ram with their routes. One would fall to a siege bow bolt every few seconds, but there were just so many.

And they weren't slipping on the grease. The bundles were a sandy loam, dumped in thick patches one after the other making a path of solid footing for the orcs to continue their assault. Angus yelled back to the elders what he thought was happening, but the only response was the occasional crackcrackcrack of the bows cocking and heavy thuds of the bolts hitting home. A deadly strategy, but not one that would work in the long run against these numbers. He began to worry about how he would do with this many orcs in the dark.

With a moment to think things through, he stepped off to the left side of the ram, so he would not be trodden on, and would try to take out the carriers on just one side, making it useless. If he could make enough hits in a very short amount of time, that was. He set himself, noting the light armor the lead orc was wearing in the new torchlight. Torchlight? He turned his head just enough to see flaming wooden golf balls lit and hit into the fray. They missed the orcs entirely and bounced off the greasy floor, one on each side.

Now when humans see their projectiles bouncing off the floor near their enemies, they might respond with groans or curses. But these dwarven codgers were cheering! Even the orcs thought it was odd, laughing at the dwarves' incompetence. Sensing that it wasn't finished, Angus took a step back from the orcs. He made his move just in time.

What had looked like simple burning fragments scattered along the balls' paths turned out to be the grease catching fire. Small fires quickly became larger, spreading exponentially. Within a second, the orcs were surrounded by flame. Most of them ran back toward the road, but some jumped forward to the non-burning area Angus was standing in. They were still drawing daggers and cudgels and handaxes when Angus struck the first one, massive crimson blade severing arm and leg below, continuing in that nigh-unstoppable arc.

A beefy orc sprang at Angus, nasty-looking daggers in either hand. The attacker was in the air with arms flung wide, daggers set to plunge into either side of Angus' neck. But axe fell first, cleaving deep into the orc's chest and stopping his momentum. The impact made the dwarf slide backwards on the smooth stone floor. As the orc fell, the axe was wrenched from Angus' hands, stuck in ribs and armor. The axe ended up under Angus' fallen opponent. It would take him precious seconds to recover it.

Seconds that he did not have. Two more came at him from either side of their cloven companion. Angus got his right hand up to block the cudgel-strike. He grabbed the club just above his opponent's grip and held fast. He stepped forward as a handaxe clanged into his backplate. Using more of the circular motion Bladin had taught him, Angus pulled the cudgel down and behind him as he pushed the orc's shoulder. That orc found his feet in the air and his weapon being twisted from his grip. The handaxe clanged off his helmet as Angus thumped the supine orc in the face; two swift blows that ended the creature's story.

The orcish handaxe landed a third time, putting the same dent back into his left pauldron. The orc was heavily backlit by the grease fire behind him; Angus didn't have to think before throwing the small club spinning end over end toward the orc's head. It was a poor throw, easily dodged. But Angus never had intended to land that strike. A lowered shoulder into the orc's chest was his real goal. The hit was enough to send the orc reeling back into the flames.

With no other enemies at hand, Angus went about retrieving his axe. He rolled the dead orc over and yanked on the handle. The blade came free with a sound like a boot being pulled out of wet mud. The smells of burning grease and charred flesh were now joined by the more agreeable scent of pine tar bubbling out of the fresh logs as they caught. He wiped the gore on one of the orc's pant legs and leaned the weapon against the door. Then he dragged the unburnt corpses to make a low berm in the path to the door, hoping that the next attempt might be slowed up by an obstacle. As the flames from the grease fire died down, Angus went back inside the fortress. There was no need to give the archers a chance at a lucky shot.

Besides – he had a headache! The armor had kept him from real damage, but a blow to the head still hurts. Angus figured a few minutes alone with a pint would help a lot. He saw the looks on the other dwarves' faces as he shut the door. Something was wrong – very wrong.

"We've just rebuffed the orcs again. I'm the only one of us who has even sustained a hit. We're winning; why do you all look so worried?" Their concern was already catching hold of him.

"As always Angus, you've proved yourself a perceptive lad," Coenor said. "We do have a problem."

"Aye, that we have." Maitian sounded downright dejected! "Lad, we've run out. We haven't any more. I don't know what we'll do." He put a hand over his beard, and Angus saw his eyes tighten.

"Well, if we're shy of siege bow bolts, let's get about making more. This is a large Holt; surely there is something we can use!"

"Nay, boy! Ye've miss'd th'point! We've bolts a-plentah." As heavy as that accent was, Angus was beginning to understand the old dwarf. "We've run ou'o a mooch moore impoort'nt sooplai; tis that!" He pointed with dramatic effect, the other dwarves following his gaze. He was pointing at... at... the keg?

"Beer? We're out of beer? That's your emergency?" Angus enjoyed a good drink as much as the next dwarf (more than the next dwarf most of the time), but it wasn't a combat necessity. "You had me worried!"

Laughing with the other elders, Coenor replied, "Aye, we're worried too! Now scuttle off to the kitchen and fetch another before we all die of thirst!" He ended with another cascade of laughter.

Angus leaned his axe against the table they had brought out. He looked over the elders, who were still chuckling. When he had looked each in the eye firmly, he joined their laughter, which came alive again. Dutifully, he fired off a quick salute and trundled along the cleared path to the kitchen to find another keg. As he jogged, he reflected on how things had once again changed. Until a month ago, he had often been the butt of the joke. He had been used to it. But somehow something had changed with his achievements. He no longer assumed that people were jibing at him. It was a change.

Then it hit him. The elders were serious; serious about enjoying life. And by introducing humor into a heavy situation, they were dealing with the anxiety that is perfectly natural. Sharing the joke just helped everyone to defuse and to reaffirm their friendships. These dwarves really knew how the psyche worked. They had seen war and peace, success and failure. The more he thought about it, the more his respect grew.

They had the valve out of the other keg by the time Angus returned, rolling the next one up. Dwarves are very efficient when it comes to drinking. Soon they were carousing – save one at all times to watch – and enjoying the rising sun. There was little talk about whether Bedwyn would make it in time; either he would, or he wouldn't. What mattered was that they each gave their best and reveled in the camaraderie. If Angus was going to die, doing so in these dwarves' company would be an honor.

Chapter 37

Knock, Knock

The dwarves congregated on the eastern end of the south-facing fortification to watch the sun sink. It was a beautiful sight, pinks and blues fighting each other in the clouds. They drank it in wordlessly as the light inevitably lost ground to the swarming darkness.

The final glimpse of direct light slipped away, and they became aware of the sound below. The sounds of marching, of work, and of hatred for all dwarves. They could not see exactly what was in store, but it couldn't be good. After using so many tactics so successfully, they were due for a loss. More than that, there just couldn't be many tricks left in the elders' bag, Angus thought.

"Stay close tonight, lad." Drailin was smiling, but his tones were serious. "The onyx floor, I think; that describes a tight arc from the main gate to the dwarf gate and nothing else. Remember the shield as they approach; they won't try simple light arrows forever. As ever, we only ask one thing; do not let the orcs get to the gate. Can you handle that, Champion Angus?"

"Well sir, we left that keg right inside the portcullis. I'm not about to share our beer with these musky fellows, now am I?" They all laughed. Then, more seriously, "I'll do my part." He glanced out the arrow slit towards the gate; it really was as small an area as it seemed when he was standing on it. It was a massive slab of onyx crystal, cut flat on one side to match the floor. As he made his way to it, Angus realized that it was the only valuable stone out there; the other parts of the design were all more mundane material. As he hefted his axe, he thought it a fitting last stand; defending a piece of ground described by onyx with a blood onyx axe, in the dark against black-hearted attackers and dreadful, dismal odds. As he stepped onto the smooth, black stone, everything felt right.

The orcs broke the plane of the plateau on a double-time march. Dozens with large shields ran off to either side of the ramp, lining the edge of the precipice. Each was carrying a heavy, lumpy bag over one shoulder, which they dropped to the ground with a clatter. When that formation was finished, there were over a hundred orcs arrayed against Angus, each holding a stone they had pulled from their bags. Angus reached for the tower shield and set it in front of him where he could duck behind it if he needed. It would be useless once he started swinging, so he just held the arm loops together in his left hand. The orcs were all staring at him. There was no doubt who their target would be when the order was given to cast.

----- -----

Bedwyn's army had made good time, but would it be enough? He was in the back of his command wagon which rumbled along the old road. The full canopy sheltered him from the elements, true; but he was more interested in keeping his maps dry and sound. He had been pouring over them for days and could not see how they could arrive in time. The Aureate would be under siege when they approached. He could only hope that this group of orcs was not one of the more intelligent.

"How could I have sent Angus?" He muttered to himself as he had so often of late. "He's too young. He's never been to the Aureate Holt before. He's too heavily armored to make good time. There is just no way that a dwarf with a beard that color could have the experience required for the task. I fear I may have made the wrong choice."

He was interrupted by the driver. "The Holt is coming into view now, General. Sir, I think you should see this."

Bedwyn climbed out of the covered part of the trailer and into the bench next to the driver. The entrance to the Aureate Holt was set up high in a south-facing valley. It was not as hidden as newer Holts would be, but you still wouldn't see it unless you knew it was there. Today, however, was a different matter. Many torches lit the small plateau where the door was, and the darkened switchback road that ascended from directly below fairly swarmed with flickering lights. Bedwyn's trained eye could see that there were organized units, and three distinctly different units that moved as one, even around the corners. He watched for a while to be sure, but the old tactician knew at once what those would be; battering rams. The Holt did not have much time.

----- -----

The marching noises had not ceased. Up the grade came a heavy tree, tossed to the side near where one of the blocking logs lay smoldering. They were rebuilding their countermeasures. A second joined it on the other side. Each time the carriers crouched down behind their woody fortifications, ready to charge when the order was given. More troops poured in, until there were hundreds – close to a thousand, really – upon the plateau. All facing Angus, and every eye fixed on him.

It was about this time that Angus noticed what was missing - the elders. They hadn't fired a single shot, sprang any traps, or shouted any directions. They were silent. Angus looked back at the arrow slits and saw nothing. He knew that they would not have abandoned him, but the thought crossed his mind for a fraction of a second. Then came a very dull vibration from underfoot. It was repeated several times, then everything was silent again except for that ceaseless sound of marching orcs with whatever passed for sergeants driving them on. Then the crude battering ram came around the corner. Not long now, Angus thought.

He was right. A harsh bark came from the back of the line, and the stones started arcing over the other orcs. Angus ducked behind the shield just in time. Hundreds of fist-sized rocks came down on him, at least a third hitting the shield. It cracked and rattled, dents forming. Corners and ends bent in under the stony hail, curling around the kneeling dwarf. Seconds later, it was over. Angus tossed the ruined shield to the side and set his axe. The ram came full speed.

The rocks strewn across the smooth stone floor tripped up the orcs carrying the ram. Some fell on their own, and some fell to Angus' axe as it swept in tight, efficient circles. Then the ram itself fell to the floor, but its momentum carried it forward, smashing into the gate. It punched through the thin gold plating and pushed on through the worm-riddled wood like a knife into a rotten apple. There was a half a moment's hesitation as the orcs realized the truth of the matter; they could walk right in. Their charge was terrible.

Angus could not count the attackers converging on him. It would happen fast; too fast to duck back inside. Not that that would help.

Out, down, back and up his axe swung repeatedly. Blows rained down on his armor from every weapon in range. He kept his feet planted instead of moving in order to avoid tripping on one of the stones or the mounting bodies. It limited where he could strike, but with this many targets, choosing shots was a moot point. The gate was swarmed with orcs now. Angus couldn't see past three feet. He knew it was over.

"Nai-OW!" Duibni's voice was loud, but barely audible over the din. Just about every orc had climbed onto the plateau and was charging the gate. Angus was being overwhelmed and the gate was crashing when the earth quaked. The ramp started to collapse, pulling the edge of the plateau down the mountain. It was a tremendous rockslide, taking a big chunk of the mountainside down with it. The edge of the plateau got smaller and smaller, hundreds of orcs tumbling along with the rocks. The roar was deafening, completely drowning out all of the screams of dying orcs. It dropped completely away, exposing more wall underneath.

----- -----

Bedwyn's knuckles were white from gripping the edge of the bench seat. He urged the driver to insane speed in the hopes of arriving in time to rescue the elders, and the ride along the old road was adding some extra curl to Bedwyn's already curly beard. "More speed!" He growled. The column was being spread out, a bad idea. And they would arrive exhausted at this pace. Looking toward the rear of his formation, he saw that they now spanned a full mile or more. Not good. Turing back to check on the Holt, he tried to focus on the scene right at the gate; but somehow, he couldn't. Every one of those fitful points of light seemed to lurch at once, a large segment of the mountainside acting independently from the rest.

After a moment, the plateau collapsed, pulling most of the torches and their bearers down with it in a terrific rockslide. Those that were still on the road that ran in a zig-zag line beneath it were swept away by the bouldery torrent. As the avalanche passed, the lights were snuffed out. Bedwyn couldn't take his eyes off the mountain for a long while.

----- -----

The only bit left standing was the onyx platform, dented and chipped by the stoning. It was still covered in orcs with one solitary dwarf standing in the middle.

Only then did the siege bows sound off. Angus never paused his hacking throughout the ordeal; orc after orc fell. And this time, when they fell, they fell much farther, bouncing in pieces off the wall and new valley below. Ten seconds later, it was silent again. Angus could hear the wind buffeting his little outcropping. He should have run right inside, but instead he fell to one knee. Only now, with the crisis over, did he feel the wounds. His armor had done its work well, but several weapons had found the chinks and struck home. He was bleeding heavily, and the adrenaline was fading fast. Angus was fading fast.

----- -----

The sun was well on its way up when Bedwyn and his entourage finally came to the ruined mountainside that had been the main entrance to the Aureate Holt. Rocks and boulders sat in a huge pile at the valley floor, covered in dust. There was very little sign of the orcish army. What little there was would be buried within a day or two. Bedwyn was sure that there were survivors among the elders since he had not found any portion of the Holtwall to be significantly disturbed.

There was activity up at the gateway. The old door had been torn down, and the portcullis had been raised. Several dwarves were setting up a transom of sorts, two tripods coming together to hang out over the drop off. In very little time a barrel was rigged with ropes and pulleys, and a dwarf was lowered slowly. Before the makeshift carriage was halfway down, Bedwyn identified Coenor, the youngest of the elders.

"Well if it isn't young General Foresight! Have you come for the work party?" Coenor's tone was light – that was likely a good sign.

"Elder Coenor, it is most excellent to see you! I and these offer you our service. Is there any pursuit to be made?" Bedwyn was as terse as he could be while following the old forms. While they had been more casual with him one on one in the past, it would not do to dismiss military dogma when leading an army to a neighboring Holt.

"Nay, Bedwyn, I don't believe that any survived this totally unforeseen and fortunately-timed collapse. If a few escaped, let them live and bring word of what happens when they decide to attack a dwarven Holt! But while you are here, we've some urgent repairs that you and yours can help with..."

"Certainly, Elder. We will stay as long as you have need of us. But tell me; did our courier make it through? A young red-bearded fellow with a stunning set of armor?"

"Ah! You must mean Angus. Yes, he made it all right, but none too soon. Orcs were hot on his trail several days ago when he arrived. And he was in terrible shape – he looked as though he had been skipped across the sod by a Giant. His timely approach kept me from having the most exciting fishing day of my long life to be sure!"

"Was he able to help with the defense of the Holt then? How did he fare?" Bedwyn could not hide his concern for the youngster.

"Help? He went out to face their entire army several times! Songs will be sung for a long time about Angus at the Aureate. Rarely have I seen a dwarf so willing to put himself in danger for the sake of a few people that he had just met. Each time he went out, the orcs were driven back. It was a defense that you would have been proud of, Bedwyn. Yes, Angus was brilliant."

"I'm concerned with the way you said he 'was' brilliant. How is he now?"

"On his final foray defending the gate, he was literally swarmed by orcs. He slew them all, but then – I'm sorry, Bedwyn. He was heavily wounded in the battle, and he fell."

----- -----

The bush moved as if stirred by a light breeze. A keen observer paying attention to that bush in particular might have seen a shadow of a shadow. But keen or not, no one was even looking that way. Black Zonka could see them, however; the nasty, hateful, evil dwarves who had just obliterated her army. With so many of them about, she would wait right here in her rag-studded cloak until dark, then slip away. It would be some time before she could mount another attack, but she was already plotting the doom of all dwarves. She swore quietly that she would see them all dead.

----- -----

"Dragonbane! Well, Angus never did tell us about that! I suppose it explains his readiness. How is it that we never knew that there was a living Dragonbane? In fact," Coenor continued, "the old treaties-"

"The old treaties are exactly why he was coming to you in the first place. I met him just last week when he brought the news." Bedwyn was reinvigorated after his first night's sleep in several days. He had slept late, a rare occurrence for him. There was a lot to do before returning to the Smaragdine Holt; they would begin work today. "I still cannot believe he fell..."

They made their way to the dining hall that had been scrubbed and put in order yesterday. There were many loud voices, laughter and shouts that overlaid the smells of eggs and spicy sausage being cooked. Conversations ran at every table, with an elder here or there. It was a very homey place now, warm and happy. Heads were turned toward the elders in different areas of the hall, listening intently to their stories. They seemed to be telling the same story from each of their points of view. Bedwyn caught snippets of each as he passed through with Coenor on their way to the kitchen.

"And he ran along the top of their battering ram, killing every orc in reach at a full run. When he reached the end and there were only those retreating left in sight, he taunted them before coming back to safety behind the wall..."

"His shield was crumpled over him by the hail of rocks; it looked like someone had taken a large, heavy sheet of paper and wadded it into the shape of a dwarf! It was concerning until he cast it aside, and we could see he was all right. Then we had a laugh!"

"When his pick became stuck in one's head, he took to brawling with the other, eventually tossing him into a fire that happened to be nearby..."

"...and he turned in the tunnel when it was clear that I wouldn't make it, facing a hundred stout and angry orcs. If it hadn't collapsed right at that moment, he would have had one hell of a fight on his hands! It must have been the sound of their thundering approach that did it..."

It was clear to Bedwyn that every story revolved around Angus and his heroism. What a waste, he thought. Clearly this dwarf had some real potential. He rounded the corner into the kitchen, making a beeline for the kegs. Eggs and sausage always went better with beer, especially after a tragic victory. There was one table in here, with Bedwyn's captains sitting around it. He saw a space open and decided that was the place for him. Coenor stayed in the dining hall.

The captains noted his entry and stood at attention as he scooped a few healthy servings onto a platter to go with his freshly filled stein. Bedwyn put them at ease as he approached. He tried to think of words fitting the sad occasion as they sat. It seemed the right thing to do to honor Angus as much privately as publicly for his sacrifice; and as a commander he knew that the tone he set here with his most trusted aides would trickle down to the troops.

He raised his head and started his speech. "As you know, we lost a good dwarf yesterday. Angus Dragonbane was a bright new talent among us, and he will be sorely missed." The reaction was not what he expected. There were raised eyebrows and guffaws. And that heavily bandaged fellow at the far end of the table was laughing outright! Bedwyn could see that the shaking shoulders and bouncing belly were opening not-yet-healed wounds beneath a sea of white gauze; but the final clue was that bright red beard. "Angus! You're alive!"

"So far, General. So far." Angus' voice was rough, and his eyes winced from the laughter induced pain. "It took you long enough to get here! I don't know how much more I could take!"

The doorway to the kitchen was packed now with laughing dwarves, as well as the dining hall beyond. Very seldom did something like this get past Bedwyn Foresight, and they all were going to enjoy it. The laughter continued for a good while.

----- -----

Angus had, in fact, been very close to death. Dwarves are a particularly resilient race, and Angus' armor was unusually protective. After his wounds had been tended and he had spent nearly twenty-four hours in bed, he was ready for a hearty meal at table. It took a full week to be well enough to travel.

"I've set aside several of my best to get you safely back to the Argentine Holt, Angus." Bedwyn wasn't happy about Angus leaving, but he understood.

"I thank you for that, but I'm not going back home just yet. I've got some business to the south that needs tending first. I would be glad of company, at least until we get back to the Smaragdine. Things are calmer south of the mountains. I think I can make my way from there, once I have my wagon."

Bedwyn was intrigued. "Business south of the Smaragdine? What kind of business would that be?"

"Well that, my dear Bedwyn," said Angus with a wink, "is another story."

Jeremy James Smith

Enjoying the Harkentale Saga?

The tale continues...

HOLTGART

PICKLED MARBLE

DREAMVINE

and many more to come.

To keep up on the development of the story,

new releases, specials, and more,

consider subscribing to the

Harkentale newsletter

at

JeremyJamesSmith.com

Made in the USA
Columbia, SC
08 July 2025